"Stay down before you get your fool head shot off,"

he commanded. "The stage is being robbed."

Maggie froze. Her gaze darted to the window, then back to him again. "The—what?"

"Outlaws are riding in." Spence drew his gun and rolled to his knees, creeping toward the window. "The stage is being robbed. Stay on the floor."

"Well, why didn't you simply say so?" Maggie demanded. Anger bubbled up inside her. "Did you think I wouldn't understand? That I couldn't grasp the concept? Did you—"

"For chrissake, lady, shut up!" He glanced back at her. "And get down on the floor!"

"Well!" Maggie glared right back at him. "Why don't *you* get on the floor?"

He rose from the crouch to peek out the window, then looked back at her. "I've already been slapped, kicked and bitten," Spence said. "I'll take my chances with the outlaws...."

* * *

Maggie and the Law
Harlequin Historical #698—March 2004

Praise for JUDITH STACY'S recent titles

The Nanny
"…one of the most entertaining and sweetly
satisfying tales I've had the pleasure to encounter."
—*The Romance Reader*

The Blushing Bride
"…lovable characters that grab your heartstrings…
a fun read all the way."
—*Rendezvous*

The Dreammaker
"…a delightful story of the triumph of love."
—*Rendezvous*

DON'T MISS THESE OTHER
TITLES AVAILABLE NOW:

#695 ROCKY MOUNTAIN MARRIAGE
Debra Lee Brown
#696 THE NORMAN'S BRIDE
Terri Brisbin
#697 RAKE'S REWARD
Joanna Maitland

JUDITH STACY

MAGGIE AND THE LAW

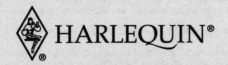

HARLEQUIN®

TORONTO • NEW YORK • LONDON
AMSTERDAM • PARIS • SYDNEY • HAMBURG
STOCKHOLM • ATHENS • TOKYO • MILAN • MADRID
PRAGUE • WARSAW • BUDAPEST • AUCKLAND

ISBN 0-373-29298-8

MAGGIE AND THE LAW

Copyright © 2004 by Dorothy Howell

This edition published by arrangement with Harlequin Books S.A.

Visit us at www.eHarlequin.com

Printed in U.S.A.

To David, Judy and Stacy with all my love forever.

Chapter One

Colorado, 1889

Men looked different when you were flat on your back.

At least, this one did.

Maggie Peyton gazed up at the man whose face hovered above hers. Dark, smoldering eyes bored into her. A corner of his lip turned back in a snarl. Hot breath puffed from his nose.

The hard floor pressed painfully against Maggie's back. His knees brushed her thighs. His long fingers pinned her shoulders down.

Bewildered, Maggie just stared at him.

For the last two hours he'd sat on the stagecoach seat across from her, rudely stretching out his legs to take up most of the room, but slouched down with his hat over his face seemingly sleeping—seemingly harmless. They were the only two passengers on board, and he'd barely spoken to her, except to introduce himself.

Then suddenly, a moment ago, this Mr. Spence

Harding had bolted upright, grabbed her, dragged her onto the floor and jumped atop her. She'd been too stunned to think, to move. Now—

"Get off of me!" Maggie swung at him. Her palm slapped against his ear and jaw with a loud crack. His head whipped around. He loosened his grip.

Maggie scrambled away, kicking at his thighs. She rolled onto her side, trying to get to her feet.

He grabbed her, easily turning her onto her back again.

A scream tore from her throat. Blindly, she batted at him, slapping his face, his shoulder, his chest.

"Settle down!" His voice, deep and guttural, boomed as he grabbed both her hands. "The stage—"

"Let me go!"

"Be still!" He stretched her hands above her head and held them down.

Maggie's thoughts raced. No one else on board. No one to help her, except perhaps the driver up top. But could he even hear her screams above the thundering of the horses' hooves, the creak of the coach, the rush of the wind?

Panic overwhelmed her. Maggie kicked wildly, blindly, furiously.

"I told you, lady, just—yeow!" Spence grimaced, then anchored his leg over hers and slapped his hand across her mouth.

Maggie's heart pounded. She struggled, desperate to escape his grasp. He'd pinned her to the floor. She was helpless, totally at his mercy.

Bile rose in Maggie's throat. Her worst fear. When she'd made the decision to leave New York, take this trip west—totally alone—her personal safety had been a concern. But she'd never expected *this*.

Maggie gulped as she looked up at Spence Harding. Beneath the brim of his black hat, his thick dark brows bunched together. His jaw tensed as his lips pressed into a thin, angry line.

The man was an animal. A beast. And he was huge. She'd noticed that the instant the two of them had boarded the stagecoach this afternoon in Keaton. Big shoulders and arms. Long legs. Meaty hands.

He'd ravish her. Murder her. Toss her body out of the moving coach. She'd never be heard from again. Her father would wait and worry, wonder what had become of his only child.

A little mewl gurgled in Maggie's throat as the man leaned down. She squeezed her eyes shut, her mind screaming in revulsion.

His leg shifted against hers. Maggie's eyes popped open. No, she couldn't—wouldn't—let this happen. She hadn't come this far, traveled for so long on such an important mission to have it end like this.

Maggie lurched, bared her teeth, and bit into his hand.

Spence jerked away. "Goddamn, son of a—"

Maggie wrestled from his grasp, groping for the seat, struggling to escape. Two big hands grasped her hips and sat her down hard on the floor. Spence glared at her, his eyes blazing.

"Stay down, before you get your fool head shot off," he commanded. "The stage is being robbed."

Maggie froze. Her gaze darted to the window, then back to him again. "The—what?"

"Outlaws are riding in." Spence drew his gun and

rolled to his knees, creeping toward the window. "The stage is being robbed. Stay on the floor."

She realized then that the stagecoach had picked up speed, bouncing and bucking worse than usual.

"Well, why didn't you simply say so?" Maggie demanded. Anger bubbled up inside her, chasing away the fear. "Did you think I wouldn't understand? That I couldn't grasp the concept? Did you—"

"For chrissake, lady, shut up!" He glanced back at her. "And get down on the floor!"

"Well!" Maggie glared right back at him. "Why don't *you* get on the floor?"

He raised from a crouch to peek out the window, then dipped his head and looked back at her.

"I've already been slapped, kicked and bit," Spence said. "I'll take my chances with the outlaws."

He turned back to the window and eased upward, his gun at the ready. Maggie rose to her knees, craning her neck to see around him.

Outside, men on horseback raced through the rugged terrain alongside the stagecoach. They would overtake the stage in moments.

Such a spectacle. Maggie stared, mesmerized by the churning of the horses' legs, the men's dusters snapping behind them, their hat brims bending in the wind, their drawn weapons.

She'd never witnessed such a sight. Not once, in all her travels with her father to the farthest corners of the world. Oh, if only he could be here to see this. How intrigued he would be.

A gunshot pierced the air. Spence returned fire, then ducked, saw her peeking over his shoulder and pulled her to the floor.

''What the hell is wrong with you, lady? Stay down.''

Another volley of gunfire sounded. Answering shots rang out, and Maggie guessed it came from the driver up top. A bullet tore through the door of the stagecoach, splintering the wood. Maggie gasped and flattened herself against the bucking floor. Spence pressed himself atop her.

''They're—they're really shooting at us,'' she whispered.

His face hovered inches above hers. Their gazes met and held in a long, lingering look. His features that had seemed so hostile, so forbidding only a short while ago, softened. The moment stretched endlessly. The two of them—strangers—caught in an age-old struggle for life itself.

''Are they going to kill us?'' she asked.

His jaw tightened. ''Not if I can help it.''

He tried to rise but Maggie grasped his shirt with both hands and yanked him down again. Visions of her life at her father's side flashed in her mind. Endless hours spent in lecture halls, dusty libraries and museums. Treks to tiny towns, remote villages, ancient ruins.

''I can't *die*,'' she wailed. ''I haven't even *lived* yet.''

Spence caught her wrists. ''Look, lady—''

''I've never married,'' Maggie exclaimed. ''Never produced a child, never even known a man!''

''I'd be happy to oblige you, honey, but all that takes a little more time than I've got right now.'' Spence pulled her hands free of his shirt and crept to the window.

Maggie pushed herself up, the meaning of his

words dawning her. Her cheeks flamed. "You think I wanted *you* to—to…right here in this stagecoach!"

Spence swore an oath, then fired his pistol out the window. Gunshots answered. He ducked, bobbed up and fired again, then dropped to the floor, his back braced against the seat.

"There're three of them coming in, covering both sides of the stage," Spence said, his fingers quick and sure as he reloaded his pistol.

The stagecoach slowed. Maggie lifted her head. "Is it really a good idea to stop now?"

He spared her a quick glance. "You're not from around here, are you?"

"Well, no. Actually, I'm from—"

A gunshot boomed outside. Maggie gasped and ducked. The stagecoach stopped with a lurch. She lifted her gaze to see Spence pointing his pistol at one of the outlaws through the coach window. He didn't fire, though, as the other man pointed a rifle back at him. She looked out the window on the other side of the stage and saw two more outlaws pointing guns at them.

"Give me that gun and come on out of there," one of the outlaws said.

Spence glared at him for a few seconds, then glanced behind him and saw the others.

Maggie gulped. They were caught in a crossfire. Their situation was hopeless. He didn't stand a chance. Yet several tense seconds dragged by before Spence tossed his pistol out the window and got to his feet.

Bending low, he caught Maggie's arms and helped her up. Her limbs felt stiff, wooden. She wasn't sure she could stand on her own.

Spence leaned into her and spoke quietly. "Do whatever they say. Give them whatever they want." His brows drew together. "And keep your mouth shut."

Maggie followed him out of the stagecoach, her heart pounding and her knees trembling. He lifted her to the ground and stepped in front of her.

Good gracious, the man was tall. Maggie couldn't even see over his shoulder. He was wide and sturdy and strong, a formidable wall of protection in front of her.

She caught glimpses of the outlaws as they went about their work. Hard, weather-beaten faces. Dusty, unkempt clothing. If not thieves, they could have been farmers or miners. What had caused these seemingly ordinary men to turn to a life of crime? Maggie wondered.

While one of the men—the leader, she supposed—remained on his horse holding them at gunpoint, the other two climbed aboard the stagecoach.

"Driver's dead," one of them called out.

Maggie's stomach lurched. Dead? The man was dead? She gulped and said a quick prayer.

An oath so vile Maggie didn't know what some of the words meant rang out from the top of the coach. "There's no strongbox."

The man on horseback cursed, then shook his head. "We'll take the team," he said, then waved his rifle toward Maggie and Spence. "See what they got on them."

Both men jumped to the ground. The bigger of the two began unhitching the horses from the stagecoach, while the other approached Spence.

"Empty your wallet," he said.

Spence shifted his weight as he towered over the robber. Maggie sensed the tension in Spence, coiled like a snake ready to strike. His face in profile, she saw his tight jaw, his eyes as they flickered from the robber in front of him to the leader holding the rifle. For an instant, Maggie was sure she saw his mind working. Calculating. Looking for a way to get the upper hand.

Then finally, Spence pulled his wallet from his back pocket and handed over a handful of bills.

The outlaw turned to Maggie. He was young, she realized, seeing his smooth jaw and the few whiskers that had pushed through. Not much taller than herself, he was thin and bony in ill-fitting clothes, a shock of unruly hair sticking out from under his battered hat. She guessed him to be considerably younger than her own twenty-two years.

So young and already his life had taken this desperate turn. Maggie just looked at him. Oh, if only her father could be here to see this.

"What's your name?" she asked.

He squinted at her. "How's that?"

"Your name," Maggie repeated.

"It's Henry," he said, and shifted uncomfortably. "Now, you gotta give me your money, ma'am."

"How old are you?"

"Huh?"

"I said, how old are you?"

Spence turned and looked at her with bulging eyes. "Shut up," he hissed.

The boy glanced at the man on horseback, then back at Maggie again. "Look, ma'am, you've got to—"

''Fifteen? Sixteen?'' Maggie asked. She looked him up and down. ''Where is your mother?''

Spence glared at her as if she'd lost her mind.

''My mama's dead,'' Henry said, and stole a furtive glance at the gang leader once more. ''Now, would you just give me your money—''

''Your mother is dead and *this* is what you've chosen to do with your life?'' Maggie shook her head, trying to comprehend. She spread her arms. ''What on earth made you do such a thing? Does it seem exciting? Did you do poorly at school? Have you no education? What was the turning point for you?''

The boy turned to Spence. ''Is she not right in the head, or something?''

''Crazy as a loon.'' Spence caught her arm and leaned down. ''Give the kid your money.''

Maggie jerked away from him. ''I am not crazy. How dare you say such a thing! I'm merely asking—''

A gunshot pierced the air. Maggie jumped. The gang leader nudged his horse and rode closer. ''What the hell is going on over here?''

Henry gestured to Maggie. ''Something's wrong with her.''

The gang leader gave her a slow once-over. ''She looks okay to me. Looks damn fine.''

Maggie flushed at the man's bold gaze. Yet she couldn't let go of her concern for the boy. ''What possessed you to employ this boy in your...organization? Have you no regard for the young mind that is, at this very moment, being warped—perhaps permanently?''

''See?'' Henry waved his hand at Maggie, as if she'd just confirmed his point.

All the men stared at her, bringing a new flush to Maggie's face and a wave of anger with it.

Her shoulders stiffened. "Now see here—"

"She's my wife's sister," Spence said. "I'm taking her to the asylum at Henderson."

"What?" she exclaimed. "How dare you suggest that I am somehow—"

He caught her arm again. "Calm down now, Sis. It's really for the best."

She jerked away from him. "What on earth are you talking about?"

"Shut up!" The gang leader waved his rifle again. "Tie them up and let's get out of here."

Henry fetched rope from his saddlebag and tied Spence's hands behind him, then turned to Maggie. He eyed her warily, as if afraid to come too close.

"Sorry, ma'am, I got to tie you up. But first, you gotta give me your money."

Maggie felt Spence's gaze boring into her. She ignored him. "My handbag is inside the stage-coach."

Henry slipped behind her and tied her wrists. Maggie pressed her lips together to keep from crying out as the rough material dug into her flesh.

She watched helplessly as the boy hopped into the stagecoach and emerged with her handbag.

"Excuse me?" she called. "But, if you don't mind, could you leave me just a little of the money?"

"For chrissake…" Spence mumbled.

Henry looked down at the handbag. "I don't think I'm allowed to do that, ma'am."

"Well, then, at least leave me the bag itself."

"I don't know…."

"Do you feel you must take it? Why?" Maggie

asked. "Is it some sort of trophy? A keepsake? Do you feel compelled to take everything you possibly can, as a way, perhaps, to make up for no longer having your mother?"

Henry frowned, then he shook his head and threw Spence a sympathetic look. "Good luck..."

"Wait!" Maggie called, as he walked away. "If you could just tell me—"

"Shut the hell up!" Spence roared.

Maggie pressed her lips together and narrowed her eyes at him, then jerked her chin and turned away.

The outlaws mounted up. Maggie's stomach lurched. They rode off with the four-horse team from the stagecoach, as well as nearly every cent she had in the world.

Not only that, but they'd left her trussed like a Christmas goose, alone in the wilderness, miles from civilization, in the company of this dreadful Mr. Spence Harding.

Perhaps if she'd thought faster she could have talked them out of leaving her here like this. If only she'd had more time to speak with them, question them, she surely could have understood them better. And with understanding came communication and, eventually, agreement—or so her father always said.

Maggie's heart sank. Still, that wasn't her biggest blunder today. She should have paid better attention to the outlaws. Studied their technique. After all, she wasn't that much different from them.

Not considering that she'd traveled all the way from New York, bound for the town of Marlow, Colorado, for the sole purpose of pulling off the most daring deed humanity had ever witnessed.

Chapter Two

Hoofbeats faded in the distance. Leaves overhead rustled in the afternoon breeze. Somewhere, a bird called.

Maggie stood by the stagecoach, dwarfed by the trees, the terrain, the man beside her…and the situation she found herself in.

Beyond that were her personal circumstances. Her dress was rumpled and wrinkled where she'd rolled around on the stagecoach floor. A lock of her dark hair had come loose from her bun and hung over her face. Her hat was askew.

Dire circumstances, certainly. Uncomfortable, too. But not insurmountable. Maggie drew in a breath and straightened her shoulders. She'd trekked to remote locations, under worse circumstances, since she was five years old and her mother had died, leaving her in the care of her father, a man whose scientific pursuits had taken him all over the world—with his daughter in tow.

Maggie glanced at Spence Harding. His face set in hard, determined lines, he worked his wrists together, struggling to loosen the ropes. Already his flesh was red and chafed.

After a few minutes, he gave up and glared at her, his gaze traveling from her waist to her hem. "You got anything under your skirt?"

An uncomfortable warmth seeped through Maggie at his bold gaze. She eased away from him. "Nothing you need to concern yourself with."

Spence grumbled. "I'm talking about a knife. Lots of women keep a knife strapped to their thigh."

"They do?" Maggie's eyes widened.

"Yeah," Spence said. "For protection."

"Oh, my…" Women arming themselves? Maggie wished her father were present to hear this. He'd be positively fascinated. "You know, there is a tribe in South America where the women customarily—"

"Look, lady, have you got a knife, or not?"

"No," Maggie said.

Spence stalked away. He backed up to the corner of the stagecoach and rubbed the ropes against the edge.

Maggie struggled with her own bindings for a moment, then gave up. The ropes were tied too tight. She didn't have to rub her skin raw to figure that out.

She huffed irritably. The least Henry could have done was left hers a little loose. Was there no consideration for a member of the female sex in the wilds of Colorado? she wondered. Why was that? Because they all wore knives strapped to their thighs? In other cultures—

"Back up."

Spence's command brought her around to face him. He'd given up scraping his ropes against the stagecoach and now stood behind her.

"We'll try to untie each other's ropes," he said.

She turned as he did and they backed up against each other. They didn't fit well together. Spence was taller, his arms longer; Maggie's bustle was in the way.

He pulled and yanked, his big, warm fingers brushing her skin as he blindly tugged on the knot. Determinedly, he struggled, but to no avail.

"Dammit," he muttered. "Try mine."

"If you can't untie my ropes, I don't know how you think I'll be able to loosen yours."

"Would you just try?" he snapped.

Maggie's arms had begun to ache. She was willing to try anything. She fumbled behind her to locate his hands, their fingers intertwining for a moment, then searched the tangled rope and finally located the knot. She struggled to loosen it, but never felt it give way.

"It's no use," she finally said, stepping away from him.

They turned and stared at each other, their circumstances turning even more dire. A wave of despair washed over Maggie.

She looked around the remote, wooded area, wondering if somewhere, something out there might help them. That didn't seem likely. In the hours they'd been on the stagecoach, no one had passed them. Not a wagon, carriage, or a single rider. She hadn't even seen a house.

"What are we going to do?" she asked.

Spence grumbled again. "I've got a knife."

Her head snapped up. "A knife? Why didn't you say so in the first place? We could have already—"

"Because it's in my pocket."

Maggie froze. Without wanting to, her gaze dropped to his feet. Worn, scuffed boots. Black trousers. White shirt. Dark vest.

She gulped. "Your *shirt* pocket, perhaps?"

"Trousers." He ground out the word between tight lips.

Her gaze dipped again, then sprang away. "*Back* pocket?"

"Front."

A little mewl escaped Maggie's lips and she fled.

"Look, lady," Spence said, striding after her. "All you've got to do is stick your hand in there and—"

She rounded on him. "For your information, Mr. Harding, I'm quite particular about where I put my hands."

"Yeah? Well, you'll be lucky to have any hands left if these ropes stay on much longer. And you'll have a hell of a time defending yourself against the next mountain lion or bear that comes along. Not to mention—"

"Oh, all right!" Maggie worked the tension out of her shoulders and drew in a deep breath. He was right, of course. Her arms ached worse by the minute and her fingers had started to tingle. They were both totally helpless, tied up like this, easy prey to whatever animals might come along.

"Look, honey," Spence said, softening his voice a little. "Just slide your hand—"

"Magdelen," she said. She'd introduced herself when they'd boarded the stage this morning, but obviously he'd forgotten. "My name is Magdelen. Magdelen Peyton. My friends call me Maggie."

He snorted. "Well, after this, Miss Peyton, we'll sure as hell be some kind of friends."

"Let's just get this over with."

Maggie sidled up next to him, delicately probing with her left hand to find the opening of his right front pocket. Heat raced up her arm, completely devouring her. Never in her entire life had she touched a man in anything even remotely resembling this situation. An arm, yes. A shoulder, once. But she'd never ventured anywhere close to—

"Are you going to take all day doing this?" he demanded.

Maggie's face flushed again. Gracious, did he believe she was deliberately drawing this out? What kind of women did he think she was?

She pulled away. Spence stepped with her, his leg bumping the back of hers. A whole new wave of heat swept through her.

"Just stick your hand in there!" he barked.

Maggie shoved her hand inside. His trousers were tight, the pocket snug—and deep. She pushed downward, farther and farther until the ropes on her wrists stopped her progress. Still she wasn't at the bottom. She pushed deeper.

"Hang on a minute…" Spence mumbled.

"I think I've got something."

"Wait—"

"Stop wiggling," she insisted.

"Hold on—"

"Yes, I can feel it," Maggie cried.

"Don't—"

"It's bigger than I expected, but—I've got it!"

"That's not my knife!"

Maggie screamed. She yanked her hand out of his pocket. It hung in the fabric. She struggled, making little whimpering noises, until she finally pulled free.

Her face burned. Her hand burned. *Everything* burned.

Mortified, she looked up at Spence. His eyes narrowed in a ferocious scowl. His jaw locked. Hot air puffed from his nose. His gaze impaled her with an intensity that scored her more deeply than anything she'd ever imagined.

"I'm—I'm sorry," Maggie whispered, her heart pounding. "I didn't realize that I'd—that is, that your—"

Spence spun away. He strode to the shade of the stagecoach and stood there, his back to her.

Maggie's head swam. She'd never been so embarrassed in her life. How would she ever face this man again?

Yet if she couldn't face him, how would they ever get themselves out of their situation?

"Mr. Harding?" she called, walking toward him.

He looked back over his shoulder with a scowl that halted Maggie in her tracks. "Just give me a minute."

She blushed anew, spun on her heel and left him alone.

He needed more than a minute, it seemed, as Maggie waited beneath a towering tree. She wasn't sure how much time passed before she finally heard footsteps behind her.

"It must be in the other pocket," Spence said, his words tight and clipped.

"Surely you don't expect me to—"

"You got any better ideas?" he demanded, leaning closer.

"Well, no," she admitted.

"All right, then," Spence said. He turned sideways, offering his left pocket. "Just get it over with."

Maggie drew in a breath, backed up against him, and slipped her hand into his pocket. Cautiously, she pushed deeper, and this time her fingers touched something metal.

"I think I've got it," she said.

"Don't drop it."

Closing her fingers around the knife, Maggie carefully pulled it out.

"Give it here," Spence insisted.

She passed the knife to him. His fingers brushed hers as he worked with the knife, then she felt the blade slice through her ropes. Her arms fell free.

Relief swamped her. She swung her arms and rubbed her wrists as she turned and took the knife from Spence. She cut through his ropes, freeing him.

He grabbed the knife and strode toward the stagecoach, working the kinks out of his arms. Maggie hurried along behind him. Spence vaulted up to the driver's seat. From the ground, she could see the driver slumped over. Spence tended to him for a moment, then jumped to the ground.

"He's dead." Spence shook his head and mumbled a curse. "Damn fool outlaws. Should have known there was no money on board since we weren't carrying a shotgun rider."

Spence looked around, getting his bearings, it seemed, deciding what to do next.

"Shouldn't we make camp?" Maggie asked. "The town of Marlow is still hours away, isn't it? Won't they send someone after us when the stage doesn't arrive on schedule?"

"They'll send somebody. Tomorrow, maybe, if

they can spare the manpower. The stage running late isn't unusual. After that rainstorm a couple of days ago, they might figure the bridge washed out. No way of knowing when somebody might ride out to find us.'' Spence nodded briskly. ''We'll walk.''

''Walk?'' Maggie gestured toward the stagecoach. ''Wouldn't we be safer here? We have shelter, it's on the road, the rescue party can find us easily.''

Spence gazed down at her. ''You know who else can find us easily? Those outlaws. I'm not taking a chance that they'll come back.''

''Come back? They've already taken everything of value. What would they come back for?''

''You.''

''Oh.'' Her eyes widened. ''Oh!''

Maggie swept into action. ''I'll gather what supplies might be on board and get my things.''

In short order, she procured blankets from the stagecoach, her two carpetbags, one she reasoned belonged to Spence, the sack of food she'd bought for herself at the stage's last stop, the one she'd seen Spence purchase, and the canteen and food that belonged to the driver. She placed the supplies under a tree, trying to avoid watching Spence as he wrapped the driver's body in a tarp, secured it with ropes and placed it inside the stagecoach.

''Shouldn't we bury him?'' Maggie asked when Spence walked over. She noted that he'd retrieved his pistol and it was now tucked into the holster on his thigh.

Spence shook his head. ''Riders from Marlow can claim him tomorrow, or whenever they show up, and take him home for a proper burial. What did you find for us?''

She gestured toward the supplies. "Food, water, blankets and our belongings."

Spence hunkered down and sorted through the items. "We'll take the food, water and blankets. That's it."

"But what about our things?"

He rose. "They'll get picked up and brought back to town along with the driver."

"No," Maggie insisted. Everything in her rebelled. She couldn't possibly leave her belongings out here. What if someone—another outlaw gang—came along and stole them? Already she'd lost her money, she couldn't bear the thought of losing her possession, as well.

"It's a long walk," Spence said. "Carrying all this stuff will just slow us down."

"No. I'm not leaving them here."

He glared at her, then huffed irritably and picked up one of her bags. "This thing weighs a ton. What the hell have you got in it?"

She shrugged. "Books."

"Books!" Spence dropped the bag.

"What if I abandon them here and someone steals them?"

He looked down at her. "Believe me, nobody is going to steal books."

Maggie shook her head. "I simply can't leave them."

He glared at her. "I'm sure as hell not hiking through miles of open country carrying a bag of books."

She pushed her chin up. "I don't believe I asked you to carry it."

Maggie turned sharply, returned to the stagecoach

and got the rope she'd found in the boot. Much to her surprise, this rear storage section contained all sort of useful items. She carried the rope back to Spence and held out her palm.

"Your knife, please?"

He just looked at her for a moment, then dragged his knife out of his pocket and gave it to her. She measured off two lengths of rope, cut them and tied each to the handles of her carpetbags, forming straps. She looped each over her shoulders, crossed them at her chest and turned to him.

"Do you think you can manage to carry the food, water, and blankets, Mr. Harding, or should I take that, as well?"

Spence just glared at her, then picked up their other supplies. He secured the food sacks onto his gun belt, then used the last of the rope to tie the blanket and drape it over his shoulder along with the canteen.

Maggie put her nose in the air. "Do try and keep up, Mr. Harding," she said, and set off at a brisk pace.

"Miss Peyton?"

Annoyed, Maggie stopped and looked back.

"Marlow is that way," he said, pointing in the opposite direction.

"Oh." Refusing to let the embarrassment she felt creep onto her cheeks, Maggie said, "I was looking for a shortcut."

"Uh-huh."

Maggie threw back her shoulders and marched right past him toward Marlow.

Chapter Three

Damn fool woman.

Spence glanced over his shoulder at Maggie on the road behind him. She'd fallen farther and farther back. All because she insisted on toting two carpet-bags—one of them full of books.

Damn stubborn woman. Spence turned his back on her and kept walking.

The afternoon sun drifted toward the horizon, promising some relief from the heat. But it was still hot, with no breeze to cool things down. Spence had already sweated through his shirt and long johns. He knew Maggie had to be even hotter, wearing all those clothes women wore, carrying a load of books to boot.

But she hadn't complained. She'd not uttered so much as a whine or a whimper. Hadn't even asked him to wait for her.

That surprised him. So had her reaction to leaving the stagecoach. She hadn't wasted time getting supplies together, just jumped in and gathered everything they needed.

An unexpected—but not unpleasurable—tingle

warmed Spence as he recalled turning around and seeing her climbing to the top of the stagecoach. Dress and petticoats flying, bending over, hiking her skirt up to jump down again.

The tingle behind his fly deepened. Spence gritted his teeth trying to shrug it off. How the hell was he going to hike all the way to Marlow if *that* kept happening?

And how the hell was he going to keep them safe if that kept happening?

He stopped and turned back, forcing his thoughts onto their dire situation. He'd learned the hard way a long time ago what happened when he let down his guard, got distracted. He wasn't about to let another woman pay for his mistake.

Maggie was farther behind now, her steps growing slower. More of her hair had tumbled down and hung loose around her shoulders. Her hat was close to falling off completely.

She didn't resemble the prim and proper lady who had boarded the stage at Keaton earlier today. In fact, she pretty much looked a mess.

His gaze dipped to the two carpetbags she'd strung across her shoulders like bandoliers. They bisected her chest, making her breasts stick out round and plump.

Spence shifted as the ache behind his fly worsened. What the hell was wrong with him? After what he'd been through today—the shoot-out and robbery—why was this happening to him?

Probably because the woman trailing him had stuck her hand into his pocket and nearly brought him to his knees. If she'd groped for another few seconds—

Spence grumbled under his breath and dragged up the one memory that never failed to clear his head.

Ellen.

Three years ago.

It felt like yesterday.

"Hell…" Spence walked back to where Maggie struggled with her carpetbags. "This isn't some stroll in the park, Miss Peyton. We're in dangerous country. You carrying those bags just slows us down, makes things worse."

She jerked her chin around at him. A fine layer of dust covered her face, streaked with perspiration. "I don't believe I *asked* you to wait for me."

Yeah, that was true. But it didn't particularly suit Spence that she'd said it. Damn fool Eastern woman. Hadn't she learned anything from that robbery this morning?

"Just give me half the provisions and a blanket, and you can go wherever you please," Maggie said, her words coming out in a breathy rush as she struggled to keep going.

Everything in Spence revolted at the very idea. Leave her? Alone? In the middle of nowhere?

"You really are crazy," Spence told her.

She jerked to a stop. Spence's stomach jolted as he saw tears spring to her eyes.

Damnation, that's all he needed. A crying woman on his hands when they should be hiking as hard as they could to get to the safety of town.

"We haven't got time for this foolishness. We're in the middle of nowhere," Spence barked. "God knows what wild animals—or outlaws—might be trailing us. We've got to—"

A little whimper slipped from Maggie's lips and two big tears rolled down her cheeks.

Spence uttered a disgusted sigh. "Look here, Miss Peyton—"

She whipped around and started walking, faster this time.

Spence grumbled another curse. Yeah, she was walking again, but at this pace she'd faint for sure. He hurried after her.

"All right, look, let me carry those bags for a while," he said, reaching for the ropes that crossed her shoulders.

"No!" Maggie whirled away. "I don't trust you. You'll toss them in a ravine, or something."

"Now you're just being stubborn," Spence told her. "Let me take them and you can—"

"No!" She swatted his hand and spun out of his grasp. But the weight of the carpetbags whirling with her proved too much. They pulled her backward. Her heel caught a rock and down she went, flat on her back in the middle of the road.

Spence stood over her looking down. She lay still, eyes closed, arms spread out beside her, her little hat dangling over one ear. He looked up and down the road in both directions. Bad enough they were out in the open like this, miles from town. Now he had a helpless woman on his hands, easy prey for who-ever—or whatever—might come along. Spence's skin crawled at the thought.

"Miss Peyton?"

"Now you've done it," she said, still not opening her eyes. "Now I'll never be able to get up."

Spence bent down, caught her under her arms, and dragged her and her carpetbags out of the road onto the grass beneath the nearest shade tree. He pulled the bags off her, then dropped the gear he carried and plopped down beside her.

Spence took off his hat and offered her the canteen. "Here. Drink this."

A few seconds passed. Maggie didn't move. Spence lifted her head and splashed a little water onto her lips. Her eyes opened and she leaned forward, taking the canteen from him. When she finished, she fell back onto the grass and closed her eyes once more.

Spence drank his fill, then capped the canteen and wiped his mouth with the back of his hand.

"I'm going to rest for a while," Maggie mumbled. "Go ahead without me...if you want."

They had to keep moving. They couldn't stay here like sitting ducks. But when he looked at her, he realized he might as well save his breath. Maggie was asleep.

Spence glanced at the horizon. Precious daylight was slipping away. Yet he didn't have much choice but to let her rest, for just a few minutes. Then they would continue, cover a few more miles before dark.

Spence scooted to the trunk of the shade tree and leaned back. He trained his gaze on the road, keeping watch, then closed his eyes, just for a second.

He awoke with a start. His hand dropped to his gun as his gaze swept the surroundings. Road, empty. Maggie, sleeping. He relaxed a little. They were safe.

Damn. How could he have fallen asleep?

The sun's rays touched the horizon, streaking the blue sky with golden rays. Spence rubbed his eyes. He'd been out for a while.

His gaze fell on Maggie once more. She was a

pretty little thing. Until this moment, he'd not noticed her soft, pale skin, her long dark lashes, or her pink lips.

A wave of guilt washed through Spence. He'd been angry with himself and he'd taken it out on her. Angry that those outlaws had overtaken the stage, that the driver had been killed, that he hadn't been able to protect any of them, that he hadn't been able to stop any of it.

That he'd failed.

Again.

The familiar guilt twisted Spence's stomach. Yes, he'd taken his anger out on Maggie. But if that's what it took to keep her alive, so be it.

Maggie's eyes fluttered open. Spence watched as she came awake. He expected her to bolt to her feet, disoriented and frightened to find herself in strange circumstances, but she did none of those things.

Maggie smiled.

A slow, gentle smile. A sleepy, seductive smile. An innocent smile that kept Spence sitting next to her, drinking in the fullness of her lips, the curve of her jaw, the blueness of her eyes as she watched him.

Reality pushed Spence to his feet. She sat up, covered a little yawn with her palm, then got to her feet and headed into the woods.

Spence started after her, then stopped, realizing she needed a few moments of privacy. He went the opposite way into the woods, then returned a few minutes later to find Maggie gazing at the horizon, shading her eyes with her hand.

"Can we cover a few more miles before dark?" she asked.

He should have been relieved that she wanted to

continue, but somehow, it annoyed him that she was being so practical while he couldn't seem to get his thoughts—or body—under control.

"It's too late," Spence said. He nodded through the trees. "I heard a creek running. We'll camp for the night."

Maggie reached for her carpetbags but Spence got to them first, scooped up all their gear, and led the way through the trees. They hiked downhill a short way to where a wide, shallow creek meandered through a narrow valley. Trees offered shade from the disappearing sun, cooling the air.

Spence selected a spot amid a stand of oaks a few yards from the creek and dropped their gear, then started gathering sticks, twigs and small logs.

"Is it safe to have a fire?" Maggie asked. "What if those outlaws spot it and come after us?"

Spence paused, a bundle of dried twigs in his hand. He wasn't sure what surprised him most: that Maggie questioned his decisions, or that she asked so practical a question.

"I doubt they headed this way, toward Marlow," Spence said. "More likely, they went up into the mountains. Besides, it'll get cold tonight. The fire will ward off wild animals. It's a risk, but we're better off with it."

She considered his words for a moment, then nodded. "I'll give you a hand with the firewood."

"I can handle it," he told her, and continued searching the forest floor. "Don't wander off."

A few minutes later, he heard water splashing in the creek. From deep in the woods, he saw Maggie seated on the creek bank, her back to him. At first he thought she was filling their canteen, then like a mule-kick in the gut, he realized she was bathing.

Bathing. Drawn forward through the trees, Spence crept closer, unable to stop himself.

Up until this moment, Maggie hadn't seemed overly concerned that she looked like something the cat had dragged in. Dusty, rumpled, hair mussed, hat crooked. Most women would have been mortified and carried on endlessly at being seen looking so disheveled. But not Maggie.

Now, she sat quietly at the creek bank. Her little hat lay beside her. Her long, dark brown hair tumbled in waves down her back.

She leaned forward, scooped water into her palms and scrubbed it over her face. Her hands worked beneath her chin. Spence's gut clenched as he realized she'd unbuttoned her dress.

Taking a handkerchief from her pocket, Maggie dipped it into the creek, squeezed water from it, then glided it around the open collar of her dress. Her shoulders rose and relaxed. Her head fell sideways, then back, as she ran the handkerchief beneath her dress, down her throat, then lower.

Spence's mouth went dry. It was one of the most private, personal moments he'd ever witnessed—yet he could see very little. But knowing what she was doing—where that handkerchief was—proved nearly too much for him.

This sure as hell was a distraction he didn't need.

Spence stomped to the creek. "Just what in the name of the good Lord in heaven are you doing?"

Maggie gazed up at him, holding her dress closed. "I'm—"

"Don't you know what kind of danger is in these hills?"

"Well—"

"Don't you have sense enough to understand our situation?"

Maggie sprang to her feet, eyes narrowed. "Don't you dare insult my intelligence another time, Mr. Harding. I simply will not allow it."

Taken slightly aback by the determined furrow of her brow and the jut of her jaw, Spence backed up a step.

"We have to make camp. Get over there under the trees." He pointed to the spot where he'd left their gear. "And stay put until I get the fire going."

They glared at each other for a moment, then Spence headed into the woods searching for firewood again.

Maggie twisted her hair into a neat bun, then closed up the buttons of her dress. That Spence Harding had to be the grumpiest person she'd ever encountered. The nerve of the man. Ordering her around, treating her as if she didn't have a grain of sense, insulting her.

Still, he had a point. They did need to make camp. She gathered stones from the water's edge and made a fire ring, then spread out their blankets and sat down.

Nearly dark now, the forest came alive with evening sounds, insects, the song of a bird somewhere high in the trees. Maggie rubbed her arms. She was a little chilly and would be glad when Spence got the fire going.

But maybe her bath at the creek wasn't the only reason she felt cold. Hiking through open country, sleeping under the stars didn't frighten Maggie. She'd done it most of her life. But this time, something felt different.

Was it the outlaws and the threat that they might return? A fear for her personal safety? Maggie considered those possibilities, but dismissed each because, actually, she felt very safe.

Her gaze drifted through the trees to Spence, his arms loaded with firewood. Strong. Capable. Fearless. How could she feel frightened with him nearby?

A strange ache tightened Maggie's stomach. She'd never met a man like Spence before. For a moment— one desperate moment—she wished to be everything she *wasn't*.

An ache of longing rose, squeezing Maggie's heart. She was a practical woman. She knew the truth. And the truth was that a man like Spence Harding would never find a woman like her attractive.

But some way, somehow, just this once, couldn't things be different?

Maggie pushed away the thought. Why was she trying to kid herself? *No* man found a woman like her attractive. Hadn't some of the greatest minds in the country told her that? Hadn't she learned it for herself already?

Too outspoken. Too forthright. Too capable. Too independent. Even too smart.

The list of reasons men did not find a woman like her appealing was a long one. It had been repeated to her often, though with the best of intentions by her father and all his colleagues. Highly intelligent men, each and every one of them. The greatest minds in the country. They *knew*.

The ache in Maggie's heart deepened a little. Did

it always have to be that way? Couldn't she—just once—fit in?

Spence walked up with an armload of wood, hunkered down and got the fire going. Maggie fetched the canteen and food while he went to the creek and washed his face and hands, then dropped onto the blanket beside Maggie.

Careful not to sit too close to her, she couldn't help but notice.

"Save some for tomorrow," she said, as he bit into a cold chicken leg. "We've still got a long hike ahead of us."

Spence cut his gaze over to her and she looked away. Goodness, she'd done it again, Maggie thought, admonishing herself for being so outspoken.

While it was true that she'd probably camped around more fires and trekked more miles than Spence—and most other people—the look on his face told her quite plainly that he didn't appreciate her advice.

Something else the greatest minds in the country had told her. Something else she'd learned the hard way.

Darkness fell. The campfire crackled, its yellow flames glowing in the night.

"Are you headed to Marlow?" Spence asked. "Or farther west?"

She glanced up at him. The fire reflected off the angles of his face making his jaw sharper, his nose straighter, his eyes deeper.

"Marlow," she said. "I'm going to Marlow. And you?"

He nodded. "Marlow."

She knew it would be best if she kept silent, but

Maggie couldn't abide the stillness or the odd restlessness that had overtaken her.

"Do you live in Marlow?" she asked.

"Yep."

"I'm visiting there. I live in the East."

He grunted. "No kidding."

Embarrassment caused Maggie's cheeks to tingle. She knew full well that she was out of her element here in Colorado. It was nothing like the other regions of the world she'd traveled. Plus, this was the first time she'd been completely on her own. Yet it bothered her that Spence held so low an opinion of her.

Perhaps the silence was better, Maggie decided.

She ate enough to take the edge off her hunger, then put the remaining food into the sack and tied it closed. As was her custom at the end of each day, she fished her journal from her carpetbag and settled by the fire again.

"You're going to read?" Spence asked.

She heard the surprise, the judgmental tone in his voice. For an instant, the temptation to drop the book back into her bag nearly overcame Maggie. Hide the thing. Get it out of sight. Don't let him see. Don't let him *know*.

"I'm keeping a journal," she said, opening it on her lap. "It's for my father. He'll be fascinated."

Spence raised an eyebrow. "Fascinated? By Colorado?"

"It's the people he'd find interesting," Maggie said. "Papa is a university professor. His field is anthropology, the study of different peoples and their cultures. He's never been west before."

A frown crossed Spence's face. "And he let you come out here by yourself? A woman, alone?"

Maggie shifted. She hadn't meant to get into her reason for coming to Colorado. Yet, something in Spence's words, his expression, was too compelling to ignore.

"Papa doesn't know I'm here…exactly."

His frown deepened. "Where does he think you are…exactly?"

"Visiting a friend in Philadelphia."

Spence looked hard at her. "Then what the hell are you doing out here all by yourself? Don't you know what could happen to a woman traveling alone? Are you deliberately trying to worry the man? Or did you just run off for the hell of it?"

Maggie's spine stiffened. "I'm here for a very serious reason, important to all mankind, I'll have you know. A matter of the utmost urgency, vital to humanity."

Spence eased back a little. "The utmost urgency?"

The skepticism in his voice annoyed her. "Yes," Maggie insisted.

"Vital to all humanity?"

"Yes."

Spence rolled his eyes.

"It's true."

Now she was annoyed with herself for letting him goad her into revealing so much.

Yet for an instant, the temptation to tell him the truth nearly overcame her. She'd carried this problem alone for so long. Spence exuded a strength, a command. If she told him, surely he could help her.

But Maggie kept her problem to herself. Absolute

secrecy was imperative. If word got out—well, she didn't want to contemplate the possibility of what might happen.

It had begun innocently enough a few months ago during a trip to South America with her father. Shortly after returning home, she realized that one of the artifacts they brought back had disappeared. Stolen, she soon discovered, because of her own incompetence. Her mistake.

Guilt ridden and fearing that her father's reputation would be ruined if word got out, Maggie traced the artifact and learned that it had been sold to a man in Marlow, Colorado, of all places. Maggie told no one—not even her father—about the theft and set off to recover the object herself. She couldn't bear the thought of how disappointed her father would be in her if he learned the truth of what she'd done. How it was all her fault. How stupid she'd been to let the artifact get stolen. Really, Papa had few reasons to find favor with her.

Spence grunted. "So you're just going to waltz into Marlow, complete this urgent, vital mission for all humanity, then head back East again?"

Maggie determinedly held her chin up. All right, when he said it like that it did sound a little silly. But she knew the magnitude of the problem she faced—knew it for a fact. She knew, too, that she absolutely could not fail. No matter what, she had to get her hands on that artifact.

Thanks to those outlaws at the stagecoach, her plans had changed considerably. She'd intended to buy back the object and return home. But now with nearly all her money gone, she was left with only two options: plead her case and hope the new owner would simply give her the artifact, or—well, Maggie could hardly bring herself to think about her only other option.

"So, how long do you think it's going to take you to rescue all of humanity?" Spence asked.

A hint of sarcasm tainted his question and it annoyed Maggie further. "I'm not sure how long."

"A day? A week? Two weeks?"

"I told you, I'm not sure."

"What, exactly, is involved in saving mankind?"

She clenched her fists and narrowed her eyes. "Be assured, Mr. Harding, that I will do whatever it takes—including resorting to crime."

Spence stilled, and Maggie was pleased that she'd shut him up. Her triumph burned hot in the pit of her stomach.

Spence's brows pulled together. "You intend to commit some sort of crime in Marlow?"

Her victory withered under his scrutiny as she realized the foolishness of her actions. "Well…"

"Yes, Miss Peyton?"

Maggie pulled herself up. "I might do just that, Mr. Harding, if it's any of your business. And—"

"Hush." Spence pushed to his feet, pulled Maggie up with him and drew his gun, forcing them deeper into the trees. "Riders coming in. Get behind me."

The outlaws? They'd come back? Maggie's heart thudded harder as four men on horses broke through the trees. She clamped her hand on Spence's arm, but he holstered his pistol and walked toward them.

"Thought you boys would never get here," he called.

The lead rider stopped his horse. Light from the campfire reflected off the badge pinned to his vest.

It was the rescue party from Marlow. Relief swamped Maggie.

"I'm so glad you're here," she said, touching her hand to her chest. "I was frightened thinking you were outlaws."

The lawman chuckled. "No need to be frightened, ma'am, not with the sheriff of Marlow himself as your escort."

Maggie froze. "The—the who?"

"The sheriff," he said and waved his hand toward Spence. "Mr. Spence Harding himself."

She whipped around. "You're the *sheriff? Of Marlow?*"

"At your service, Miss Peyton." Spence touched the brim of his hat and leaned down. "Now, you were saying something about a crime you intend to commit in my town?"

Chapter Four

The gazes of the men in the rescue party and that of Sheriff Harding burned hot against Maggie's skin. Embarrassment rolled through her.

Bad enough that she'd allowed herself to be goaded into revealing her intention once she reached Marlow. But she'd told the sheriff. The *sheriff.*

How stupid of her.

How *like* her.

Maggie's humiliation burned hotter. She felt the men staring at her. They'd be laughing at her soon, when Spence told them how he'd tricked her, how she'd shot off her mouth.

Her stomach twisted into a familiar knot. She should have known better than to come here, to attempt to recover the artifact on her own. She should have known she'd do something stupid like this. She should have *known.*

Spence continued to glare down at her, waiting for an answer to his question, waiting for her to divulge exactly what sort of crime she planned to commit in Marlow.

Anger spiked through her embarrassment. Anger

at that awful Spence Harding as she realized this predicament wasn't all her fault. It was *his* fault, too,
for deceiving her by not revealing his true identity.
If he'd told her who he was, she'd never have di-
vulged her plan, let alone bragged about it. Maggie's
anger doubled.

Spence squared his shoulders. "Miss Peyton, I
asked you what you intend—"

"You, Sheriff Harding, are a disgrace to the law
enforcement profession. You have misrepresented
yourself in the most egregious fashion imaginable."

His brows pulled together, apparently taken aback
momentarily. "I'm a—what?"

"You should have told me you were the sheriff.
Why aren't you wearing a badge? Isn't there a law
requiring it?"

His frown deepened. "Well, no, not that I—"

"Then there should be. I intend to contact the gov-
ernor and insist upon it." Maggie raised her chin.
"Stand aside."

Spence didn't move, so she ducked around him.
She stomped to the creek, retrieved her hat and
shoved it into her carpetbag along with her journal
and other belongings.

"Smother the fire," she barked as she jerked up
one of the blankets. "And don't leave your food for
the animals."

Her anger gave her unexpected strength. She
pushed past him, hoisted both her carpetbags and
headed for the horses.

Silent, eyes wide, the men of the rescue party
watched as she tied her bags onto the saddlehorn of
one of the extra horses they'd brought with them.

"Let's go!" She jerked the reins from the man holding the horses.

The deputy shifted in his saddle. "Who's rescuing who?" he asked, causing the other men to chuckle.

"Miss Peyton?" Spence laid a hand on her elbow as she reached for the saddlehorn. "Let me give you a hand."

Maggie jerked away and narrowed her eyes. "For your information, Sheriff Harding, I've ridden a goat, a dogsled, a donkey, a mule, a camel and an African elephant. I'm quite certain I can manage this horse. And I'm quite sure I *don't* need any help from *you.*"

Spence stood silent as Maggie pulled herself into the saddle. He stepped forward and caught the bridle.

Anger roiled inside her. "I told you I don't—"

"Miss Peyton," Spence said softly. "Marlow is the other way."

Embarrassment ripped through her. She yanked on the reins, turned the horse and galloped into the woods.

By the time they reached the town of Marlow, hours had passed and fatigue had replaced Maggie's anger. It had taken no time at all for the rescue party to catch up with her. She'd ridden at the rear, no one—certainly not Spence—speaking to her.

She'd overheard parts of their conversations, though, enough to gather that Spence had been away from Marlow for several weeks, that there'd been problems in his absence, but nothing serious. He told the men about the stagecoach robbery and the dead driver, and made sure someone would ride out tomorrow with another team of horses to recover the body and bring the stage to Marlow.

As Maggie listened to Spence's account of the robbery, she wondered if the two of them had been at the same holdup. He told the bare facts—number of outlaws, extent of the theft, their escape. No mention of his daring deeds.

No mention of her hand in his pocket.

Warmth rushed through Maggie at the memory. Embarrassment, surely.

Spence was a man used to being in charge. She'd sensed that on the stagecoach this morning as he faced the outlaws and during their trek toward Marlow. She saw it now in the glimpses she got of him in the moonlight as he dealt with his deputies, in the bits of their conversation she overheard, the way they reported to him, waited for his answers.

Strange, this sheriff of the West. Maggie reminded herself to make a note of it in her journal.

Her first impression of Marlow wasn't much. As she rode behind the rescue party down what she assumed was the main street, Maggie saw wooden buildings—stores, shops, a bank—fronted by boardwalks, hitching posts and water troughs. Few lights burned in the windows. She saw only two people on the street at this late hour.

When they stopped in front of the Marlow Hotel, Spence bade good-night to the other men as they rode away, then dismounted and tied off his horse.

"You'll stay here tonight," he said to Maggie.

A room. A bed. A soft mattress. Sleep. It all sounded so wonderful. She was tired and chilly, desperate for a place to lay her head, but knew it couldn't be here.

"I can't stay at a hotel," Maggie said, a little annoyed at him for bringing her here, knowing full well she couldn't afford it. "I don't have any money."

"Don't worry about it," he said, standing beside her horse.

"I can't accept a room knowing I have no way of providing payment."

Spence sighed wearily. "Look, Miss Peyton, it's all right. Just come on and—"

"No, I won't—"

Maggie gasped as Spence reached up, caught her waist and pulled her from the horse. Before she could get her feet under her, he pressed her back against the saddle, his hands gripping her waist.

Spence leaned down, his breath hot on her cheek. "Okay, then, you can bunk with me over at the jail."

Breath left Maggie in a startled wheeze. Heat from Spence washed over her, plumed inside her. The idea. The very *idea*. She should be insulted. Offended. Outraged.

So why did she feel excited?

Stunned by her own thoughts, Maggie pushed them away. Insulted. Yes, that's what she felt. Insulted.

How dare he suggest such a thing? Even if she had been on the trail with him. Even if she had intended to sleep out in the open with him.

Even if she had put her hand in his pocket and touched—

"What's it going to be, Miss Peyton?"

His gazed seemed to see straight inside her, know her thoughts. Maggie felt her cheeks heat and looked away.

"The hotel, of course," she said, trying to keep

her voice from trembling. "I'll figure a way to re-imburse the owner for the room."

"You're hardly the first person to get robbed and need a place to sleep," Spence said. "That's the way we do things around here."

He stepped back, allowing a rush of cool air to swirl over Maggie, then took her carpetbags from the horse and led the way down the alley alongside the hotel.

Maggie followed and waited while he pounded on the back door. Finally, a light appeared through the curtains and the door opened. A tall, thin man dressed in trousers and a rumpled shirt, and holding a lantern squinted out at them.

"What's going on?" His eyes narrowed further. "That you, Sheriff? When'd you get back in town?"

"Evening, Mr. Taylor." Spence nodded toward Maggie. "Got a woman here needs a room."

"At this hour?" he complained.

"Stage was held up. Just got into town."

"I heard the stage was late." Mr. Taylor grunted. "Guess you're gonna tell me that she's got no money."

"Christ, Ezra, have you got a room or not?"

He glanced back over his shoulder. "Well, now, Sheriff, you know if it was just me I'd say it was all right, but—"

"Ezra! Ezra, what in tarnation is going on out there?" came a shrill voice from deep inside the hotel.

Mr. Taylor cringed. "It's nothing, Lula, nothing a'tall. Just—"

"Don't tell me it's nothing. I know when it's nothing, and this is not nothing." A stout woman in a worn wrapper and white sleep cap planted herself next to Ezra. She spotted Spence and a smile came to her face. "Why, Sheriff, I didn't know you were back. What can we do for you?"

Before he could answer, the woman swung her gaze to Maggie. "Well, now, what have we here?"

"This is Miss Peyton," Spence said. "She was on the stage from Keaton when it was held up this afternoon."

"Held up? Why, that's awful. Just awful." Mrs. Taylor's mouth opened, then snapped shut. "I guess you'll be needing a room, then, won't you, dearie?"

Maggie gulped. She knew she didn't make much of an impression. Her dress was rumpled and soiled. She didn't even have on a hat.

"Yes, Mrs. Taylor, I'd desperately like to have a room here," Maggie said. "But, truth is, I don't have any money."

"Now, don't you give it another thought." Mrs. Taylor waved Maggie forward. "Why, Mr. Taylor and I are pleased as can be to do our part to make Marlow the kind of town where everyone is welcome, no matter what. You just come on inside, Miss Peyton, and don't worry about a thing."

"Thank you," Maggie said, heaving a silent sigh of relief. "Thank you so much."

"Ezra, bring her bags. Miss Peyton, follow me." She took the lantern from her husband and left, leaving him to struggle with her carpetbags as he trailed along behind her.

Maggie hesitated at the door. She knew she should thank Spence for finding her accommodations for the night—even if he had insulted her in the process. But before she could say anything, he rested his thumbs on his gun belt and blocked her from following the hotelkeepers.

"We didn't finish our conversation from the campsite, Miss Peyton. I want to know what you're up to here."

Even with only the pale moonlight through the doorway to illuminate the room, Maggie saw the determination on his face, his eyes dark and accusing beneath the brim of his hat.

"I have nothing to say to you," she said, surprised that her anger at him should still simmer, that it could present itself so quickly. "And I'll thank you to get out of my way."

He didn't. Instead, he eased closer.

"Look here, Miss Peyton, I'm not going to allow you to come into my town and cause trouble. You may as well tell me now what you're up to."

Maggie forced her chin a little higher. "I've already told you, Sheriff, I have nothing to say to you."

Spence shifted his weight, drew even closer. "You'd better think that over, because I'm going to stay no more than two feet off your sweet little fanny until I find out what you're up to."

Maggie flushed and drew back.

Spence leaned down. "Get used to it."

He glared at her for a long moment, then spun away and left, closing the door behind him.

A shiver passed through Maggie. Good gracious, the town's lawman was going to watch her every move? As if she were a common criminal? And she'd deliberately provoked him. Refused to cooperate. What had come over her?

"Miss Peyton!"

Mrs. Taylor's screeching voice jarred Maggie back to reality. She hurried through the hotel guided by the faint glow of the lantern, and caught up with the Taylors as they climbed the steps to the second floor. Mr. Taylor dropped her bags in the center of a room at the front of the hotel, and left. Mrs. Taylor lit the lantern on the bureau.

"I can't thank you enough for what you're doing, Mrs. Taylor," Maggie said. "I appreciate—"

"Oh, you can thank me, all right." The warm, welcoming smile she'd worn downstairs in front of Spence disappeared, an ugly sneer taking its place. "You can thank me by finding a way to pay me for this room."

Surprised by the venom in her words, Maggie stammered, "But—but my money was taken by those outlaws, and—and—"

"And I have bills to pay," Mrs. Taylor told her. "How do you expect me make ends meet if I give you a free room?"

"I—"

"Just remember this," Mrs. Taylor said, pointing her finger. "Marlow's having its Founders Day festival soon and folks will be coming to town. I'll not have one of my rooms tied up for a charity case. You'd better come up with some money or else find another place to stay. And quick!"

Mrs. Taylor shut the door behind her, the thud echoing in the silent room.

Stunned, Maggie sank onto the bed. Fatigue washed over her, bringing with it every ache and pain she'd suffered this harrowing day. Her dire circumstances flashed in her mind but she pushed them away, clinging to her one bit of hope.

She could leave tomorrow. Tomorrow. All she had to do was contact the man who now possessed her father's artifact, get it back, and board the first eastbound stage.

Of course, she was hopelessly short on funds, thanks to those outlaws. The few coins she always kept sewn in a tiny pocket in her skirt for emergencies when she traveled wouldn't be nearly enough to pay for her ticket home.

But surely the stagecoach company would take pity on her and grant her free passage. She knew they routinely did that in cases such as hers. After all, they were the reason she was nearly penniless now. And perhaps the minister at the local church might be persuaded to give her sufficient funds so that she could eat on the journey—which she'd reimburse promptly when she reached New York.

A wave of relief washed over Maggie. Yes, she could do this. She could make this journey, retrieve the artifact and return home, all on her own. Once she presented the statue to her father and explained what she'd accomplished, he'd forgive her stupidity at letting the artifact get stolen in the first place. Why, he may actually be proud of her.

Oh, how wonderful the idea seemed. How easy, how simple. Maggie rose from the bed and drifted to the window, the excitement of her accomplishment burning in her stomach. There was nothing now that could stand in her way.

She glanced out the window. Below, across the street, a man stood outside the general store gazing up at her.

Maggie narrowed her eyes, then gasped, fell back and plastered herself against the wall.

It was Sheriff Harding.

He was watching her.

Chapter Five

"Sheriff? Sheriff, are you listening?"

Spence glanced up at Dex Hopkins, one of his two deputies, who stood in front of Spence's desk in the jailhouse.

"Yeah, Dex, I'm listening," he said.

"Uh, okay, then," Dex said, finding his place once more on the ledger he held. "Saturday, nine-fifteen in the morning, Mrs. Frazier came to the office complaining about Mrs. Tidwell's dog digging in her flowers…"

Spence's thoughts drifted away again as his deputy continued reciting the report he'd taken upon himself to write, containing everything that had happened in Marlow during Spence's absence. Young, slim, Dex was a stickler for details—and a trial to Spence's patience at times.

The chair creaked as Spence sat back and glanced around the room. A jailhouse, but his home, too. A familiar comfort washed over him at being here again, seeing the rifle racks and Wanted posters on the walls, the little stove in the corner. Down the hallway were two cells and the room he slept in. The place smelled of gun oil, wood and leather.

He'd been relieved to come to the jailhouse last night and see that the cells were empty, that Dex hadn't arrested half the town in his absence. From the sound of the report he was hearing, only a few arrests had taken place in the weeks he'd been away, and those were for minor offenses.

As Dex droned on, Spence sat forward and sorted through the stack of papers that had collected while he was away. Thank God nothing more serious had happened. It had been difficult enough to leave town in the first place. He wouldn't have gone at all if his ma hadn't been so sick. Spence couldn't bear the thought that something might have happened—somebody had gotten hurt or killed—and he hadn't been here on duty to prevent it.

The door opened and Ian Caldwell, Spence's other deputy, came inside along with a fresh breeze and a slice of morning sunlight. He was a big fellow, dependable, more levelheaded than Dex. It had been Ian who'd ridden out with the rescue party yesterday.

"Morning, Sheriff," Ian greeted him as he strode inside.

"Dang it, Ian," Dex complained. "I'm right in the middle of reading my report and—"

"Shut up, Dex." Ian stopped in front of Spence's desk.

"Looky here now," Dex protested, "the sheriff needs to know what all was going on—"

"Spence can read for himself." Ian plucked the ledger from Dex's hand.

"Just because you got your nose out of joint over Lucy Hubbard—"

"That's enough," Spence told him.

"It's true," Dex insisted. "Ever since her husband got back to town, Ian's been—"

"Enough," Spence repeated.

Dex sulked for a moment. "Fine, then. I'm going out on rounds." He pulled a little tablet and nubby pencil from his shirt pocket, glanced at the clock on the wall, made a note, then threw Ian a contemptuous look and left the jail.

Silence hung in the room as the door slammed shut. Spence saw the familiar hurt in Ian's eye at the mention of Lucy Hubbard's name. Ian was in love with the woman, and Spence suspected she felt the same. But Lucy was married, true to her vows—and to that worthless husband of hers.

Spence didn't think much of Dex throwing the hopeless situation in Ian's face. As deputies went, Dex wasn't everything a sheriff could hope for. But he kept up on the official record of arrests and fines that Spence hated to do, hung the new Wanted posters, and he didn't mind fetching meals for prisoners or cleaning up after them.

"Things were pretty quiet while you were gone," Ian said and dropped the ledger Dex had been reading onto the corner of Spence's desk. "A few drunk cowboys, couple of fistfights, and, of course, Mrs. Frazier complaining about everything under the sun."

Spence snorted, glad the awkward moment had passed. "Sounds like business as usual."

Mrs. Adelphia Frazier was the wife of the town's richest man, Trent Frazier, a rancher with a big spread just west of Marlow. Adelphia didn't live on the ranch, however, she had a house—the town's biggest, of course—where she stayed with her young nephew who'd recently arrived from the East. The arrangement between the Fraziers had seemed odd to Spence, at first, but after his initial run-in with the woman, he understood completely. Apparently, her own husband couldn't get along with her any better than anyone else.

"Hank Townsend over at the dry-goods store thinks somebody's been stealing his merchandise," Ian reported. "I think he's having trouble keeping up on his inventory since his son left town."

"Could be," Spence mused. "Let's keep a closer eye on the store just the same."

"You thought anything about who you want to deputize for the festival?" Ian asked.

Spence rose from his chair. "I've been thinking on it."

"I'm heading out," Ian said and nodded eastward. "Nate Tidwell is riding with me. Jonah down at the livery is loaning me a team to bring the stage back. I already sent the telegram to Keaton, letting them know about the driver."

Spence shifted as a familiar knot drew tight in his gut. If only he'd realized those outlaws were riding in sooner—just a few seconds sooner—maybe no one would have to notify the family about the driver's death.

"Did you get Miss Peyton settled at the hotel last night?" Ian asked.

Spence's stomach jerked again, this time into a different sort of tangle, the kind that welled an odd warmth inside him.

Ian chuckled. "She's a pistol. Must have been a hell of a hike with her yesterday."

Spence's gaze came up quickly, annoyed with the grin on Ian's face, but not sure why.

"Well," Ian said after a moment, "I'm heading out. Be back quick as I can."

After he left, the silence of the jailhouse closed in around Spence. An uneasiness crept over him, the same restlessness that he'd felt weeks ago before he'd left town to visit his family. A craving of some sort, but just what he was craving he didn't know. He'd thought that being home again might help. It hadn't. He'd thought returning to Marlow would smooth things out. It didn't.

Spence sighed heavily. Hell, he didn't know what was wrong.

Opening the ledger containing Dex's report, Spence flipped through the pages. Not much going on in Marlow, which should have pleased him, but didn't for some reason.

The only thing requiring his attention at the moment, it seemed, was lining up temporary deputies to handle the crowds that flocked to Marlow during its Founders Day celebration. Ranchers, miners, settlers from the surrounding area flooded the town for the weeklong festivities. But along with them came con artists, pickpockets and outright criminals. Spence needed extra deputies to keep a lid on things.

He shut the ledger and sighed deeply. Seeing that he wouldn't need those men for a while yet, the biggest threat to the security of Marlow at the moment was one slip of a woman. Maggie Peyton.

She didn't look like much of a danger. She looked like a lady. She looked…pretty.

Last night when he'd finally fallen into his bunk, tired and weary from the long day, Maggie had floated through his mind. If things had gone differently at the stagecoach robbery yesterday she could have wound up shot by those outlaws for her outspokeness. Damn fool woman, he'd told her to keep quiet.

Obviously, she was an Easterner who had no idea of how to conduct herself in Colorado. And her rambling on about a mission to save humanity? A crime she intended to commit?

Spence had a good eye for criminals, for suspicious people, and he couldn't picture Maggie pulling something off. If anything, she was more a threat to herself than anyone else.

Spence sighed and fetched his Stetson from the peg beside the door. Women sometimes ran off halfcocked, did strange things for crazy reasons. Who knew what she might have planned?

Still, Spence couldn't stand idle and let her hurt someone...or herself. The sooner he got to the bottom of this and found out exactly what Maggie was up to, the better.

Spence pulled on his hat and left the jailhouse.

Maggie stepped out of the hotel and got her first look at the town of Marlow in the morning sunlight. It was bigger than it had seemed last night. The main avenue extended into the distance, and two side roads—one at each end of town—led off from it, housing all manner of businesses, most in rough, wooden buildings. Freight wagons, buggies and horses crowded the dirt street.

The people she saw reflected the ruggedness of the land and the town. Grizzly-looking men in stained buckskins, slouch hats, with unkempt beards. Cowboys in Stetsons and spurs. All of them with a pistol strapped to their side.

Yet among them were businessmen in suits. There were women in bonnets and simple dresses, and others dressed much as Maggie was, in stylish gowns with overskirts, bustles and small hats perched atop their heads.

Such diversity. Through her extensive travels with her father she had come to appreciate the differences in people, cultures and places. For a moment, Maggie wished she weren't leaving this place so soon.

But time was of the essence, she reminded herself as he headed off down the boardwalk. She had to reclaim her father's artifact and return it to New York as quickly as possible. The longer she delayed her return, the more likely the theft would be detected, the more likely her father's reputation would be ruined…and the more likely he would be disappointed in her. Again.

She couldn't let anything—or anyone—stop her.

Sheriff Harding sprang into her mind.

A little ball of anger grew in Maggie's stomach as she recalled the gall of that man. First, not divulging that he was, in fact, the sheriff, then insulting her last night, threatening her, and finally keeping watch on her hotel room.

Maggie knew that if she was to succeed in her mission here she must, at all costs, avoid the sheriff.

The townsfolk moved past Maggie on the boardwalk as she continued through town. Some nodded pleasantly, a few men touched their hat brims as they passed; others eyed her suspiciously. Some of the men, the big, burly ones, frightened her. Just because she appreciated diversity in people didn't mean some of them weren't dangerous.

Stopping at the corner of one of the buildings, Maggie pulled a folded piece of paper from her skirt pocket. It was the report prepared by the detective she'd hired to investigate the theft, and on it was the name of the man who'd come to possess the artifact. According to the report, this Mr. Otis Canfield had a business of some sort nearby.

Maggie slid the paper into her pocket once more and gazed around, squinting her eyes against the morning sun. All she had to do was find the place. It couldn't be too difficult in a town this size.

Upon leaving New York on this trek, it had been her plan to simply buy back the statue. Mentally she rehearsed the speech she'd been practicing since she woke this morning. Mr. Canfield was a businessman so certainly he understood money. Unfortunately, thanks to the robbers who'd held up the stage, an outright purchase was no longer possible.

So that left the next logical possibility. She would simply tell the new owner the truth, rely on his decency as a human being to do the right thing and allow her to take the artifact with her, then send him the money after she returned to New York.

A nervous flutter quivered in Maggie's chest at the thought of Mr. Canfield's possible refusal. A vision of the familiar look on her father's face—the one she'd seen all her life—floated through her mind. Disappointment. Her very earliest memory of him.

Maggie drew in a determined breath. She could not—absolutely could not—leave this town without that statue.

No matter what it took.

So far she'd seen no storefront with Mr. Canfield's name on it. She looked up and down the street in both directions, wondering—

She gasped. The sheriff. That awful Sheriff Harding was heading straight toward her.

For a second Maggie stood frozen on the boardwalk, hoping she was wrong. But there was no mistake. Taller than most of the other men, wide shoulders, black hat, perpetual scowl, he walked in her direction, his head moving back and forth as he took in both sides of the street.

Maggie ducked into the alley and pressed herself into the shadow of the large building beside her. Her heart raced. Was he coming after her, asking more questions, making more demands? Had he even seen her?

No, she didn't think so. After all, the boardwalk was crowded and she'd been standing there for only a few minutes. He couldn't have seen her.

She tried to shrink herself to her smallest size as she kept her gaze trained on the boardwalk. Any second now the sheriff would walk past, and when he did, she'd head in the opposite direction, avoiding him completely. A perfect plan.

Seconds ticked by. Maggie stood still, scarcely breathing, concentrating on the boardwalk, waiting. Any moment now…any moment…any time now Sheriff Harding would walk past and then she'd—

"Miss Peyton?"

Maggie shrieked and whirled around. Spence Harding towered over her, frowning.

She clamped her hand over her racing heart. He'd sneaked up on her! Circled the building in a surprise attack! Was there no decency in this man whatsoever?

"You scared me half to death," she told him, bracing her arm against the side of the building to steady herself. "What's the matter with you? Sneaking up on unsuspecting women? What on earth are you doing here?"

Spence shifted his weight, crowding her against the building. "I'd like to ask you the same thing, Miss Peyton."

She was hiding from him, but she certainly wasn't going to admit it. Maggie drew in a few deep breaths, calming herself.

She pushed her chin up and tried to muster an indignant look. "What I may or may not be doing here, Sheriff Harding, is none of your business."

He hung his thumbs on his gun belt. "You damn well better know it's my business when you're sneaking around the alley outside the bank."

"The—what?" Maggie followed his thumb as he jerked it toward the side of the building and saw First Union Bank painted there in big black letters. She gulped. "This—this is the—the bank?"

"Don't play dumb with me, Miss Peyton."

Maggie cringed. Of all the alleys she could have ducked into, all the buildings she could have stood beside, why did she have to stumble upon this one? The *bank* of all places? Embarrassment heated her cheeks.

"You're only making this harder on yourself," Spence said. "You'd best go ahead and tell me what you're up to, get it over with."

A stab of guilty conscience pierced Maggie's thoughts, bringing with it the temptation to tell

Spence the truth. Perhaps he could help her retrieve the artifact. After all, it had been stolen. Her father was the rightful owner.

But she had no proof of her claim. Nothing to bolster her assertions, just her own word. And there was no reason to think Spence would believe her. After all, she was an outsider and Mr. Canfield was quite likely a respected businessman here in Marlow. Plus, if she told Spence the truth and he didn't believe her, did nothing to help her retrieve the artifact, he'd be onto her. He'd know exactly what she was up to, why she was there.

And it wouldn't take him long to figure out what she might be forced to do next.

Maggie disregarded the idea and replaced it with outrage.

"I am not *up* to anything," she informed him. "Since when is it against the law for a woman to walk through an alley?"

"It may not be against the law, Miss Peyton, but it's not very smart." His gaze swept her from head to toe, then landed on her face again.

Heat sprang from him, arced to her, covering her with its intense warmth. Her stomach coiled and she flushed from the inside out.

A thousand thoughts jetted through her mind. Her pink dress, freshly ironed, one he hadn't already seen her in. The morning's hot bath, despite Mrs. Taylor's complaint about the cost. Knees trembling for no apparent reason. Bodice suddenly a fraction too snug.

A moment dragged by and Maggie could think of nothing to say—not a sentence, not one word. All she could do was stare up at Spence.

He'd bathed, too. The smell of cotton and soap

wafted from him. A heady scent, somehow masculine. His jaw was clean shaven, smooth.

Touch it.

The idea raced through Maggie's head. Touch his cheek. What did it feel like? And the black hair curling from the opening at the top of his shirt. Was it coarse? Soft? Was there more of it? Was his chest covered with it? His—

Maggie broke eye contact with Spence and averted her gaze. Good gracious, what was she thinking? What was wrong with her? Spinning fantasies. A woman like herself concocting wild notions about a man like Spence.

Ridiculous.

She forced her mind back to the situation at hand. "I can assure you, Sheriff Harding, that I have no intention of robbing the bank."

"I'm glad to hear that."

"So would you please just leave me alone?" she asked.

Spence shook his head. "You're up to something and I intend to find out what it is."

Maggie huffed impatiently. "Surely you have more serious criminal activity that requires your attention."

"Nope. Just you."

She certainly hadn't wanted to hear that. She tried another tack. "You're wasting your time."

"We'll see about that."

Maggie fumed silently. Obviously, this conversation was doing her little good. Better to move on.

"Good day, Sheriff." She didn't wait for a response, just pivoted and headed down the boardwalk, desperate to keep her chin up, her back straight, and her knees from shaking, yet sure she felt Spence's gaze burning into her back.

He'd made good on his threat to keep an eye on her. Now, more than ever, she had to make Mr. Canfield give her that statue. With the sheriff breathing down her neck, watching her every move, the only alternative left to her would be nearly impossible.

Maggie continued down Main Street, pretending to window-shop. At the dress store she glanced back. Spence stood at the corner of the bank, watching. When she got to Townsend Dry Goods, Spence was across the street, gazing her way.

For a moment, Maggie glared at him. He stared right back. Then, thankfully, a man approached Spence, drawing him into conversation.

Maggie darted onto the side street. East Street, according to the crude wooden sign at the corner. Buildings housing shops and stores lined both sides of the street. A bathhouse, another general store, a—

She stopped still on the boardwalk as the name *Canfield* leapt out at her from a sign above one of the shops. This was it. This had to be it.

Maggie glanced back toward Main Street. Seconds ticked by. No sign of Spence. She breathed a sigh of relief. She'd lost him.

Hiking up her dress, she darted across the street between a freight wagon and three men on horseback, and stepped up on the boardwalk in front of the building bearing the sign Professor Canfield's Oddities of the World Museum.

The man was a professor? Maggie hadn't known this. Odd that the investigator hadn't mentioned it in his report. A new thread of hope wove through her.

Professor Canfield was a man of science, obviously, so surely he would be sympathetic to her plight. He, of all people, would understand the need to return the artifact to its rightful owner. Her hopes soared. Yes, she could be on the stage eastward perhaps as early as this afternoon.

Maggie grasped the brass doorknob and pushed, but it didn't open. She threw her weight against it and shook hard, but still the door remained closed tight.

Moving to the display window beside the room, Maggie cupped her hands and peered inside. No sign of life, just an eclectic collection of exhibits. She pressed her face closer to the glass, scanning the room.

The artifact. There it sat on a shelf at the back of the shop. Only a foot tall, the statue had been chiseled with distinctive outstretched arms and a loving smile.

Maggie tried the doorknob again.

"He ain't here."

She turned toward the voice and saw a man wearing a shopkeeper's white apron, holding a broom, standing on the boardwalk in front of Norman's General Store.

"The professor," the man said. "He's gone."

"Gone?" Panic rippled through Maggie. "Do you mean, sir, that he's merely away for a few moments? Or is he—"

"Gone. He's gone. Plain and simple."

Maggie gulped. "Gone where?"

He pointed vaguely with the broom handle. "Off on one of those expeditions, he calls them, gathering up stuff for this museum of his."

A knot jerked in Maggie's stomach. "He is coming back, isn't he?"

"Oh, sure. He'll be back in time for the Founders Day festival. Nobody wants to miss that."

"When is it?"

"In a few weeks."

"A few weeks?"

"Yep," the man said, and started sweeping the walk in front of his store again.

Maggie's head spun. A few weeks? She couldn't wait weeks for Professor Canfield to return. She had to reclaim the artifact now, get it back to her father before anyone realized it was missing. She couldn't stay *here* for weeks.

As she clenched her fists, an unexpected wave of calm overtook Maggie. There was only one solution to this situation. She'd known it since those robbers ran off with her money.

She'd have to take the statue by force. She'd have to steal it.

Chapter Six

Was it easier to commit robbery on a full stomach?

Maggie thought surely it must be, as she slipped quietly out the rear of the hotel into the alley under the cover of darkness, her stomach rumbling.

Under Mrs. Taylor's constant glower, Maggie hadn't dared ask for anything to eat at the hotel today. For breakfast, she'd eaten the food she'd brought with her from the stage, then purchased two apples at Norman's General Store and a biscuit and chicken leg from the Pink Blossom Café. With less than a dollar to her name, Maggie hadn't dared splurge on a full meal.

She paused at the corner of the hotel, letting her eyes adjust to the darkness, then headed east through the alley following the route she'd planned this afternoon.

She'd chosen this way to Professor Canfield's Oddities of the World Museum so as not to advertise her presence on the streets in the middle of the night. If stopped, how would she explain herself, much less the fireplace poker and empty flour sack she'd borrowed from the hotel kitchen and now carried? Maggie hoped her growling stomach wouldn't give her away.

At the rear corner of a building, Maggie glanced toward Main Street. Well after midnight, no one was out. Decent people were home in bed. Faint on the breeze, she heard a piano and guessed the sound drifted from the saloons on the west end of town. She'd seen them—and everything else in Marlow— as she'd walked the streets most of the day.

Maggie darted across the alley and skirted the rear of another dark, sleeping building.

After her initial visit to the museum this morning, she'd returned to Professor Canfield's and gone around to the rear of the shop; she was becoming more familiar with Marlow's alleys than the main thoroughfares. She'd spotted the back entrance to the museum, assessed its strength and plotted her crime.

The night air seemed colder as Maggie continued eastward, and she wished she'd brought a wrap. But perhaps it was the memory of yesterday's stagecoach robbery, which suddenly presented itself that chilled her.

Did her intended action this evening put her on the same level as those thieves? They looked like hardened criminals and she certainly wasn't that. Circumstances had pushed her to this moment, this robbery. She remembered the young boy, Henry, who'd been part of the gang, and wondered if he, too, hadn't turned to crime because of circumstances. Their encounter had made for an interesting entry in her journal.

Maggie reached the rear of the buildings that faced East Street and slipped silently between two of them. At the front corner, she spotted Professor Canfield's museum across the street. Dark. Not a sign of life in the building, or in the shops situated on either side.

She'd have to cross the street to reach the museum, expose herself in the open. There was no way around it.

She glanced up and down East Street and saw dim light shining in a window on the second floor of one of the shops down the block; all the others were dark.

Her greatest fear was that someone might see her. But would they recognize her? Almost no one in town knew who she was. She had to chance it. Drawing in a breath and checking the street one final time, Maggie crossed to the museum and slipped into the shadows at the corner of the building.

Quickly, she whirled around, her gaze darting back and forth. No shadows on the lighted window. She began to breathe again, not realized she'd held her breath.

Footsteps silent in the dirt, Maggie hurried to the rear of the museum and peered into the alley. As with most of the businesses she'd seen here in Marlow, a privy, outbuildings and barns, and a small corral sat a few yards in the distance. Maggie smiled. Lots of shadows to help cover her movements, even with the cloudless sky and golden moonlight.

Awkwardly, she wedged the poker between the museum's back door and the frame, and pushed hard. Wood splintered, sounding like thunder in the silent night. She dropped the poker. The door popped open. A sick knot jerked Maggie's stomach tight and her mouth went dry. She wasn't meant for a life of crime.

She stood still, listening, waiting for the sound of shouts, running feet. Her heart pounded in her ears. Long moments dragged by.

No one came. In fact, no one seemed to have noticed the noise or her presence. Maggie drew in a breath and swung the door open. Still, she couldn't make herself go inside.

Oh, Papa.

What would he think if he saw her now? Would he be pleased that she'd gone to such lengths to get his prized artifact back, save his reputation, right the wrong that she'd created with her own stupidity? Would he admire her ingenuity, her gumption, her determination? Would he tell her that, finally, she'd done something right?

The idea filled Maggie's mind and she reveled in the fantasy. To know that she'd succeeded, that she'd pleased her father was worth the risk.

Moonlight flowed through the open doorway illuminating Maggie's way as she crept inside. On her visits to the shop earlier today, she'd peered through the front window and seen exactly where the statue sat on the shelf. But she'd had no way of knowing what lay in this, the rear portion of the shop, closed off from view by a curtained doorway.

She hurried though what appeared to be Professor Canfield's living quarters, suddenly desperate to grab the artifact and leave. Perspiration dampened her palms. Her heart thumped in her chest.

How did those outlaws do it? How did young Henry manage to pull off one crime after another? Maggie's stomach ached and now she was glad she hadn't eaten.

Pushing back the curtains, Maggie stepped into the museum. Scant moonlight filtered through the front window, casting the room in near darkness. The odd mix of exhibits rose around her, casting grotesque shadows.

She threaded her way through to the shelf in the back and looked up at her father's artifact. A chill ran up her spine, as it always did when she gazed upon the statue.

Thousands of years old, mined from an ancient quarry. Only a foot tall, the statue was short, squat, with an oversize belly and feet. Its face was a primitive carving, large eyes and a gentle smile, a loving expression that belied the dangerous powers the artifact possessed. Its thick, outstretched arms urged all who gazed upon it to come closer, a mystic, deceptive lure, almost impossible to ignore.

Who had fallen prey to the artifact, Maggie wondered, since it had been out of her father's care? How many lives had it touched, changed, permanently altered? She doubted if even Professor Canfield, a man of science, knew the power the statue possessed.

Maggie slipped the empty flour sack over the artifact, careful not to touch it. Even though the cloth, the stone was warm, its curves worn smooth from centuries of caresses. She peeked into the sack. The statue seemed to glow in the faint light.

More anxious than ever to be out of this place and done with this misdeed, Maggie hurried to the back entrance of the museum. She paused, listening for murmured voices out back, but heard nothing. She stepped outside, snatched up the fireplace poker—the final evidence of her crime—and pushed the door closed. Eventually—tomorrow, perhaps—someone would notice the damaged door and guess there'd been a break-in. Maggie intended to be long gone before that happened.

A rush of exhilaration surged through her. She'd done it. She'd pulled it off. She'd retrieved her father's artifact, and tomorrow—thank God—she could leave this town.

Thoughts sped through Maggie's mind as she hurried away. Pack her belongings. Hide the artifact in her carpetbag. Present herself at the stage depot at first light. Beg, if necessary, for a ticket east. Prevail upon the church minister for a small loan. Make sure she—

A man leaped from the corner of the building. Huge, black-clad, he towered over her, blocked her path. Maggie froze. He reached for her.

A scream gurgled in her throat as she whirled and ran. Footsteps pounded the ground behind her. A hand grabbed her elbow and pulled her around. She swung the poker at him.

He ducked, tore the poker from her hand and heaved it away.

"What the hell are you doing?" he demanded.

Maggie gasped. That voice. She knew that voice. She squinted up at him.

The sheriff. That horrid Spence Harding. He'd caught her red-handed. And she'd tried to bean him with a fireplace poker!

She jerked her arm from his grasp and ran. She had to get away. She couldn't be discovered—not by the sheriff.

He caught her in three strides, latched on to her arm and yanked her to a stop.

"Settle down!" he roared.

Maggie leaned back, keeping herself as far away from him as she could with him still holding her wrist. Her mind spun. What could she tell him? How could she explain being here? Good gracious, the evidence of her crime was in her hand. She eased the flour sack behind her.

"What the hell are you doing out at this time of night?" Spence demanded. Concern tinged his words. "A back alley is no place for a lady. What were you thinking?"

"I—I—"

He peered around her. "What have you got in that sack?"

"Nothing." The words came out in a tiny squeak. Maggie cringed. She sounded guilty, even to herself.

He looked hard at her, and slowly the concern disappeared from his face, replaced by suspicion. Spence's gaze swept the area, landed on the museum's broken door and frame, then jumped to the fireplace poker lying on the ground, shining in the moonlight like a lighthouse beacon.

His gaze impaled her. A wave of guilt crashed over Maggie. Her knees weakened. He *knew*.

"Give me that sack." He didn't wait for her to hand it over. His fingers still locked tightly around her wrist, Spence reached for the sack.

Maggie backed away. "It's—it's nothing you need to concern yourself with."

"Hand it over."

"No," Maggie insisted, "it's—"

She backed into the side of the museum. Spence bumped into her. His chest met her breasts. His gun-belt buckle pressed against her belly. His legs brushed her thighs.

Maggie gasped. Heat—a strange heat she'd never felt before—rolled off Spence, covering her. His breath fanned her cheek. She gazed up at him, unable to move, unable to speak. He was tall and strong and sturdy. She'd never felt so weak and frail in her life, as if his nearness had somehow robbed her of strength, willpower and thought.

"You're—you're hurting my wrist," she finally said, yet managing nothing more than a whisper.

Spence dropped her arm so quickly it startled her. He stepped back, yet didn't release her from his gaze.

Cool wind swirled between them, bringing Maggie back to her senses. Somewhat.

"These…these are my belongings," she said, still keeping the sack behind her.

"Let me see."

She tried to look indignant. "They're personal."

Spence shook his head. "I don't know why you bother to lie, Miss Peyton, it's a waste of effort."

He reached around her for the sack. Maggie scooted sideways, but he was too fast. Spence grabbed the sack.

Maggie held on tight. "No!" she shouted, and tugged it toward her.

He yanked it the other way.

"No! You mustn't—" She pulled it again.

With a final heave, Spence jerked the sack from her hand. It flipped over and the statue tumbled to the ground.

Horrified, Maggie stared down at it. "Oh, no…"

"What the hell…?" Spence knelt.

"No!" Maggie dropped to her knees. "No! Don't touch it!"

Spence reached for the statue. "What is it?"

"You mustn't touch it!" Maggie batted his hands away and grasped the artifact.

Spence uttered an irritated grunt and grabbed one of the statue's arms.

"No!" Maggie stared in horror at her hands clutching one arm of the artifact, Spence's hands on the other. "I told you not to touch it! I told you not to!"

"What the hell is wrong with you?"

"This statue is an ancient love goddess. We've both touched it," Maggie said. "Don't you see? Now we'll have to get *married*."

Chapter Seven

"Married…?" Spence let go his end of the statue and rocked back on his heels. "What are you talking about?"

The artifact seemed to suddenly weigh a ton. Maggie let it drop to the ground. "This is an ancient South American artifact. A love goddess. It has special powers. Everyone who touches it falls in love."

Spence rose slowly. He eyed Maggie warily, looked at the artifact, then at Maggie again. He swiped his palms down the front of his shirt.

"It's true," Maggie insisted, getting to her feet. "My father discovered it on our last trip to South America. According to tribal lore—"

Spence waved his hands, silencing her. "What has any of this got to do with you being back here?"

"I'm retrieving the artifact," she told him, as if it should be obvious.

"Retrieving?" Spence glanced at the broken door on the museum. "Maybe where you come from, Miss Peyton, that's called 'retrieving.' But around here, we call it stealing."

"I was merely reclaiming what belongs to my father," Maggie insisted.

Spence pointed at the artifact. "Pick that thing up. Put it in the sack."

Maggie knelt and put the love goddess into the sack. "If you'll just let me explain—"

"You can do all the explaining you want," Spence told her. "Down at the jailhouse."

How humiliating.

Maggie managed to keep her chin up as Spence escorted her though the streets of Marlow to the jailhouse. Of course, he paraded her down Main Street. He didn't even have the decency to take the back way. It was a small consolation that no one was out at this time of night. Still, there could have been. And how would that have looked?

Spence's hand cupped her elbow. Warmth radiated up and down her arm. The same sort of warmth that had overpowered her when he'd fallen against her outside the museum. His presence at her side was disconcerting.

But only because he was taking her to jail.

For an instant, Maggie considered making a break for it. But where could she go? Nowhere that Spence couldn't find her. Besides, he had the love goddess tucked under his arm. She couldn't leave without it.

Inside the jailhouse, Spence sat her in one of the chairs in front of the desk, then lit the lanterns. Maggie gazed around. Rifles. Wanted posters. A stove with a coffeepot. Just enough clutter to make the room look homey. This was a jail, but somehow, there was a warmth here missing from her hotel

room. Once again, she wished her father could
see this.

Spence hung his hat on a peg by the door, then
placed the statue of the love goddess—still in the
flour sack—on a high shelf between the rifle racks.

"Do you live here?" Maggie asked, gazing around
the room. "In the jail, I mean."

"I've got a room in the back," Spence said, and
dropped into the chair behind his desk.

"Is there a kitchen?"

His brows pulled together. "No."

Maggie forced a little smile. "I've never been in
a jail before," she explained.

"And I don't get too many criminals in here wearing little hats with flowers on them," Spence answered.

"That's because I'm not a criminal," Maggie said.
She pushed her chin higher. "Actually, I'm on a hu-
manitarian mission."

Spence raised an eyebrow, then sat back in his
chair.

"Where did you get that fireplace poker?" he
asked, gesturing to the spot where he'd leaned it
against the door.

"From the hotel," Maggie said, then realized how
the admission made her look guilty. "I borrowed it."

"Like you 'borrowed' that statue?"

"The artifact belongs to my father. It was stolen.
I came here to get it back."

"Stolen? By Professor Canfield?"

"No," Maggie said. "It was stolen in New York.
I hired a private detective agency to trace it, and they
located it here in Marlow. It had been sold to Professor Canfield."

"So why didn't you have this private detective come after it?"

Maggie pressed her lips together. She wasn't about to tell Spence about her blunder, which caused the artifact to be stolen, nor would she confess the low opinion her father would have of her if he learned what she'd done.

"The artifact has mystical powers," Maggie explained. "I couldn't leave it in the hands of just anyone."

Spence uttered a skeptical grunt. "Mystical powers?"

"Oh, yes," Maggie said. "As I told you, my father discovered the love goddess on our last trip to South America. It was quite a find. As tribal lore goes, any man and woman who touch it will fall in love. People come from miles around to see it, touch it, revel in its special powers—and have for centuries."

"You're trying to tell me that a hunk of stone can make people fall in love with each other?"

"You touched the statue yourself. It's not ordinary stone. It's different."

Spence waved his hand, dismissing her words. "This is the biggest load of horse—that is, Miss Peyton, I find your story a little hard to believe."

"But it's true."

"I'll tell you what's true, Miss Peyton." Spence leaned forward. "First off, you stole a fireplace poker from the hotel—"

"I borrowed it."

"You broke into Professor Canfield's museum."

"I had no choice. He's out of town," Maggie said.

"And you attempted to assault a peace officer with a poker."

"It was dark. I didn't know it was you."

He touched his vest. "I was wearing my badge."

Maggie glared at him, refusing to respond.

"Have you got anything that proves that statue belongs to your father?" Spence asked.

"Well...no," Maggie admitted. "It's an ancient artifact discovered in a remote South American village. It doesn't have a bill of sale."

Spence sat back in his chair and gestured toward the statue. "What's something like that worth?"

"It would be hard to put a value on it," Maggie said. "It's thousands of years old. Practically priceless—"

She stopped, realizing that he'd just talked her into divulging another reason why she might be stealing the love goddess.

"This is ridiculous," Maggie declared. "My father is a renowned university professor. I'm from a well-respected family."

"Then you should know better than to steal." Spence opened one of the desk drawers, pulled out a ledger and flipped it open.

Fear rippled through Maggie. Good gracious, was he making an official report on her? Giving her a criminal record?

She scooted forward to the edge of her chair. "What—what are you doing?"

Spence tapped the page. "This is where I keep a list of all the fines, arrests and jail time."

"A fine? But you know I don't have any money."

"I guess that just leaves jail time."

Maggie gasped and fell back in her chair, feeling

slightly light-headed as Spence's hard gaze impaled her from across the desk.

How could her simple mission to recover her father's artifact have gone so horribly wrong? How could she have gotten herself into an even worse situation?

Maggie gulped back the lump that rose in her throat. Because she never should have attempted this trip in the first place, that's why. She should have known she couldn't handle it. She shouldn't even have tried.

"You're serious?" she asked, her voice just above a whisper. "You'll put me in jail?"

Spence's expression softened a fraction. "No. I'm not going to put you in jail. *This time.*"

"So I can leave?"

"You can leave."

"And I can take the artifact with me?"

"Hell no."

"But—"

"Listen, Miss Peyton, I can't give you that statue without Professor Canfield's say-so. You'll have to wait until he gets back to settle ownership."

"But—"

"Or you can leave town without it."

"Leave?" Maggie sprang to her feet. "I can't possibly leave without it."

Spence rose from his chair. "That's your choice. In the meantime, that statue is staying right here."

Maggie's immediate thought was that the sheriff was being pigheaded and obstinate, but decided it would do her no good to point that out. She'd have to abide by his decision. For now.

She gestured to the statue. "You must be careful with it."

"I'm not expecting a big rush of people in here to look at the thing."

"You must make sure no one touches it," Maggie said. "Who knows how many lives have been affected by it already?"

"Besides yours and mine?" Spence asked, as he moved around the desk and stood next to her.

He was so big. His nearness overwhelmed her, intimidated her.

Called to her.

Maggie didn't back away.

"The lore of the love goddess is true," she said. "Whether you believe it or not, she can change lives."

"Yeah? Well, so far, all that block of stone has done is get *you* into trouble with the law, and *me* nearly killed with a fireplace poker." Spence moved around her and plucked his hat from the peg beside the door. "I'll walk you back to your hotel."

Maggie was anxious to get out of the jail, and even more anxious to be out of the company of Sheriff Harding.

"I'll walk myself to the hotel," she told him.

Spence settled his hat on his head. "I'll walk you. Just to be sure nothing in any of the shops catches your eye along the way."

Heat flushed her cheeks. She turned away from him and reached for the fireplace poker. Spence stepped in front of her.

"I'll carry this," he said and picked it up.

The night air was chilly as Maggie stepped out onto the boardwalk, Spence beside her. He didn't grasp her elbow this time, yet walked close enough that she could once again feel the heat that surrounded him.

Neither of them spoke as they walked to the rear entrance of the hotel. Spence opened the door she'd left unlocked. She expected him to turn and leave, but instead he followed her into the kitchen.

The room was dark. It smelled faintly of tonight's dinner. The silence, the late hour, Spence's presence brought an intimacy that Maggie couldn't ignore.

The moment outside the museum when their bodies had come together sprang into Maggie's mind. Was Spence thinking of it, too, she wondered? Had he felt that jolt of energy, that sudden heat?

A man like Spence Harding probably felt those things all the time, Maggie realized. But with other women. Not someone like her.

"I don't want you walking the streets late at night again," Spence said, his voice low.

"I don't have a reason to anymore, now do I?" Maggie said, and turned away.

He touched her arm, stilling her. "That's not what I mean."

The concern in his voice turned her around.

"The streets are no place for a lady like you. It's dangerous. Some drunk cowboy could come along and—" Spence eased closer. "Promise me, Maggie. Promise me you won't do such a foolish thing again."

"I promise," she whispered, the words slipping out before she realized she'd even thought them.

Spence gave her arm a little squeeze, then presented her with the poker. "Put this back where you found it."

He stepped outside. "Be sure to lock up," he said, and closed the door.

Maggie stood there for a moment, listening to the heavy thud of his boots as he walked away. Her head spun slightly. Spence seemed to take all the warmth, all the air out of a room.

She turned the key in the lock, left the poker by the hearth, and went upstairs, a strange ache in her stomach. Hunger, surely.

In her room, Maggie lit the lantern on the bureau. She eyed the window for a moment, then, unable to stop herself, she crossed to it.

Below, on the street in front of the general store stood Spence gazing up at her.

A love goddess?

Spence stared at the statue on the shelf between the rifle racks, the flour sack puddled around its big feet, its arms stretching toward him.

Ancient lore? Mystic powers? He'd never heard such nonsense in his life.

He turned away from the statue with the intention of blowing out the lanterns and going to bed. After leaving Maggie at her hotel a short while ago, he'd taken a turn around town, rattled doorknobs, checked alleys, then walked past the saloons one final time. He'd returned past the hotel and seen that Maggie's room was dark. Now, in the jailhouse again, the familiar restlessness claimed him, and he couldn't bring himself to go to bed quite yet.

He supposed it was the crazy story Maggie had told him about the supposed artifact. Hard to believe. Yet she seemed convinced it was fact. Would she have traveled all this way to retrieve the thing if it weren't true? If the statue didn't actually have special powers?

Spence knew Indian ways, knew some of their beliefs included strange things that other people didn't understand. And he'd seen a few things in his life that couldn't easily be explained.

But a hunk of stone that caused people to fall in love? Hell, no.

And him falling in love with Maggie Peyton?

Well…

Spence paced to the stove in the corner, pulling on his chin. He felt something for the woman. He could admit that. But it wasn't love.

Concern. Yes, concern. He turned and retraced his steps to the opposite side of the room. Maggie didn't have any business being here in Colorado, so far from everything she knew and understood. The woman was a danger to herself. So, yes, he felt concern.

Was that all?

A little nagging voice buzzed in Spence's head, stopping him in his tracks. There was something besides concern.

Lust?

Spence shifted as a familiar craving stirred. Lust was a possibility. After all, Maggie *had* stuck her hand in his pocket and found something more than the knife she was fishing for. And it had been a while since he'd known the pleasures of a woman. He'd spent the last three weeks visiting his family in Texas and he'd had little time or opportunity to see to life's necessities.

Spence grumbled aloud. He and Maggie? Together? She was the very last woman he could ever picture himself keeping company with, let alone marrying.

Still, there was something about her....

A familiar ache settled around Spence's heart.

There'd been something about Ellen, too.

Now Ellen was dead.

Spence grabbed his hat. He'd never sleep now. He headed out the door.

Chapter Eight

Stranded.

Maggie lay in bed staring up at the ceiling as the first rays of the morning sun filtered around the edges of her window shade. She'd been awake for some time now, her situation robbing her of sleep.

Stranded. She was stranded in this little town. Alone, thousands of miles from home, from all that was familiar. Nearly penniless, unsure of where her next meal would come from, or how much longer Mrs. Taylor would allow her to occupy this hotel room.

Last night and the jail sentence she'd momentarily faced flashed in Maggie's mind. Frightening as it had seemed at the time, at least in jail her lodging would be paid for and she'd have gotten three meals a day.

Maggie pushed the coverlet away and sat up. Her long brown hair fell over her shoulders and she pushed it away; she'd been too tired to braid it last night.

She crossed the room to the window and pulled back the corner of the shade. Just past dawn, no one was on the street yet. The spot in front of the general store that Spence had occupied so often was empty. A knot of disappointment settled in Maggie's stomach, then she chided herself for it.

Had she really expected to find Spence standing on the boardwalk across the street, staring up at her room? Had she really hoped for it?

She turned away and drew in a breath. How silly of her to have such thoughts. Especially now, when she had an important decision to make.

Stay and recover her father's artifact? Or return home empty-handed?

Maggie sank onto the end of the bed and contemplated her two choices. Returning home would solve all of her immediate problems. She'd be with people who loved and cared about her, people who didn't think she was a common thief. She'd have the familiarity of her life once more.

She'd also have her father's disappointment. Forever.

Maggie visualized returning home, seeing her father, telling him about the theft. Telling him how it was all her fault. She'd have to confess that she'd lied to him, that she'd never been in Philadelphia visiting friends at all, that she'd been in Colorado— of all places—attempting to recover the love goddess.

Attempting. Attempting and failing.

Her father was a goodhearted man. He'd forgive her. That had never been in question.

But the matter wouldn't end there. Friends, fellow professors, colleagues—everyone—would find out, eventually, how she'd made such a stupid mistake to begin with, then how she'd bungled the recovery plan. With the best of intentions, everyone would tell

Maggie how she shouldn't have tried such an out-rageous thing. They'd ask why she'd even attempted it. She wasn't up to it. Didn't she know better?

Without a doubt, Maggie knew she'd never hear the end of this. Ever. It would haunt her for the rest of her life.

Maggie drew in a long breath. Maybe she deserved to hear those things. After all, they were true.

Yet, somehow, Maggie couldn't let that happen. Not now, not after all she'd been through already. She had to try—at least once more—to accomplish what she'd set out to do.

Rising from the bed, Maggie pressed her fingers to her lips. She didn't relish the idea of living here in Marlow for several weeks until Professor Canfield decided to return. So perhaps she could locate him. If she could contact him, surely he'd return so they could settle this dispute. He was a man of science. He'd understand the significance and importance of returning the artifact to its rightful owner.

Maggie spirits lifted. Someone in town knew Professor Canfield, knew his plans, knew where he'd gone. She'd just have to find that person.

Of course, even if she ascertained the professor's whereabouts immediately, it might be a while before he could make the return journey to Marlow. In the meantime, she'd have to provide for herself some-how.

Maggie dashed to the rocker in the corner and picked up her corset she'd tossed aside last night, the day ahead suddenly filling her mind. She'd find a job. That way she could pay for her food and lodging until Professor Canfield returned.

Excitement swept through Maggie. Her problem

was solved. All she had to do was find a job. She could accomplish that by noon and then she could—

Her feet stilled as her enthusiasm ebbed. What if that awful Sheriff Harding intended to tell everyone how she'd been caught breaking into the Oddities of the World Museum? Even if she explained it to a potential employer, it would look bad for her. Why, they might not believe her, after hearing the sheriff's side of the story.

With a sigh, Maggie sank onto the bed again. She had to find out what Spence's intentions were. She had to go talk to him.

Back to the alleys, Maggie thought, as she crept out the rear of the hotel. She'd dressed hurriedly and rushed downstairs, trying to get to the sheriff's office before the citizens of Marlow came awake and filled the streets. She'd decided it best to take the alley and slip through the back entrance of the jailhouse. She didn't want to be seen going inside via the front door. That would do her reputation no good, whether or not Spence had already told anyone that he considered her a thief.

At the rear of the jail, Maggie paused. No sound from inside. She turned the knob and the door opened. She hadn't expected it to be locked. Surely, no one broke *into* a jail.

Closing the door behind her, Maggie found herself in a darkened hallway. Straight ahead was the deserted office. She glimpsed the desk she'd sat in front of last night. On her right were two jail cells—empty, thankfully. On the left was a single doorway. It had to be Spence's room.

She listened, her ears straining for any sound. Nothing.

Darn, she'd thought sure she'd find Spence here. She hadn't imagined he'd be out on rounds—or whatever it was a sheriff did all day—at this early hour. She couldn't guess where he'd be unless—

A little mewl slipped through Maggie's lips. She slapped her hand over her mouth.

What if Spence was in bed?

Maggie's heart rate picked up slightly. Suppose, at this very moment, only steps away, he lay sleeping. *In bed.*

Did he wear a nightshirt? The thought flew into her head. Her father wore one. All men did. Didn't they?

The image blossomed in her mind. Spence sleeping, tangled in a blanket. Long legs, big arms. Wide chest. Nowhere in that vision could she picture a nightshirt. More likely, he slept in…nothing.

Nothing? Maggie fanned her warm cheeks with her open hand. How could she have thought such a thing? A woman—a lady—with her upbringing?

There would certainly be no mention of *this* in her journal.

Maggie drew in a breath and realized she still hadn't heard a sound from anywhere in the jail. Disappointment calmed her runaway heart. Spence wasn't here. Now she'd have to hunt him down, approach him on the street or in one of the shops, draw attention to herself. Certainly not what she wanted to do.

But just to make sure, Maggie crept down the hallway and peered into Spence's bedroom. A bunk stood in one corner, the covers knotted, a pillow lay halfway on the floor. There was a washstand with a wadded towel, a straight razor and shaving cup on it. A hairbrush, coins and a scrap of crumpled paper rested on the bureau. Shirts and a vest dangled from a row of pegs on the wall.

A man's room. Maggie stepped inside, drawn there by some irresistible force that called to her, urged her on. The window stood opened, allowing the faint breeze inside. Somehow, though, the room still smelled like Spence. The scent, his belongings, the very notion of where she was touched something in Maggie. A yearning. A yearning she'd never experienced and didn't really understand.

She did understand, however, that nowhere in the room were Spence's boots and gun belt. Sure proof that, already, he was up and gone.

Maggie left the room, forcefully pushing aside the odd feelings, and went into the jail's office. If Spence wasn't here and she couldn't speak with him, at least she could check the ledger he kept in his desk drawer and see if, in fact, he'd entered her name and her alleged crime into the official records of the town of Marlow.

Maggie glanced out the front windows. Still no one on the streets. She knelt behind the desk. Unsure of which drawer she'd seen him take the ledger from last night, Maggie opened the bottom one on the right. Papers. She scrounged through them. No ledger.

Opening the next drawer, she saw three ledgers stacked atop each other. Which one had Spence used last night? She lifted all three from the drawer and spread them on the desk. She'd have to check them all and see which of them—

Footsteps.

Maggie perked up, her senses on alert. Footsteps. She heard footsteps in the hallway, coming closer.

She cringed. If Spence was returning, he'd catch her red-handed going through his desk. Goodness knows what sort of crime he would drum up and accuse her of then. She couldn't let him find her here.

Her gaze darted to the door. No time to make an escape. Maggie pushed the drawer closed, grabbed the ledgers and dived headfirst into the desk's knee-hole. She inched forward on her hands and knees until her head bumped the desk. Her hat slid sideways. She squeezed her legs closer to her arms, making herself as small as possible, hoping nothing was sticking out. Silently she prayed that Spence—or whoever it was—intended to simply pass through the jail and out the front door, not come to the desk. Could she be that lucky?

"Miss Peyton?"

Spence's voice. Maggie cringed. Footsteps—*his* footsteps—crossed the room and circled to the back of the desk.

"You want to come on out of there, Miss Peyton?"

How embarrassing. Maggie felt her face flush. Here she was on her hands and knees, her behind up in the air sticking out from under the desk.

How had he known it was her?

Maggie inched backward out from under the desk. Spence's boots appeared, scuffed, worn, braced wide apart. Her gaze traveled upward. Black trousers. Long legs. Her neck craned upward. Long, long legs. His holstered pistol. His gun belt slung low on his hips. And—

Maggie plopped back onto the floor.

No shirt.

Washboard muscles rippled across his stomach. Dark hair swirled across his wide chest. Big arms hung from straight shoulders. All with nothing more than the narrow width of his dark suspenders covering them.

Maggie's heart thudded into her throat, cutting off her words. Yet, she didn't know what she would have said, had she been able to speak.

She'd seen men in diminished states of dress before. On her many travels with her father there'd been privacy issues to deal with. Other cultures they'd visited had their own fashions, often more revealing than what she was accustomed to. But this…

Maggie blinked as she saw that Spence had extended his hand to assist her to her feet. She reached up quickly, afraid that it had been hovering in front of her for a while now and she'd been too busy looking at his chest to realize.

His long fingers closed around hers—good gracious, his hand was warm—and he pulled her to her feet with an ease that startled her. That put her on eye level with his bare chest. She gulped and forced her gaze upward.

He hadn't shaved yet. Stubbly whiskers darkened his chin and jaw. Nor had he combed his hair, except perhaps with a swipe of his fingers. A lock of his dark hair hung over his forehead, rousing in Maggie the desire to smooth it in place. And those eyes of his. Blue. Deep blue. Bluer than—

Spence released her hand. Had he held onto it a little longer than was really necessary? she wondered. Or had it been her clinging to him?

"How—how did you know it was me?" Maggie asked, desperate to get her thoughts onto something else.

"I saw you come inside," Spence said, and jerked his finger toward the rear of the jail. "I was out back."

She'd arrived while he was in the outhouse? Fingers of fire crept up Maggie's neck. How much more embarrassing could this morning get?

She cleared her throat. "I thought you were gone."

"I figured that," Spence said. "I've got to admire your guts, Miss Peyton, sneaking into the sheriff's office, attempting to steal that statue you claim belongs to you."

Maggie's head came up quickly. "Steal the artifact? You think I came in here to steal it?"

Spence lifted his shoulders. "Makes me think, too, that you're not as innocent as you let on. Makes me think, maybe, you're a professional."

"A *professional thief!* I most certainly am not!" Maggie flung out both arms. "I came here to discuss a matter of official business with you!"

"I don't know how things work back in New York, but around these parts when people want to talk to me they come in through the front door, stand upright and speak aloud."

"I was only under your desk because I—" Maggie clamped her lips shut. If she told him about rummaging through his desk and looking at his ledgers, heaven knows what he might accuse her of next.

She straightened her shoulders. "Is crawling under a desk against the law in this town?"

Spence looked at her for a long moment. "No," he finally said.

"Then I'm free to go?" she asked.

He didn't answer immediately, just gazed at her intently.

Maggie couldn't have moved even if he'd said she could leave. His closeness, his scent—something— cast a spell over her that kept her standing in front of him. An air of expectation hung between them. Maggie's knees trembled slightly and her stomach wound into a tight knot. She'd never felt anything so terrifying—so joyous—in her life.

He eased closer. Maggie's heart thumped harder. Was he going to kiss her?

"Your hat is crooked."

She gasped. Her hat? He'd been looking at her because her hat was askew? And she'd been imagining all sorts of silly things. How stupid of her. How *like* her.

Maggie reached up to straighten her hat, suddenly desperate to be out of this man's presence. Spence reached for her hat, too. Their fingers entwined. The sensation seemed to startle Spence as much as herself. Both of them froze.

Standing in the circle of his outstretched arms, Maggie was mesmerized by the blue of his eyes. He gazed down at her, unblinking, his expression seeming to see straight into her soul. And tell her...what?

He leaned in, lowered his head and kissed her. His warm lips met hers gently, delicately, yet covered hers completely. Maggie's knees nearly buckled while some unseen force held her upright, caused her to stretch upward to receive his kiss.

"Morning, Sheriff, I—"

Maggie gasped and spun around to find a man she didn't recognize standing in the open doorway, staring at the two of them. He gaped, his mouth slightly open, obviously as stunned as she.

"What the hell do you want, Dex?" Spence barked.

"Uh, well, uh…" He ducked his head. "Sorry, Sheriff, I didn't know you were…uh, occupied."

Maggie blushed. She knew she looked guilty—because she *was* guilty. Here she stood inches from Spence, her hat crooked, her dress slightly disheveled from crawling under the desk. And she *had* been kissing him.

Beside her, Spence tensed. He took her arm and escorted her past Dex, and out the front door. To his credit, he didn't attempt to explain their situation.

On the boardwalk, Spence held her arms loosely and stared down at her. She didn't know what to say. Apparently, Spence didn't, either.

For a moment, she was tempted to tell him the reason she'd come to the jail this morning, but couldn't quite muster the words. She supposed he'd figure it out once he found the ledgers she'd left under his desk.

"I have to go." Maggie eased her arm from his grasp.

For a few seconds they gazed at each other. Then Maggie turned and hurried down the boardwalk.

A fresh wave of embarrassment wafted through her. She'd come to the jail this morning to ensure her reputation as a honest person remained intact. Not only had she bungled that completely, now she had to worry what tales the deputy might tell about her.

Maggie walked faster along the boardwalk, not sure where she was going. All she knew was that she had to get away from the jail, away from Spence.

In fact, she realized, she'd be better off if she stayed as far away from Spence as possible. Her question about his intention to tell anyone about her break-in at the museum would have to go unanswered. She'd have to take a chance that he wouldn't tell anyone. If she could find a job quickly enough and establish her reputation with her new employer, perhaps anything Spence said later wouldn't matter.

At the corner of the bank building, Maggie paused. Unable to stop herself, she turned back.

Spence still stood outside the jail, watching her.

A little tremor passed through Maggie, then disappeared with a jolt. He probably wanted to make sure she didn't do anything else illegal. Why else would he watch her?

Men like Spence didn't watch women like Maggie. She'd do well to remember that. Although, she couldn't really explain why he'd kissed her.

Her roiling emotions boiled down to one simple fact: she had to do whatever it took to recover the love goddess and leave Marlow. Forever.

Chapter Nine

"Dang, Sheriff," Dex said, as Spence walked into the jail again. "Was that the lady Ian told me about? Miss Peyton? I didn't know that you and she were—"

"We weren't doing anything," Spence barked, pushing the door closed with a thud.

"I'm not saying that you were," Dex said quickly. "It just looked like, well, like maybe you were."

"Well, we weren't," Spence told him. He was tired because he'd been up most of the night, and grumpy because—hell, he didn't know why he was grumpy, except that he'd gotten caught kissing Maggie Peyton. But he wasn't in a frame of mind to keep his foul mood to himself.

He pointed at Dex. "Keep your mouth shut about this."

The deputy held up both hands in surrender. "Yes, sir, Sheriff, whatever you say."

He'd said what Spence wanted to hear, yet Spence couldn't help but wonder if Dex would do as he was told. Dex wasn't as discreet with official matters—or gossip—as Spence would like.

"What are you doing here this early?" Spence asked, as he crossed the room.

"Norman Kirby came knocking on my door first thing," Dex said. "The window of his store got busted out last night."

Spence turned around as suspicion crept through him. Already he had a good idea of who might be responsible.

"What happened?" he asked.

Dex pulled the tablet from his shirt pocket and consulted his notes. "At six-thirty this morning, Norman says he got up, went into his shop and saw that his front window was broke all to pieces. He came right over to my place, seeing as how I live just down the street."

"Anybody hurt?"

"No, sir."

"You been down there yet?"

"Thought I'd better get you first," Dex explained.

"I'll be ready in a minute," Spence said and headed down the hallway to his room.

When he'd rolled out of bed at first light, he'd pulled on his trousers, boots and gun belt; he never went anywhere without his gun, not even the outhouse. Now he washed quickly and finished dressing. Spence glanced at himself in the mirror above the washstand as he closed the last button on his vest. He didn't have time for a shave. He'd stop by the barber later.

He strode into the office and stopped. "Dex?"

The deputy popped up from behind the desk. "Over here."

Spence mumbled a curse. Why the hell was everyone under his desk this morning?

Maggie sprang into his mind, a tremor of warmth presenting itself along with her image. Forcibly, he pushed both away.

"What are you doing?" Spence demanded.

"Found these." Dex got to his feet and showed him three ledgers.

"What the…?" Suspicion of another sort flared in Spence.

When he'd spotted Maggie going into the jail this morning, he'd intended to fuss at her for sneaking around in the alleys again. But when he'd walked into his office and found her under his desk—her bottom up in the air—every other thought had flown completely out of his head. He hadn't even found out why she was here.

He couldn't let that happen again.

"Let's get down to Norman's place," Spence said. He followed Dex to the door, then stopped and turned back. There, where he'd left it on the high shelf, sat the statue of the love goddess.

"You go on," Spence said. "I'll be right behind you."

Dex gave him a questioning look but didn't say anything. When he was gone, Spence crossed the room and gazed up at the artifact.

In the morning light, the thing looked even more harmless than it had last night. Just a hunk of rock, carved with an odd human face and exaggerated features. Spence didn't believe it had any special powers, no matter what Maggie said.

Still, he used only his fingertips to pull the flour sack over the statue, then carried it at arm's length to his bedroom, where he shoved it under the bed.

"Damn lot of nonsense," Spence mumbled, then

cursed aloud as he caught himself wiping his fingers on his shirt front.

He strode out of the jail annoyed with just about everything that had happened to him already today. Spence was almost glad he had a vandal to take it out on.

Dex waited on the corner and fell into step beside Spence as he strode by. Few people were on the street at this early hour, mostly shopkeepers opening their businesses for the day.

"Who you reckon would do such a thing?" Dex mused. "Who'd want to bust out Norman's window?"

"I've got a pretty good idea," Spence said.

When they reached the corner of East Street, Spence nodded south. "Go on down to Mrs. Bishop's boardinghouse and get Ian."

Dex looked a little disappointed that he was being sent away, but hurried down the block without commenting. Spence turned the other way, crossed East Street and stepped up onto the boardwalk in front of Norman's General Store.

Without wanting to, Spence's gaze darted to Professor Canfield's Oddities of the World Museum. Maggie flew into his mind. Last night. The two of them out back in the dark. The moment when she'd stumbled backward against the building and he'd run into her.

Soft curves. Her sweet scent. Spence realized then that he'd wanted to kiss her at that moment. For a bare instant, it had seemed like the most natural thing to do.

Was that why he'd kissed her this morning?

"Hell…" Spence swung around and eyed the general store's broken window. Shards of glass littered the boardwalk, twinkling in the early morning sunlight. Norman Kirby stomped out of the store, a white apron tied around his wide girth, frowning.

"What the devil is going on in this town you're running, Sheriff?" Norman demanded. He gestured wildly at the broken window. "A man can't run a business around here, with this sort of thing going on. How am I supposed to make a living? Huh? Tell me, how am I supposed to do that? And what about my family? I've got a wife and daughter living here, remember?"

Spence ignored his accusations. Norman was just letting off steam and, really, Spence couldn't blame him. He let the shopkeeper run on while he assessed the damage.

Footsteps sounded on the boardwalk and he turned to see his two deputies approach. Ian looked grim; Dex had his tablet out, scribbling furiously. With all three lawmen on the scene, Norman started up again, but Spence cut him off.

"Dex, take Norman inside and see what else he has to say," Spence said. Dex nodded briskly and hustled Norman inside the store. Ian stepped up next to Spence and eyed the broken window.

"Vandals," Ian said after a moment. He motioned toward the window. "Nothing stolen. Stock still setting on the shelves. Big rock in the middle of everything. Vandals."

Spence nodded. "And I've got a good idea of who that might be."

Ian's gaze met his for a moment and he nodded, too. "You're thinking what I'm thinking?"

"Yep."

"Damn..." Ian's shoulders slumped a little. He shook his head. "You're going to go talk to her?"

"I am," Spence said, and by Ian's reaction, Spence knew his deputy didn't envy him.

But, to his credit, Ian drew himself up. "I'll go with you."

"Sheriff? Sheriff!" Dex hurried out of the general store, his tablet still clutched in his fist, Norman Kirby striding along behind him.

"What is it, Dex?" Spence asked.

He consulted his tablet. "At around midnight last night, Mr. Kirby says he got up and heard something through his open bedroom window. A ruckus of some sort."

Spence turned to Norman. "What did you hear?"

"Voices," Norman reported. "Two of them. I couldn't hear what they were saying. Sounded like arguing. Coming from the alley."

Spence's stomach tightened. He and Maggie. Norman had heard them in the alley. Spence pulled his brows together and drew his lips into a hard line.

"I'll bet it was the vandals," Dex declared. "We ought to check around, see if anybody else heard voices in the alley, or saw somebody sneaking around back there."

That's the last thing Spence intended to let happen. "Did you hear glass breaking at that time?" he asked.

"Well, no," Norman admitted.

Spence heaved a silent sigh of relief. "Then whoever was in the alley wasn't the vandals. Besides, I've already got a notion about who did it."

"You do?" Dex asked, his brows climbing up his forehead.

"Give Norman a hand getting this mess cleaned up, Dex, then head on over to the jail and write up a report." Spence glanced at Ian and nodded down the street. "Let's get this over with."

They walked down the street together, then turned the corner onto Main, Spence making a mental note to have the museum's back door repaired today.

"There's no good way to handle this," Ian said.

Spence couldn't argue the point.

"She'll throw a hissy-fit the minute you say anything," Ian pointed out. "She thinks that nephew of hers is pure as the new-driven snow."

Spence knew that, too. Fact was, he'd rather go up against a gang of cutthroats in a one-sided shoot-out than confront the woman. Finesse, good manners and a degree of diplomacy were needed for this confrontation, and Spence wasn't in the mood to display any of those things this morning.

But he knew in his gut who'd broken Norman's store window, and Mrs. Adelphia Frazier was going to hear that he suspected her nephew, whether she liked it or not.

The delicious aroma of food wafted around Maggie as she sat at a table by the window in the Pink Blossom Café. A serving girl walked by, her arms loaded with teeming plates of hot vegetables and meats, and saucers of flaky pies oozing fruit fillings.

Maggie looked down at the cup of coffee and crumbs from the single biscuit she'd devoured, and her stomach growled. She couldn't remember when she'd had her last full meal.

But that would change soon, Maggie told herself, forcing her eyes onto the little slip of paper in front of her. On it was the list of Marlow's businesses she'd compiled, places where she intended to seek employment. She gave herself a little shake, mentally assuring herself that by the end of this day her circumstances would be much improved.

First, a job. Then, payment to Mrs. Taylor for her hotel room. She'd be set. Everything would be in place to allow her to stay in Marlow until Professor Canfield returned. Why, by then she'd probably have saved enough money from her job to buy the love goddess outright. She could return to New York, her mission accomplished.

All she had to do was forge a life for herself in Marlow for a while. How hard could that be? All she needed was—

Maggie gasped as a familiar figure caught her eye out the café window. With an instinctive reflex, Maggie drew back as Spence strode down the boardwalk, his deputy at his side. For an instant Maggie feared he'd seen her in the restaurant and intended to barge in, accuse her of another crime. But he didn't. He and the deputy kept walking.

Maggie leaned closer to the window and followed him with her gaze, relieved that he wasn't coming after her again. The man was a thorn in her side, the one person standing in her way of retrieving the love goddess.

He was also the first man to kiss her—really kiss her.

A warmth spread through Maggie at the memory. Her heart beat a little faster. For an instant, she lost herself in the recollection of his strength, his lips, his taste, then came to her senses.

What was she thinking? Sitting alone in a restaurant, spinning fantasies about a man who couldn't possibly have any interest in her?

How stupid of her. Stupid and foolish. She'd let her imagination run away with her, pretending that she was desirable—to a man like Spence. That he would want someone like *her*. Stupid.

Maggie grabbed the list of businesses she'd made and hurried out of the restaurant.

Chapter Ten

On the boardwalk, Maggie drew herself up as she took in the storefronts of Main Street. Yes, she was undesirable—she'd known that for a long time. Yes, she seldom fit in—anywhere. But she was going to find a way to stay in Marlow, get her hands on her father's artifact, and return triumphant to New York. At that, she simply would not fail. Regardless.

Maggie turned sharply and set off down the boardwalk toward Townsend's Dry Goods store.

Her determination faltered almost immediately as she approached the shop adjoining the dry-goods store. Loitering on the boardwalk outside the Marlow Bake Shop was the most scary-looking man Maggie had seen in her life—and that included her travels to foreign countries. She'd seen this man on the streets of Marlow before—he seemed to be constantly roaming the town—and each time she'd managed to cross the street or duck into a shop to avoid him.

He was a mountain of a man. Tall, with shoulders wide as an oxen yoke, dressed in stained buckskins and a slouch hat. His golden hair hung in a wild mass past his shoulders, and mingled with his chest-long beard. A thick, fuzzy mustache drooped past his lips.

Frightening. The man was terribly frightening. Once again, Maggie crossed the street to avoid him, and searched out the next business on her list.

Three hours later, Maggie found herself back at the same spot outside the Marlow Bake Shop. Thank goodness the scary-looking man was gone, because she'd worked her way through nearly her entire list of employment possibilities—with no luck at all.

It had been the same everywhere she went. The manager of the First Union Bank told her—quite indignantly—that he had no need for a woman teller. At the school a very kind Miss Whitney told her that the town had funds for only one teacher—her. Mr. Townsend at the dry-goods store had sensed immediately that she'd never worked with the public, and sent her on her way. With a great deal of trepidation she'd gone to Norman's General Store—though it was a bit too close to Professor Canfield's museum and her brush with the law for comfort—where the owner hadn't even bothered to be nice when he'd told her he wasn't hiring. At the Pink Blossom Café she'd been quizzed on her cooking skills, and having none, was sent on her way. Much the same had happened at Mrs. DuBois's Dress Shop where she was forced to reveal that she could barely thread a needle and, of course, wasn't hired.

It was some comfort that no one had turned her down because of any rumors they'd heard about her. Maggie was glad about that. Spence, apparently, hadn't told anyone about her supposed attempted robbery of Professor Canfield's museum. She wasn't a marked woman—yet, anyway.

Now, her list of possible employers wilted and tattered, hot, weary and hungry, her feet aching, Maggie gazed at the front door of the Marlow Bake Shop. If she didn't find work here, all that was left on her list was Marlow's feed store, the blacksmith shop and the undertaker.

Drawing in a fresh breath, Maggie did her best to plaster on a smile as she pushed her way into the bakery. The delightful smell of baked goods covered her like a much-loved blanket, reminding her once more of how many hours had passed since she'd last eaten.

Red checked curtains covered the shop's sparkling windows, glass cases displayed cookies, pies, cakes and other baked goods. The woman behind the counter was young—no older than Maggie—quite tall, and surprisingly slender, given the rich desserts constantly at her fingertips.

"Afternoon," the woman called. "Can I help you?"

Maggie straightened her shoulders and approached the counter. "Yes. Yes, you can. My name is Maggie Peyton and I'm here seeking employment."

"Emily Delaney," the woman said, wiping her hands on her white apron. "You must be new to Marlow."

"Yes. I arrived here only recently."

"How do you like the town?" Emily asked.

Maggie was taken aback by the woman's friendly question, but didn't dare tell her the truth. "I love it here," she proclaimed, forcing an even wider smile on her face.

Emily's brows drew together. "Really? It took me

a while to get used it. I moved here from New York and—''

''New York?'' Maggie gasped, feeling a joyful bond spring up between them. ''You're from New York? Me, too.''

Emily's smile widened. ''How about that. What are you doing here in Marlow? Did you come because of the railroad?''

''The railroad?''

''The town's been expecting it through for a while now. There's been a delay—again—but the town's growing in anticipation.''

Maggie thought it prudent to give a shortened, modified explanation for her presence. ''I came here to visit an…an old family friend. Professor Canfield. But there must have been some sort of mix-up because he's not in town.''

''I came out last fall to live with my brother,'' Emily explained. ''Jack Delaney. He owns the Lucky Streak Saloon.''

Maggie remembered seeing the name on one of the saloons as she'd walked the streets of Marlow.

''He's gone back to New York to visit the family,'' Emily explained. ''He got married and wanted to show off his new bride. She's from here in Marlow. Rebecca Merriweather. She owned the Marlow Tea Room and Gift Emporium along with her aunt. All of them went to New York together.''

Maggie had seen the tea shop also, and wondered why it was closed. It would have been a perfect place for her to work. Though her domestic skills were lacking, she could certainly pour tea.

''You didn't go with them?'' Maggie asked.

Emily gestured, encompassing the bakery. ''I'd

just opened this place, and I couldn't face that long trip again.''

It was all Maggie could do not to disagree with her. At the moment, she'd fight tooth and nail to take advantage of an opportunity to head east again—as long as she had her father's artifact with her.

"I don't suppose you know where Professor Canfield might be?" Maggie asked. "A way I can contact him?"

Emily shook her head. "No. Sorry."

Maggie hadn't expected any help in locating the professor. She'd asked about his whereabouts at every place she'd been today and everyone said the same. He had no family in town, and wandered seemingly aimlessly about the country until he took a notion to return.

"Since it seems I'm going to be in Marlow until Professor Canfield returns," Maggie said, "I decided I should get a job to keep myself occupied. I was hoping you might need some help."

Emily gave her the kindest rejection smile she'd seen all day. "Sorry, Maggie, but I'm really not busy enough to hire anyone else."

Maggie's shoulders slumped, despite her best effort to hold them up. "Well then, perhaps you know someone else who is hiring?" Other than the feed store, the blacksmith or the undertaker, she hoped.

Emily thought for a moment. "I understand that business always picks up in town as the Founders Day Festival draws closer. But that's weeks away, still."

"I need a job right away," Maggie said.

"You might do what Lucy Hubbard does," Emily suggested. "Her husband was out of town on business for several months, and she supported herself by taking in laundry, doing mending, cooking and baking pies. I buy pies from her myself. Lucy makes the best pies in town.''

Washing? Mending? Baking? The prospect of supporting herself in Marlow evaporated before Maggie's eyes.

''Well, thank you,'' she began. ''I appreciate—''

The bell over the door clanged. Maggie saw the expression change on Emily's face and turned to see who had walked in.

It was the giant. The mountain man. Maggie's stomach tightened as fear spread through it. Was he following her?

''Ma'am,'' he said to Maggie, touching the brim of his hat respectfully. He turned to Emily then. ''Afternoon, Miss Delaney.''

Maggie had expected the man to have a loud booming voice, one that fit his size. But instead he was soft-spoken and moved with a gentle slowness.

''Good afternoon,'' Emily responded, and smoothed her apron with both hands, then patted the back of her dark hair. She fiddled with the glass jars on the counter, straightening them, squaring them off.

''Smells mighty good in here,'' the man said, almost in a whisper, gazing intently at Emily.

''Thank you,'' she said, then gave him a quick smile and gestured toward Maggie. ''Have you met Miss Peyton? She's visiting from back East. Maggie, this is Mr. Seth Grissom. He owns a carpentry shop here in town.''

Seth turned to her, and for the first time Maggie noticed his eyes. Blue. Startling blue. Beautiful. And he was young, which came as an even greater surprise. Probably no older than thirty.

"Pleasure to meet you, Miss Peyton," he said softly and dipped his head slightly. "Welcome to Marlow."

"Thank you, Mr. Grissom," she replied, and found herself smiling at him.

He turned back to Emily. "Might I trouble you for a couple of your oatmeal cookies, Miss Delaney?"

She smiled. "Sweet tooth working overtime today?"

"Yes, ma'am."

"Mr. Grissom is my most loyal customer," Emily said, as she took the cookies from the display case and folded wax paper around them.

Seth fished money from his pocket, the coins tiny in his meaty hand, and laid them on the counter. A moment passed before he picked up the cookies. Another few moments went by while he looked at Emily, and she simply looked back at him. Finally, he nodded to both women, and ambled out the door.

Seth Grissom seemed to take the warmth, the air, the very life out of the room with his departure. Maggie turned back to Emily and saw that her cheeks were pink.

"Well, thank you for your help," Maggie said, suddenly anxious to be on her way.

"What?" Emily shook her head as if clearing her thoughts. "Oh, yes, of course. Good luck to you."

"Thanks," Maggie replied and slipped outside. On the boardwalk, people moved past her, people with homes to go to, people with jobs, surely.

Disappointment over the day's events crept into Maggie's thoughts. Doubts threatened to overwhelm her. She should have known she wouldn't find a job. She'd been told her whole life that she had little to offer anyone outside the academic community.

Her stomach rumbled loud and long, reminding Maggie of her hunger, and—yet again—of the miserable failure she'd been today. Not one single job prospect—and few possibilities left to explore.

Bone tired from the long day, Maggie headed back toward the hotel. At least she still had a room to sleep in. And much as she hated to, she'd have to ask Mrs. Taylor to let her have something to eat.

Tomorrow was Sunday, so none of the town's shops would be open for business, making it impossible to look for work. If she could just hold on until Monday, she'd start job-hunting again. She'd ask for work as a scullery maid, if necessary, anything to stay in Marlow. Anything to get back the love goddess.

The Marlow Hotel looked warm and inviting in the late-afternoon sun and, as she approached, Maggie picked up her pace, anxious for the feel of the soft feather mattress beneath her aching body. She circled around back and let herself into the kitchen through the rear door. Mrs. Taylor stood at the stove.

The aroma of boiling potatoes and the sizzle of frying chicken made her mouth water. Maggie would offer to clean up after the meal—clean the entire hotel—if Mrs. Taylor would let her have a plate of food.

"Mrs. Taylor, I would—"

The older woman's gaze came up from the pots she tended on the stove and landed on Maggie. The small semblance of a smile she'd worn disappeared as her brows pulled together and her mouth twisted angrily.

"There you are!" Mrs. Taylor shook a wooden spoon at her. "Decided to come back, did you?"

Maggie just stood there, stunned.

"Let me tell you something right now," Mrs. Taylor said. "No guest of mine—certainly not a freeloader like you—is going to sully my reputation and the reputation of my hotel."

"What—what do you mean?"

Mrs. Taylor's eyes narrowed. "I know you were out last night, walking the streets at all hours, doing God knows what."

Maggie gasped.

"And I know that you brought a man back here with you—I heard his voice right here in this very kitchen."

Spence had been with her last night when he'd walked with her from the jail. It had been his voice Mrs. Taylor had heard.

"I can explain," Maggie said, though she wasn't sure how she could do that—without making the situation worse.

"So you admit it." Mrs. Taylor's expression changed to smug satisfaction.

"If you'll just let me tell you—"

"No, *I'll* tell *you*." She drew herself up. "You're no longer welcome in my hotel. I want you out of here."

"Out? But I—I don't have anyplace to go," Maggie pleaded. "I don't know anyone who would take me in."

Mrs. Taylor pressed her lips together. "I won't have you on the street, spreading tales about me, telling everyone I kicked you out. You can stay the night. But tomorrow, I want you gone. Do you understand? Tomorrow, you're to leave—and I don't want to see you again!''

Chapter Eleven

Sunday. A day for prayer and worship. Maybe a miracle, too?

Maggie slipped quietly down the staircase and out the hotel's front door knowing that a miracle was exactly what she'd need if she was going to find a way to stay in Marlow long enough to retrieve the love goddess.

She'd slept little, tossing and turning fitfully on what, perhaps, would be her last night in a real bed. Awakening early, Maggie listened at the top of the stairs until she heard the Taylors leave the hotel, headed for church, no doubt. She didn't want to face Mrs. Taylor again so she'd waited, giving them a head start before leaving for church herself.

A miracle, Maggie thought as she walked along Marlow's quiet streets. Yes, a miracle would do quite nicely right about now. She'd seen miracles before. One didn't traverse the globe to distant lands under oftentimes dire circumstances without witnessing incredible events.

But as she strolled toward the church on the edge of town, Maggie conceded that an outright miracle wasn't necessary today. At least, not at this moment. Right now she'd settle for a friendly face, some fellowship, the serenity of the church, the inspiration of a sermon and an uplifting hymn or two.

She'd seek guidance in prayer, Maggie decided, seeing other people on the boardwalk ahead of her, headed in the direction of the church. Surely, something would come to her. A voice from on high telling her how she'd possibly survive marooned in this town with less than a dollar to her name, no place to live, no job and no prospects.

Maggie's stomach rolled. Maybe a miracle was what she needed all right.

Her footsteps slowed as the church came into view. Its white clapboard and tall steeple looked peaceful amid the sparkling green grass and sheltering trees. Already, the townsfolk had gathered in the yard waiting for the service to begin. They grouped together in little knots, everyone dressed in their best, talking, chatting, sharing news and the latest happenings in Marlow.

Maggie's feet dragged to a stop. Was *she* one of Marlow's news items?

She spotted familiar faces. The schoolteacher Miss Whitney who had turned her down for a job. The banker, the shopkeepers, the café owner who'd all done the same. Were they exchanging stories about the outsider—qualified to do absolutely nothing—who'd been foolish enough to apply for work?

And Mrs. Taylor. What was she telling? Maggie saw the woman among the churchgoers, in a large group of women crowded together near the church stairs. Maggie's stomach knotted. Surely Mrs. Taylor hadn't hesitated to tell everyone what she perceived to be Maggie's egregious indiscretion.

Maggie summoned her courage. Regardless of whatever the people of Marlow chose to say about her, the church was a refuge, a sanctuary, the one place where she could find peace and acceptance. She wouldn't let them keep her away.

Drawing up her strength, Maggie took a step forward. Then stopped. Even if she went into the churchyard, held up her head and ignored the talk, what would she do?

She couldn't very well join in a conversation with the other women. They had babies and husbands, homes to tend and meals to prepare. What would Maggie say to them? She had no recipes to share. She'd be totally lost trying to discuss children, homes or husbands.

The vision of herself standing alone among so many people froze Maggie on the spot.

All these people were friends. They knew each other. She was an outsider. She'd always been an outsider. She didn't fit in. Certainly not here.

Overwhelmed by her shortcomings, Maggie turned and hurried away.

Where was she going?

Standing alone under the trees in the churchyard, Spence watched as Maggie turned tail and lit out back toward town. Why was she leaving? Where was she going in such a hurry? Had something happened and he'd missed it?

Not likely, he admitted to himself as the voices of the townsfolk floated around him. Spence hadn't been at church five minutes before he realized that he'd been scanning the crowd more than usual. He always kept an eye out for trouble, even here. But this morning he'd been looking for something else—Maggie.

It had startled him when he'd realized it, and he forced his gaze to the other churchgoers. He knew everyone in town. When his gaze had crossed with Mrs. Frazier's, she'd given him her evil eye. He'd expected as much.

He and Ian had paid her a visit yesterday, told her about Norman Kirby's broken window and asked to talk to her beloved nephew Andrew. The woman had become enraged. No nephew of hers, certainly not her refined, well-bred nephew from Boston, would have anything to do with vandalism. She harangued Spence for once again suspecting little Andrew of breaking the law, and she'd threatened to go to the mayor and town council if Spence didn't stop harassing him.

Spence had expected as much from her. In her eyes, the boy could do no wrong. But Spence saw things differently. Andrew was a thirteen-year-old hellion who'd already caused trouble in town several times, but was too devious to get caught red-handed. Having an aunt who was the grand dame of Marlow and stood up for him regardless, didn't help things.

So as Mrs. Frazier had stared at him across the churchyard this morning, Spence had stared right back. Until Maggie walked up, that is. But how could he not look at her?

She was a pretty little thing, all fixed up in her Sunday clothes, with her hair curled and a little hat sitting at a jaunty angle. He knew she smelled good, too.

For a moment, Spence considered sitting next to

her in church. For once, he might forego his usual spot—the back pew, right beside the door—and sit with her.

But now she was leaving. Spence went after her.

He wound through the crowd, lengthening his steps until he caught up with her.

''Miss Peyton?''

She didn't stop, but he thought he heard her gasp.

In two more strides, he was beside her. Spence touched her arm. ''Miss Peyton?''

Maggie stopped abruptly and looked up at him. Spence's stomach bottomed out. Tears stood in her eyes.

''What's wrong?'' he asked, the words coming out more harshly than he'd intended.

She gulped and swiped at her tears. ''Nothing. Nothing's wrong.''

''Something sure is wrong,'' he told her, again sounding gruff. But he couldn't help it. Something had happened to her. He wanted to know what, who was responsible. He wanted to fix it. Right now.

''It's—it's nothing,'' she said, sniffing. She looked away, not meeting his eyes. ''I—I just don't feel well. That's all. Please, I have to leave.''

Maggie hurried away, forcing down her emotions, forbidding herself to break into a run. When she reached town, she was tempted to look back, make sure Spence wasn't following. If she saw him again, she knew she'd break into tears.

Maggie stepped into the alley, out of sight of the few people who might be on Main Street instead of at church. She gulped, holding a tight rein on her emotions. Falling to pieces—anymore than she already had—wouldn't help anything.

But telling Spence her troubles might.

The thought came to Maggie, bringing with it the only comfort she'd experienced in days. Something about this tall, sturdy man urged her to lean on those wide shoulders of his, unburden herself, knowing he'd make things better for her.

But Maggie shook off the idea, drawing in a determined breath. She couldn't tell him anything. He already thought ill of her, and that was troubling enough. She wouldn't willingly lower his opinion of her by pouring out her problems.

For the first time since arriving in Marlow, she was tempted to forget the idea of recovering the love goddess and just leave. Her circumstances here were dire, with no relief in sight. If she really wanted to, she could leave tomorrow on the stagecoach. Go home.

And show up empty-handed?

The image of her father floated through her mind. No, she couldn't do that.

She was on her own. Maggie pushed her chin up. Time to get on with solving her problems.

A job, she thought. A job, a job, a job. If only she could find a job she could stay here. Maggie thought about the places she'd been yesterday. Of course, there were other employment possibilities in town, but surely they wouldn't pay as much as those she'd tried already. A cleaning woman or a maid were possibilities, though she wasn't qualified to do those things, either.

Regardless, she had to find work today. Mrs. Taylor wouldn't let her stay another night in the hotel. Unless she wanted to sleep in a doorway somewhere tonight, she had to find a job.

But what was open on a Sunday?

Maggie rose, straightened her skirt and gazed up and down Main Street. All the shops were closed, except for the Pink Blossom Café, of course. Since she'd already been refused work there, what was left to her?

She thought back to her conversation yesterday with Emily Delaney in the bakery. Her brother owned the Lucky Streak Saloon. Even though he was back east right now, perhaps if she mentioned Emily's name to the man running the place he would give her a job.

She'd seen women working in the saloons. The costumes they wore were scandalous, but it was better than starving to death. Apparently, no particular skills were needed for a job here. How difficult was it to serve drinks? Even Maggie could do that.

She drew in a breath. Desperate times called for desperate action. Maggie headed toward the Lucky Streak.

Yet when she arrived, she hesitated. She rose on her toes and peeked over the bat-wing doors. Two cowboys stood at the bar, a woman between them, and several men sat at the gaming tables. The place looked clean, Maggie thought, it looked as if—

She gasped aloud at the picture hanging over the bar. A portrait of a woman lying on a rock near a waterfall. An unclothed woman. Scandalous. Yet very well done. Even from this distance Maggie could see that it was good quality work, reminding her of some of the paintings she'd seen in European museums.

Even with only a few men inside, Maggie couldn't quite bring herself to walk through the swinging doors and ask to see the acting manager. Better to try the rear entrance, she decided. She turned, then stopped in her tracks. Spence headed straight toward her. He didn't look happy.

Maggie mentally cringed, but stood her ground as he walked up and planted himself squarely in front of her.

"What are you doing here?" he asked, sounding more than a little out of sorts.

That annoyed her. And, somehow, it felt good to experience an emotion this morning that didn't bring her to tears.

"What I'm doing here is none of your concern," Maggie told him, pushing her chin up a little.

Spence glanced at the doorway to the Lucky Streak. "I'm making it my business."

She huffed irritably. "Let me assure you, Sheriff Harding, that I have no intention of stealing anything from this establishment. And, frankly, I resent your nosing into my business like this."

He leaned in a little and looked her hard in the eye. "You'd better tell me what you're doing here, right now."

The steel in his voice caused Maggie to back up a step. He was a man to be reckoned with, she'd known that from the start. At the moment, it seemed prudent not to antagonize him further.

Yet she managed another irritated harrumph, just so he'd know he'd annoyed her again, and said, "I'm here seeking employment."

Now Spence backed up. He straightened, his brows drawing together in a deep frown.

"You're here looking for a job?" he asked carefully.

"Yes," she informed him.

"Here. At the Lucky Streak. You're trying to find a job here."

For a moment she thought perhaps he'd suddenly gone thick in the head. "Yes. I. Am."

He pressed his lips together in a hard line. "What type of work are you looking for her, Miss Peyton? Exactly."

"I'm doing what all the women here do," she told him.

His brows bobbed upward. "And that would be…?"

She huffed again. "Serving drinks."

He just looked at her.

"Drinks," she said to him. "Serving drinks. Surely you've been in a saloon before and seen women serving drinks."

His mouth opened slightly and he continued to stare at her.

How rude. Maggie squared her shoulders. She'd wasted enough time with Spence already.

"So if you'll excuse me," she said and ducked around him.

Spence caught her arm, stopping her. "Uh, just a minute, Miss Peyton."

She glared up at him. "What is it?"

"Uh, well…" Spence shifted uncomfortably. "Well, you see, Miss Peyton, the women who work in these places, well, they don't serve drinks."

"Of course they do. You can look inside and see them—"

"That's not all they do," Spence said.

Something about the tone in Spence's voice

caused a little knot to jerk in Maggie's stomach. "What...what else could they possibly do?"

Spence drew in a breath and blew it out. He glanced away, then back at her again. "Well, you see, Miss Peyton, the women here, they also...well, they see to the...needs—the personal needs...of the men."

"But—"

"For money."

"Oh." Maggie looked up at him. "Oh!"

She felt the color drain from her face. Good gracious, the women here were prostitutes. She'd very nearly waltzed into the saloon and asked for a job as a prostitute.

Heat plumed up Maggie's neck and onto her cheeks, warming them until they burned. Humiliation boiled inside her. She'd never been so mortified in her life.

"Well, thank you for your...help," she whispered, then turned quickly and dashed away.

Well, if this wasn't the perfect ending to a perfect morning, she couldn't imagine a better one, Maggie thought. What a fool she'd been. And right in front of Spence, too.

A fool. A complete fool. Again.

She tucked into the nearest alley, plopped down on the edge of the boardwalk and burst into tears.

Chapter Twelve

The tears poured, and Maggie let them. Seated on the edge of the boardwalk, her hands over her face, she cried, sobbing out the loneliness, the hurt, the humiliation she'd lived with for so many days now. She could have sat there forever, she thought, and done so happily, but footsteps behind her intruded. From the corner of her eye she saw boots stop beside her.

Maggie glanced up, not bothering to wipe her tears or even try and stop them. Spence stood over her, staring down at her from beneath the brim of his black hat.

"There are laws against women crying in this town," he told her.

Maggie just looked at him.

His face softened a little. "Crying alone, that is."

Spence sat down beside her and looped his arm around her shoulder. Maggie pulled away, but he tightened his grip and drew her against his chest. She snuggled closer and sobbed harder.

Even wracked with tears, Maggie sensed the

warmth Spence gave off, his strength as he held her. For some reason, it made her cry harder.

When she finally settled down, she sniffed and straightened away from him. Spence pulled a handkerchief from his back pocket and offered it to her. She wiped her tears, and drew in a ragged breath.

"In many ancient cultures, prostitutes were revered among the citizens," Maggie said quietly as she toyed with the handkerchief and gazed down the alley. "The Romans...the Greeks...they saw nothing wrong with it."

Spence touched her chin and turned her toward him. "Why are you crying?"

"Because I'm a complete failure at everything." The words flew from Maggie's mouth and she didn't try to stop them. It felt good to say them aloud, to no longer hold back, pretending everything was all right.

"I can't get a job anywhere, and I've been thrown out of the hotel, and—and I haven't had a meal in days, and I don't have any money, and I want to go home but I have no way to get there, and even if I did I couldn't go, and—and—"

"Come on." Spence rose suddenly, took her hand and pulled her to her feet. He plucked the handkerchief from her grasp, wiped away the last of her tears, caught her hand and again headed down the boardwalk.

Maggie sniffled as he led her down the alley and around to the rear entrance of the Pink Blossom Café. Spence opened the door without knocking and strode inside.

A woman stood at the stove and another at a worktable peeling potatoes. Maggie recognized them from yesterday when she'd come here to ask for work.

"Morning, Sheriff," the cook said, smiling. "You're a little early. You know we don't open until after church."

"Just bring us whatever you've got ready," Spence said and crossed the kitchen into the dining room, Maggie in tow.

The restaurant was deserted but Spence chose a table in the back corner. Maggie was glad because soon church would be over and the place would fill up. He seated her with her back to the room, then eased into the chair across from her and laid his hat aside. A moment later, the serving girl came out with cups of hot coffee and two plates filled with thick slices of ham, sweet potatoes and ears of corn.

"Biscuits will be ready soon," she said, placing everything on the table. "Chicken is frying now. Do you want—"

"Bring it," Spence told her and she disappeared into the kitchen again.

Maggie nearly swooned at the scent of the food wafting up from the plates. Her stomach growled and her mouth started to water, but she held back.

"I don't have any money," she said.

Spence looked up at her, his fork poised at his lips. "Just eat."

"But I can't pay for this."

"The town's also got a law against letting a woman starve to death," Spence said.

And then he grinned.

Maggie very nearly did swoon this time. She'd never seen Spence with anything but a grim or serious expression on his face, and now she knew why.

Dimples.

This hardened, no-nonsense, rough-hewn lawman had dimples. Huge ones, in both cheeks. They transformed his face, softened his expression, made him appear accessible, open and kind.

No wonder he never smiled. What outlaw would take a face like that seriously?

"Eat," he said, chewing and pointing at her plate with his fork.

Maggie ate. She cleaned her plate, and when the serving girl bought out fried chicken and potatoes smothered in gravy, she ate that, too. Biscuits dripping with butter and with honey. Cups of steaming, sugar-laced coffee. Everything tasted wonderful, better than any meal she'd had in her entire life. She couldn't stop herself. When the serving girl bragged that they had one of Lucy Hubbard's apple pies, Maggie devoured a large slice of it, too.

Scraping the last of the flaky crust from the plate, Maggie sat back, a little embarrassed to realize that Spence had finished eating already, and looked as if he'd been sitting and watching her for quite some time.

She dabbed at her mouth with the napkin and pushed her plate away. "Everything was delicious. Thank you."

He nodded, then waited in silence while the serving girl poured more coffee and took away their plates. Spence rested his arms on the table.

"Now, suppose you tell me what's going on with you."

When he'd looked at her that way before, Maggie had struggled to resist. But now she saw no reason to. He'd seen her at her worst—many times over. No sense in keeping secrets now.

"Since most all of my money was stolen at the holdup," Maggie began, "I haven't had any way to buy food."

"Mrs. Taylor at the hotel isn't feeding you?" Spence asked, and sounded both troubled and surprised.

"Mrs. Taylor asked me to leave the hotel."

Spence's brows drew together. "She what?"

"I don't think she likes me very much," Maggie said. "I've tried to find a job, but it hasn't gone as well as I hoped."

Spence looked surprised. "You ought to be able to find a job in town somewhere. What sort of things are you good at?"

Maggie shifted uncomfortably, wishing she didn't have to admit the truth—to Spence, of all people.

"My past has been a bit…different…from other women."

Spence stilled. "Different?"

She leaned forward slightly. "I'm not like other women."

His gaze did a quick sweep from her face to her bosom to the top of her head and back to her face again. His frown deepened. "Different how?"

Maggie glanced around, then lowered her voice. "I have a…"

Spence looked alarmed now. "A what?"

"A…a university education."

He rocked back in his chair and rolled his eyes. "Hell, Maggie, I thought you were going to tell me you had an extra leg, or something."

"At least with an extra leg I could display it at carnivals and make some money," she blurted out, a little annoyed that she'd told him her secret and he'd not seemed to appreciate the magnitude of her revelation.

Spence looked at her for a long moment, seeming to see her in a different way now. He leaned forward once more. "You've really been to a university?"

She felt her cheeks flush slightly. "Yes."

He nodded, seeming to approve. "What made you decide to do that?"

"It was my father's idea," Maggie said. "As I told you, he's a professor of anthropology. It made him happy that I attended university. I've traveled the world with him on expeditions since I was a child."

"No kidding," Spence said, looking genuinely interested. "Where have you been?"

"Europe, of course. The Far East. South America. That's where we found the love goddess."

"Oh, yeah. The love goddess. How did that thing get away from you, in the first place?"

"Because I was stupid," Maggie said, mentally cringing, recalling what had happened back in New York. "I trusted someone I shouldn't have, allowed him into my father's workshop where the artifacts were being cataloged, didn't watch to see what he was doing. Stupid of me, really."

"I think you must be pretty smart, if you got yourself a university degree," Spence pointed out.

"Well, it's not doing me any good here in Marlow," Maggie insisted. "Since I can't find a job, can't feed myself, can't keep a roof over my head. And I'm stuck in this town, under these dire circumstances until Professor Canfield returns, unless—"

Spence seemed to read her mind. "No."

"Unless you let me take the love goddess now and return to New York."

"No," he said again.

Maggie sat up straighter. "This is all your fault, really."

He raised an eyebrow. "My fault?"

"Yes. If you'd just let me—"

"Let's go." Spence rose from his chair, put on his hat and slid her chair away from the table.

"Go? Go where?" she asked, forced to her feet.

"Since this is all my fault, I guess it's up to me to make it right."

Maggie's spirits soared. "You're going to give me the love goddess so I can go home?"

"No, Maggie." He looked down at her. "I told you, I can't let you take that thing without first talking to Professor Canfield."

"Then where are we going?"

"To get you a job."

"But I've been everywhere in this town and nobody will hire me."

"Just trust me on this," Spence said, and grinned at her.

Maggie's stomach quivered, and she desperately wished she could loosen the stays of her corset. With that smile of Spence's and the big meal she'd just consumed, she might really swoon.

Spence gestured toward the door but Maggie stayed put.

"You won't tell anyone, will you?" she asked. "About my attending the university."

"Why don't you want people to know?" he asked. "You ought to be proud of your accomplishment."

"People treat me differently, sometimes."

He shrugged. "That's their problem, not yours."

"But I don't like being treated differently," she said. "I just want to…to fit in."

He looked as if it didn't really suit him, but he nodded. "All right. If that's what you want."

"Promise?"

He nodded. "I promise."

Satisfied, Maggie allowed him to escort her from the restaurant.

More people were on the street now, coming from the direction of the church. Services, apparently, had ended.

Maggie and Spence went to rear of the Townsend Dry Goods store. She waited in the alley while Spence pounded on the back door. After a while, Hank Townsend appeared, dressed in a rumpled shirt and frowning.

Spence and he spoke. Maggie wasn't close enough to hear their words but she saw Hank look past Spence to her, then shake his head. Their talk continued for some time. Hank kept shaking his head. Spence kept talking. Finally, the shopkeeper threw out his hands—an obvious sign of surrender. He disappeared into the store briefly, came back and handed something to Spence who walked away sliding whatever it was into his pocket.

"You start work tomorrow morning," he reported as they headed down the alley.

Maggie glanced back. "Are you sure? Mr. Townsend didn't seem as if he really wanted me to work there. I'd been by his store yesterday and asked him about a job and he said no. What did you say to him?"

Spence stopped then. "Hank's giving you a job. That's all you need to know."

"He owes you a favor?"

"You might say that."

Maggie couldn't imagine what sort of "favor" would result in Mr. Townsend allowing her to work for him. But Spence didn't give her a chance to ask. He took her arm and started walking again.

They went down Main and turned onto West Street. There were a few businesses here, along with two lovely homes. Near the end of the street was a little cottage, obviously abandoned for a while.

Spence took a key from his pocket, unlocked the door and led the way inside. With a little trepidation, Maggie followed.

It was a two-room cottage, with a parlor, kitchen and dining room together in one area, and a small, separate bedroom. Large pieces of furniture remained, shrouded in white cloths. Dust covered most everything. The windows were grimy, draped with curtains that needed washing.

"Townsend's son lived here with his wife," Spence explained. "Her pa died and they had to move to Texas and take care of her ma and younger brothers and sisters. They left a couple of months ago. Hank said you can live here now."

"Here?" Maggie's eyes widened. "All by myself?"

"Nobody's using the place," Spence said. He gestured around the room. "It just needs a little cleaning, some fixing up. A woman's touch."

Maggie gazed at the room. "A woman's touch...?"

"There's a little garden out back where you can

put in some vegetables. Might be something left in the root cellar, too.''

''A root cellar?''

''Be at Townsend's store first thing tomorrow morning. He'll show you around, explain about the stock and what you're supposed to do with the customers. He'll give you an advance on your week's wages, too,'' Spence said. ''I'll stop by the hotel and have Mrs. Taylor pack up your things and send them here.''

''But…''

''I've got to get over to the jail.'' Spence headed for the door.

''Wait!'' Maggie hurried after him.

He paused in the doorway. ''You're all set now. Everything will be all right.''

''But, I—''

Spence hesitated, gazing down at her as if he wanted to say—or do—something more. But instead he gave her a brisk nod and left, closing the door behind him.

For a moment she was overwhelmed with the need to run after him, cling to him, insist that he come back into the house with her.

Maggie didn't, though. She turned in a slow circle taking in the room. She'd have to learn the stock in the mercantile, figure out how to wait on customers, and please Hank Townsend so she didn't get fired? *And* clean the cottage, turn it into a home, plant a vegetable garden, and cook for herself?

This was Spence's idea of solving her problems?

Maggie's shoulders slumped. How would she ever manage?

Chapter Thirteen

Maggie hurried into the Townsend Dry Goods store the next morning, fearful that she was late for work on her very first day. Since she had no supplies in her new home, she'd gone to the Pink Blossom and spent her very last nickel on breakfast. The ladies there were nicer to her, and she couldn't help but wonder if it was because Spence had treated her to supper yesterday.

The look on Hank Townsend's face told Maggie that she was, in fact, late for work. He stood behind the counter wearing his white shop apron, writing in a ledger. He scowled as she walked up.

"I told Spence I'd give you a try here," Hank told her. "But that doesn't mean I have to keep you on."

Maggie tried to smile. "Yes, Mr. Townsend. Thank you. I appreciate your giving me a chance, and I'll do my very best."

He harrumphed as if he doubted that her "very best" would be good enough.

"I don't know why you'd come all the way to Marlow to see that Professor Canfield," Hank complained. "The man's always gone. If you ask me, it's a waste of good store space having that museum of his right there on East Street. That's where the train depot is going."

Maggie didn't know what to say so she remained quiet.

Hank grunted, then went on. "Here's what you need to do. Greet the customers when they come in. Ask what they want, show them where it is, bring it to the counter for them. Got it?"

Maggie glanced around at the hundreds of items crowding the shelves. "Yes, sir."

"Be nice to them. I want them to keep coming back."

"Of course," she replied, but couldn't help but wonder how he had any repeat business at all if he was this gruff with his customers.

"And get them to buy something more," Hank said. "Got it?"

"Yes," she said, trying to sound confident.

"Keep your hand out of the till. I handle the money, not you." He reached under the counter, then slapped money down. "Here's your week's wage. You'd better earn it, or it's the last wages you'll see from me. Got it?"

It was all Maggie could do not to lunge for the money. She'd never been so glad to see anything in her life. She gathered it quickly and dropped it into the pocket of her skirt.

"All right, then," he said and turned back to his own work. "Business will be slow today, but stay busy."

Maggie unpinned her hat and placed it on a shelf behind the counter. Now that she had some money, and if she budgeted right, she could buy herself a handbag to replace the one stolen at the stage holdup. It just didn't seem right walking around town with nothing clutched in her fingers.

Hank ignored her as she walked up and down the store aisles, familiarizing herself with the stock. She'd have to be able to assist every customer who walked into the store, regardless of their needs, if she wanted to keep this job. And she desperately wanted to keep this job.

But Hank's intrusive throat-clearing signaled her first failure when she looked up and noticed that a customer was already in the store. Maggie hurried over, asked if she could be of assistance and was told a simple ''no'' by the man who went directly to Hank at the counter. Hank's scowl conveyed his disappointment in her.

With one eye on the door and the other on the shelves, Maggie caught the next customer who stepped into the store. She hurried over and greeted the woman.

''I'm here about the soap,'' she said.

Soap, soap, soap. Maggie's mind raced trying to remember where she'd seen the soap. She touched her fingertip to her temple. ''Yes, of course, I know we have it here someplace. I just—''

''I'm Lucy Hubbard,'' the woman said, as if that explained everything. Apparently the blank look on Maggie's face prompted her to continue. She touched the market basket on her arm. ''I make soaps and Mr. Townsend sells them for me.''

''Oh.'' Now the woman's name meant something to Maggie. Emily at the bakery had mentioned her. This was the woman whose husband had been out of town for months and she'd supported herself baking, sewing and mending.

But this Lucy standing before her didn't match the mental image Maggie had of a woman strong enough to support herself in time of need. She'd imagined her older, stronger, and harder-looking. To the contrary, Lucy was a young slender woman with dark hair and a pretty face.

"I had one of your pies at the Pink Blossom," Maggie said, remembering her supper with Spence. "It was delicious. Everyone says you make the best pie in town."

"Thank you," she said and blushed modestly. "I don't think we've met. Are you new in town?"

Maggie introduced herself and told her the same story she'd told Emily, that she'd come to town to visit Professor Canfield.

"I hope you'll still be here for our Founders Day Festival," Lucy said.

Maggie sincerely hoped that she would not be, rather wishing she'd find a way to return to New York before then, but didn't say so. Instead, she decided to try out her new role as shop assistant.

"Is there anything else I can help you find?" she asked, gesturing around the store.

Lucy looked around longingly, her eyes lingering for a moment on a display of fabrics. But she shook her head. "No, I'd better not buy anything. My husband is home and I have to get back before he—"

She stopped suddenly as Seth Grissom filled the shop's doorway. Maggie shrank back from the golden-haired giant, giving him plenty of room to pass by, forgetting completely that she was supposed to wait on him.

"Morning, ladies," Seth said softly as he walked past.

"Good morning, Mr. Grissom," Lucy said, though Maggie managed little more than a weak smile.

When he stopped at the counter talking to Hank, Maggie whispered to Lucy. "He frightens me."

Lucy nodded. "He frightens everyone. But he's very artistic. You should see some of the cabinetry work he does."

Maggie's brows lifted. "Really?"

"Oh, yes. Paintings and sculpting, too," Lucy told her. She leaned in and lowered her voice to a confidential tone. "I think he's enamored with Emily Delaney. I see him going into her shop all the time."

"Is she—?"

"I doubt it," Lucy explained. "But who can blame her reluctance? I mean, look at him."

Maggie turned her gaze on Seth Grissom once more. Under those stained buckskins, tangled beard and wild hair might be an attractive man. But what woman could get over her fright long enough to find out?

"I'd better get these soaps to Mr. Townsend," Lucy said. But instead of heading over to the counter, she stood still, her gaze on the front door.

Maggie's stomach jumped as she, too, saw Spence walk into the store, his deputy at his side. The two men seemed stunned to find the women there, because they halted in their tracks.

The air seemed to grow unbearably hot, despite the cool morning breeze that flowed in through the open door. Ian Caldwell's gaze landed on Lucy, burning hotter than the midday sun. Her face flushed. Then, after an intense moment, Ian turned and disappeared out the door. Lucy gulped, offered not a word, and dashed to the counter with her market basket.

Maggie turned a questioning look to Spence. He eased up beside her, bringing a new sort of warmth with him. "The two of them are..."

"In love?" Maggie asked, though it was obvious. "But isn't Lucy married?"

Spence scowled. "Married to the most worthless excuse for a man I've ever seen. They hadn't been married but a short while when they moved here. He took off, supposedly looking for investments, left her behind to fend for herself for months. Didn't write, didn't send money. Nothing."

"That's terrible," Maggie agreed.

"Worthless bastard," Spence muttered. "Just about the time she'd decided to file for a divorce, he showed up again. He hasn't worked a day since he got back. Lucy's the one who keeps food on the table for them."

"Why doesn't she leave him? Especially if she's truly in love with Ian."

"For the same reason Ian won't ask her to," Spence said. "She took vows before God. She's married, and that's that."

"So she'll stay with her husband forever? Regardless?"

Spence shook his head. "The day will come when she's had enough of him. I just hope it won't be too late."

A sadness settled around Maggie's heart. In the academic world she'd lived in all her life, matters of love and marriage had seldom been mentioned. Seeing the look on both Ian and Lucy's faces, hearing their story, knowing the futility they faced brought on a hurt Maggie hadn't experienced.

"Are you getting settled here all right?" Spence asked.

Maggie looked up at him. Tall, handsome. She understood now why he smiled so seldom, but couldn't help but wish she could see those dimples of his again.

"I'm doing fine," she told him, though she didn't feel that way at all. "I never thanked you for finding me the job, or a place to live."

Spence shrugged. "It's the least I could do, considering your predicament is all my fault."

He grinned then, and a thousand imaginary butterflies took flight in Maggie's stomach.

"Is the love goddess still safe?" she asked.

"Yeah, I'm guarding that hunk of rock with my own life," he told her, his grin widening.

"I know you don't believe in its powers, but you should take them seriously."

"I take rock very seriously," he assured her.

Maggie giggled, because it was so obvious that he was simply appeasing her, and to her delight Spence's grin blossomed into a full smile. And how good it felt, looking up at this handsome man, laughing together, enjoying something only the two of them shared.

Hank's throat-clearing intruded, dragging Maggie's attention away from Spence. To her horror, she realized three more customers had entered the store and she'd not even noticed.

"I'd better get to work," she said to Spence.

The spell broken, his stern expression in place, he

backed away. "I've got things to do," he said, and disappeared out the door.

For an instant, Maggie wished she could go with him. How much more delightful the day would be, walking the sunny streets at Spence's side, talking, laughing occasionally, than to be stuck in this store.

Reality hit home when Hank called her name—none too politely—and she hurried to wait on the customers.

When she left the store at the end of the day, Hank Townsend didn't even tell her goodbye. He handed her a market basket filled with supplies, which Spence had arranged for, she was sure, then ushered her out the front door, pulled the shade and locked up, obviously not pleased by her performance today.

Maggie couldn't blame him. As she walked toward the little cottage that was her home, she knew she hadn't been much help to him. Somehow, customer after customer had gotten by her that she hadn't greeted. She couldn't remember where most of the stock was located. In her haste to assist two miners buying blankets, she'd knocked over a display of blue-speckled coffeepots, raising a ruckus as the enameled cookware clattered to the floor. She was sure Mr. Townsend regretted whatever favor Spence had done for him that resulted in a debt so great he'd been forced to hire her.

Of course, Maggie hadn't really enjoyed working there, either. Everybody who came into the store already knew Mr. Townsend as well as most of the other shoppers. No one had much to say to Maggie. She's stood off to the side, watching the conversations, the laughter. The few woman who'd entered the store brought babies and children with them.

Children who ran down the aisles, babies who screamed. Two little boys—twins—had tormented her, purposely, she was sure.

The prospect of returning to the store tomorrow was a dismal one.

Almost as dismal as going into her new home, Maggie thought as she walked up the path to the cottage. The sun had almost set, leaving the little house in deep shadows that did nothing to improve its appearance—or Maggie's enthusiasm at living there.

She fished the key from her pocket and let herself in through the front door. Her spirits flagged once more, looking at the dust and grime on everything. Yesterday, she'd done nothing more than hunt out clean bed linens from a chest in the bedroom, thankful that Mr. Townsend's son and daughter-in-law had left so many things behind. Apparently, they knew most everything they'd need waited at their destination. She'd also put away her belongings that Mrs. Taylor had sent from the hotel, but hadn't mustered the energy to write in her daily journal.

She placed her market basket on the table, the silence in the house roaring in her ears. She'd slept alone before, of course, in her room at home in New York, in tents and grass huts around the world, in hotel rooms like those she'd occupied on her journey west.

But she'd never been this isolated before, as she was now in this little cottage on the edge of town. Someone had always been within earshot of a distress cry. There'd been a connecting wall she could pound on, if needed. For the first time, she was totally alone. Anxiety grew in Maggie. She didn't like the feeling.

Perhaps Spence would come by.

The notion flew through her mind, lifting her spirits. How nice it would be to see him standing in her doorway, to have him come inside, for the room to fill with his presence, his warmth.

But she knew that wasn't likely. Surely, the man had important things to do—things much more important than checking on the likes of her. He'd done so much for her already.

Maggie busied herself unloading her supplies from the market basket onto her kitchen sideboard. Unexpectedly, a shiver passed through her. She jerked around and gazed through the streaked kitchen window to the rear yard.

The woodshed, the outhouse, a small barn and corral, the withered remains of the vegetable plot. Nothing more. Yet Maggie's senses remained on alert. Cautiously, she approached the window. She scanned the yard carefully but saw nothing out of the ordinary, just the usual—

A shadow. Maggie gasped and drew back from the window. That shadow. Had it moved? Was somebody outside, watching her house? Or was her imagination playing tricks on her?

Maggie's heart thumped harder in her chest. Spence flew into her mind once more. Oh, if only he'd come by.

Spence stood at the corner of Main and West Streets trying to decide what to do. Just down West stood the little cottage Maggie had moved into. She was home now; she had to be since Townsend's store was closed.

Somehow, the little house called to him, urged him to walk over, knock, go inside—or rather, its occupant did the imaginary calling.

Maggie, inside alone. The idea caused his gut to tighten predictably.

She might need his help with something, he told himself, searching for an honest reason to call on her. The house was a mess, so something heavy might need to be lifted or moved. Maybe she needed more firewood chopped?

Somehow, he felt a need to look out for her, help her, though she'd never asked him to. If anything, she kept her problems to herself and soldiered along, never uttering a complaint.

Maybe that was reason enough to stay away from her. The truth of that realization slammed hard in Spence's gut. Maggie took up too much of his thoughts. She was too much of a distraction. Just yesterday, he'd left church without really looking around, seeing if anything was a problem. He just took off after Maggie when she walked away, overwhelmed with the need to catch up with her, find out what was wrong, fix it.

Today he'd caught himself walking past Townsend Dry Goods over and over, glancing at the doorway, the window, sure there was something he needed to buy.

Yet how could he do his job, watch for trouble, keep everyone safe if Maggie was on his mind all the time? What if he missed something and—

Ellen.

Spence gritted his teeth at the memory. She, too,

had taken up much of his thoughts, his attention, his time.

What if *that* happened again?

Spence couldn't bear the idea. He turned sharply and headed back down Main Street. Better to stay clear of Maggie, keep his mind on his job. Better for everyone.

If Ellen could look down at him from heaven right now, she'd surely say the same.

Chapter Fourteen

Early morning in Marlow had always been Spence's favorite time. Quiet. Almost no one out. A time when he could walk the streets of his town and relax, just a little.

Spence's boots thudded on the boardwalk as he headed east toward the rising sun. Marlow hadn't come awake yet. Few people were out, and that was normal. But Spence found no comfort in the solitude of the early morning hours.

Maybe because he felt like hell, Spence thought. The emptiness, the restlessness he'd felt for weeks hadn't eased. Instead it had gotten worse. It was as if he was hungry all the time and couldn't get enough to eat. Or his senses were heightened, waiting for something to happen.

He hadn't slept well, either. Night after night he tossed and turned, finally dozing off only to wake and realize the sun was rising. It was starting to wear him down.

Last night had been the worst. All he could think about was Maggie, alone in the new house. He'd wanted to go over there, check on her. But he'd told himself that she was fine. If she'd truly traveled the world, as she'd said, then staying in the little cottage here in Marlow wouldn't cause her any distress. So if he went to see her, it was only because he wanted to be there, not because she was in any sort of danger. And what if he indulged himself and something happened elsewhere?

Spence pushed the thought from his head, determined to find some solace in his early-morning walk through town. Thankfully, things had been pretty quiet in Marlow lately. A few drunk cowboys, a fist-fight or two, and of course, Mrs. Frazier's usual complaints about everything and everybody. But nothing serious had happened. Even Mrs. Frazier's hellion nephew was no longer a concern, thanks to Ian's good work.

Spence turned the corner onto East Street and saw that the door to Norman Kirby's general store stood open. For an instant, Spence wondered if something had happened but nothing seemed amiss, from the outside anyway. It wasn't unusual for Kirby to open early; the man would keep his doors open all night as long as he had a single customer in the store.

Just to be on the safe side, Spence crossed the street and walked past the store, glancing inside. His breath caught. Maggie stood at the counter. His belly warmed and an odd craving came over him, pulling him toward her.

She looked out at that instant, saw him, and to Spence's surprise, she whipped around and dashed down one of the store aisles, back out of sight. A guiltier look on anyone's face, Spence had never seen.

"What the hell...?" He pulled his hat lower on

his forehead and stepped into the store. Since he was tall, seeing over the aisles wasn't difficult. He spotted Maggie feigning interest in the canned goods, and walked over. No one else was in the store, not even Norman Kirby.

"What are you up to?" he asked.

Maggie looked up, trying not to cringe outwardly. Darn her luck. Did Spence have to show up at all the wrong times in her life? Where was he last night when she was trembling in her room, frightened by every sound she heard, when she really needed him?

The suspicion that had come over her last night that her house was being watched, only grew stronger as darkness fell. She'd crept into her bed and pulled up the covers, sure she heard footsteps outside, scraping noises at the door. Once she'd thought a shadow had moved across her window. When she finally fell asleep, she dreamed that someone was inside her house. She woke panicked, gasping for breath.

By the time she'd dressed, eaten a little something, Maggie had decided she wouldn't spend another night like that. She'd left early and gone straight to Norman's General Store, relieved to find the man already outside sweeping the boardwalk. He'd been only too happy to assist her with her purchase.

But now if Spence didn't leave right away, he'd ruin everything.

"I'm shopping," she said, waving her hand around the store, indicating that her purpose here should be only obvious.

"It's mighty early to be shopping," Spence said, watching her in that lawman way of his that she'd seen all too often already.

"As you well know, I have a job now that occupies much of my time," Maggie explained. "Mr. Kirby was nice enough to open his store for me this morning."

"What are you shopping for?"

She paused, shifted her gaze away from him. "Something ...personal."

"What is it?"

She pushed her chin up a little trying to muster enough irritation to send him on his way.

"I told you, it's personal."

"Look, Miss Peyton, I know you're up to something, so you may as well tell me what it is."

Maggie stewed for a moment, hoping she looked angry rather than guilty. "All right, fine. I'm here to buy a...handbag. Mine was stolen and I need a new one. There. Now you know. Are you happy?"

Spence gazed across the store. "I don't recall Kirby carrying ladies' handbags."

"Well, he does," Maggie told him, and flung her hand toward the stockroom behind the counter. "Mr. Kirby just received a new shipment and he's getting them for me now. So, if you'll just go about your business, I'll go about mine."

Maggie glared up at Spence, willing him to turn and leave the store before Norman Kirby walked out of the stockroom.

Spence nodded thoughtfully. "I don't believe I've ever seen a woman pick out a handbag before. Might be kind of interesting to watch."

He knew she was lying. Maggie read it in his expression. But she couldn't back down now.

"There's nothing interesting about it," she said

quickly. "Really, Sheriff, I'm sure your time would be better spent—"

"Here you go, Miss Peyton," Norman announced, bustling through the curtain from the stockroom. He placed a box on the counter and swept off the lid. "A Colt .45 Peacemaker. Just like you asked for."

Maggie cringed, wishing she could slip between the cracks in the floorboards and disappear. She dared to glance up. Spence's jaw was locked, his gaze murderous.

No sign of those cute little dimples now.

"Forget it," Spence called to Norman. The shop-keeper looked up, confused, but Spence ignored him. He grasped Maggie's upper arm with just enough strength that she knew he meant business, and ushered her out of the store.

On the boardwalk, Spence looked down at her, horrified.

"What the hell do you think you're doing buying a gun?" he demanded.

"It's none of your concern," Maggie told him.

"The hell it isn't. What are you planning to do? Bust into the jail? Take that statue by force?"

"What?"

"There's no way in hell you're buying a gun." Spence pointed his finger at her. "I kept quiet about you breaking into the museum and stealing that thing, but I'm not letting you arm yourself, even if it means going to every merchant in town and telling them what you did."

"You wouldn't dare!" Maggie clamped her arms at her sides.

Spence leaned down. "Try me."

Maggie pursed her lips and narrowed her eyes in

what she hoped was a menacing sneer. She managed to hold it for only a few seconds, no match for Spence's anger.

She buckled. "I was frightened last night."

His anger vanished as if it had been whisked away with a broom. "What happened?"

"I kept thinking someone was trying to get in, and—"

"Damn…" Spence backed off. "I knew I should have gone over there."

Maggie's stomach jolted. "You wanted to come over?"

"Dammit," he swore again, the curse directed at himself. "I had a feeling something was wrong. I thought about you all night…."

"I thought about you, too." The words popped out of Maggie's mouth before she realized they'd formed.

Spence stilled. "You did?"

"Yes," Maggie admitted. "I was frightened, and I kept hoping that you'd come by."

He shook his head. "I should have."

"Then why didn't you?"

"Because—" Spence stopped suddenly, as if he'd been about to say something—something personal, maybe?—but had changed his mind. He waved his hand as if to wipe away his own thoughts. "Tell me what happened."

Maggie thought back to last night, wondering now if telling the story might sound a little silly. After all, nothing had actually *happened*. She pushed ahead anyway, knowing Spence wouldn't let her not tell him.

"I heard noises out back, and I had a feeling

someone was watching the house. During the night, I was almost sure I heard something scratching at the door," she explained, and to her relief, Spence seemed to take her concern seriously.

"Could have been animals looking for food," he speculated. "Might be a den underneath the house."

"Do you think so?" Maggie asked, hoping that's all it was.

"I'll go over and have a look around," Spence promised.

Maggie gestured toward Norman's General Store. "Don't you think I should get the gun, just in case? I'm a very good shot."

"No."

"But what if it's not animals and—"

"No."

"Mr. Kirby was nice enough to let me have the Colt on credit," Maggie said. "I think it would be very rude of me not to buy it."

"Hell, no, you're not buying a gun," Spence told her. "You'd better get over to Townsend's place. He'll be opening soon."

As Maggie walked at his side it occurred to her that she'd never been afraid in Spence's presence. When they reached the dry-goods store he left her standing in front of the closed door, and headed toward West Street.

She watched him leave, glad for the few minutes she had for herself until Mr. Townsend opened the store. She was still a little annoyed that Spence had kept her from buying the gun, but comforted to know that he was on his way to her house to have a look around.

A thread of warmth wound through her as she

watched his wide shoulders and broad back striding away from her. He'd said he thought about her last night. Worried about her. He'd been tempted to come check on her, but hadn't allowed himself to give in to the desire.

For a moment, Maggie allowed herself to believe that he'd been troubled because he cared about her. After all, he had kissed her. But could it be true? Could a man like Spence Harding really worry about *her?*

The warmth in Maggie's stomach turned into a cold knot as a wave of fear swept through her.

There was only one reason Spence could have spent a sleepless night because of her.

The love goddess.

Chapter Fifteen

The morning dragged by for Maggie, her mind on the situation with the love goddess rather than the customers coming into the store. She straightened shelves, lost in thought.

Of course, it shouldn't come as a surprise to her that Spence had worried about her last night and been tempted to come to her house and check on her. The two of them had touched the love goddess simultaneously, bringing hundreds of years of ancient forces to bear.

Spence didn't really *care* about her. He was under the influence of the love goddess. An unexpected lump of emotion rose in Maggie's throat. She pushed it down, reminding herself that it was silly to think otherwise.

A man like Spence truly interested in a woman like her? Of course not.

But what about other people in Marlow? Maggie fetched the broom from the stockroom and went out onto the boardwalk. The town had come to life. People went about their business, filling the streets, the shops and stores.

How many of them had been affected by the powers of the love goddess?

Just down the street, she saw the mountainous Seth Grissom lumbering toward the Marlow Bake Shop. Maggie gripped the broom handle. When she'd visited Emily Delaney and Seth had come into the shop, Maggie had gotten the distinct impression that something more than the sale of a couple of cookies had passed between the two of them. Had Seth and Emily somehow touched the love goddess at the same time?

And what about Ian Caldwell and Lucy Hubbard? Had they fallen to the same fate? Had they experienced an encounter with the love goddess, a brush that had altered their destinies?

Maggie's stomach twisted. Lucy was a married woman. Had Maggie's carelessness with her father's artifact ruined a marriage?

And what of Ian? Had a chance exchange ruined him for all other women?

Alarm spread though Maggie. Who else in town might have succumbed to the love goddess's spell—and not know it?

Spence sprang into her thoughts with such force that she whirled around on the boardwalk. Sure enough, there he was crossing the street toward her. She'd sensed his nearness. Maggie's stomach knotted again. The powers of the love goddess were working on her, too.

And for a moment, she gave into them. The knots in her stomach turned into tingles, an awareness washed over her, concern rushed through her over her appearance. Maggie let them all come.

So this was what it felt like to be attracted to a man. And not just any man. Sheriff Spence Harding.

Handsome, capable, strong. Maggie felt her cheeks flush.

Spence stepped up onto the boardwalk. "I was at your place just now, and I—"

"I have to talk to you." Maggie propped the broom up against the store. "Privately."

She clamped her hand around Spence's arm and headed for the alley, then just as quickly, jerked to a stop. Spence wouldn't move.

"Come on," she said, tugging on his arm. He just stood there, as if rooted to the spot. "It's about the love goddess."

"Oh, Christ…" Spence rolled his eyes and allowed her to pull him into the alley beside the store.

"How long has the artifact been in Marlow?" Maggie asked.

"Don't you know?" he asked. "You paid an investigator to find the thing."

"He was a little vague on some points," Maggie admitted, except, of course, on the extravagant fee she'd had to pay him for his investigation. "Anyway, all I cared about was learning its whereabouts so I could retrieve it."

Spence lifted his shoulders. "Until you showed up in town, I didn't even know the thing was here."

"Oh, dear…" Maggie pressed her lips together. "This is terrible, just terrible."

"Why?"

"Don't you see? Many, many people could have gone into Professor Canfield's museum and touched the love goddess. Who knows how many?"

"There wasn't exactly a steady stream of people going in and out of his place," Spence said.

"But people did go in there. Suppose they were affected by the artifact's powers?"

Spence snorted his doubt.

"You don't believe in the love goddess, do you?" Maggie challenged.

"Hell, no."

"Then how do you explain Ian Caldwell and Lucy Hubbard's attraction for each other?"

"Simple," Spence said. "Lucy's married to the biggest jackass in town, and Ian's a good man."

All right, that made some sense, Maggie had to admit. "But what about Seth Grissom and Emily Delaney?"

Spence raised an eyebrow. "What about them?"

"They're attracted to each other."

"They are not." Spence shook his head, then looked down at Maggie. "Are they?"

"Yes, I believe they are," Maggie reported. "And how could Emily possibly be attracted to a man like Seth if not for the powers of the love goddess?"

"What's wrong with Grissom?"

Now Maggie rolled her eyes. "He's the most frightening-looking man on the entire earth—I know this because I've seen a good portion of it."

Spence thought for a moment. "Grissom's never been in trouble with the law. There was a little problem a few months back with the men in town giving Seth a hard time about having to paint Jack Delaney's wife's storefront pink, but that passed. He runs a good business, goes to church, helps out when anybody needs him. What's wrong with that?"

"He's unkempt and slovenly and—"

"And that means Emily couldn't care about him?"

Maggie drew in a quick breath. "You—of all people—should know exactly what I'm talking about."

Spence's brows pulled together. "Why's that?"

"Because you kissed me," Maggie explained.

He drew back a little. "So?"

"You couldn't help yourself," she said.

"I couldn't?"

"You find me irresistible."

Spence just looked at her in that questioning way of his, bringing a blush to Maggie cheeks as she realized what she'd said.

"It's because you're under the influence of the love goddess," she hurried to explain. "We both touched it, remember?"

Spence looked hard at her. "You think I kissed you because of some hunk of rock?"

"Yes," Maggie insisted. She shifted and looked away. "I mean, why else would you? Someone like me is hardly…hardly the type of woman that would be interesting to a…a man like you."

Spence leaned around, catching her gaze. "Who told you that?"

"My father," Maggie said, meeting his eye. "And his friends, the other professors. Brilliant men, all of them. A woman with an education. What man would find that attractive? And they were right, too. I've never been overwhelmed with gentleman callers, except for a few who sought favor from my father. Never because of…me."

"So you think having a university education scares men off?" Spence asked.

Maggie nodded with the full knowledge of her father's advice and her own experience. "It's true."

Spence squared his shoulders. "Do I looked scared to you?"

"Well, no," Maggie admitted. She couldn't resist dropping her gaze to his big chest and wide shoulders for an instant. "I can't imagine that you've ever been afraid of anything."

"It must have taken a lot of hard work and dedication to make it through your studies. You must be really smart," Spence said. "I admire all those qualities."

"Even in a woman?"

"Especially in a woman," Spence said. "Although, I think you're putting way too much stock in this love goddess statue."

"I don't believe I am," Maggie said, shaking her head.

He nodded thoughtfully. "So if what you're saying about the powers of that hunk of rock is true, that must mean you have feelings for me. Right?"

Maggie blushed anew. "Well…"

"A man like me? *Without* a university education?"

"But I don't care about things like that," Maggie told him, and it was true. "You're smart about other things. In ways that are truly important. You're strong and hardworking. You're not afraid to draw a hard line, yet you're kind and understanding. You have integrity and—"

Maggie snapped her mouth closed seeing the smug look on his face and how much he was enjoying her tribute to his many good qualities. Honestly, the man had a way of letting her talk herself into the most embarrassing moments.

"I have to go back to work now," she told him,

then put her nose in the air, whipped around and headed back to the store.

"Don't you want to hear what I learned when I was at your house?" Spence called.

She was forced to turn and face him again. But he didn't speak right away, just stood there looking at her, making her heart beat a little faster.

"I found footprints around the outbuildings and at the back of the house," Spence said.

"So somebody *was* there?" she asked, a little alarmed now.

He lifted a shoulder. "We've had no rain or wind in the past few days so I couldn't tell how long the tracks had been there."

"The cottage has been empty for a while. Do you think perhaps a transient has been living there?"

"I doubt it. I always know when there's somebody new in town."

"Then who—"

"I'll check around some more, see what else I can find out," Spence said. "Don't worry. You'll be safe there. I'll see to it."

The man had a way of inspiring confidence that Maggie couldn't deny. She knew that if Spence said he'd make sure she was safe in the little cottage, that's exactly what would happen.

"Thank you," she said.

Hank Townsend, the store, the stock, the customers waited, but Maggie couldn't bring herself to leave the alley. A moment, then another, crept by while she stood there just looking at Spence. He seemed all right with it, because he stood there, too.

Finally, he walked forward. She fell in step beside him and went with him to the door of the dry-goods store. He touched the brim of his hat, catching her gaze and favoring her with a small grin—complete with dimples—then continued down the boardwalk.

Maggie stood there another moment, watching his purposeful, long strides as he weaved his way through the pedestrians, heading toward the jail. A little sigh of longing slipped through her lips.

She gasped and slapped her hand across her mouth. Maggie glanced around quickly. Had anybody heard her? Had someone seen her watching Spence?

She'd have to be more careful about her conduct, and remember that she was in the clutches of the ancient love goddess. Why, if anyone had just witnessed her behavior they'd likely think she had genuine feelings for Spence. And she didn't, of course. It was the spell of the love goddess.

Maggie took one final look at the jailhouse as Spence went inside.

Yes, it was only the love goddess.

She hurried into the store.

Chapter Sixteen

If anything, Maggie's job performance was worse this day than the day before. Hank Townsend hadn't pointed it out, but Maggie saw those thoughts in his sour expression.

The customers who came in the store still avoided her, preferring to discuss their purchases with Hank Townsend himself. The children who accompanied their parents were as disruptive as ever, asking for things, whining, tugging at their mothers' skirts, begging to leave. The twins, Jack and Jake, came in again, making faces at her, running off with her feather duster. Maggie wondered how mothers ever got their shopping done.

Finally, a bright spot in the afternoon lifted Maggie's spirits when Lucy Hubbard came into the store. Maggie observed her in silence, looking for outward signs of the love goddess's influence. She saw none.

"More soaps?" Maggie asked, walking over and gesturing toward the basket Lucy had on her arm.

"Eggs today," she reported. "I started raising chickens a few months ago. Mr. Townsend buys the eggs. So do Emily's bakery and the Pink Blossom."

My, but this woman was industrious, Maggie thought. She would have told her so, but Lucy seemed troubled today, not in the mood for small talk. She certainly couldn't ask her if she'd been to Professor Canfield's Oddities of the World Museum along with Deputy Ian Caldwell, much as she wanted to.

"Mr. Townsend will be finished with his customer soon," Maggie said, waving her hand toward the counter. "Let me know if I can help you otherwise."

"Thank you," Lucy murmured.

Maggie busied herself straightening the canned goods that Jack and Jake had amused themselves with while their mother shopped, while Lucy ran her hand along the bolts of fabric stacked nearby. When Mr. Townsend was available, she concluded her sale with him quickly and headed out the door. But a man stepped in, blocking her path. From the expression on both their faces, Maggie realized they knew each other.

"Where've you been for so long?" the man asked Lucy, a slight edge to his voice.

"I told you, Raymond, I was delivering eggs this afternoon," Lucy said.

Maggie couldn't help but overhear their conversation as they stood just a few feet away. She dared to glance up and look at the man, whom she assumed to be Lucy's husband. Raymond Hubbard wore a white shirt, and a coat and tie. He would have looked quite dapper, had the collar and sleeves not been frayed. He had dark hair that was a trifle too long, in need of cutting. He was handsome enough, yet something about him made Maggie uncomfortable.

Perhaps it was the things Spence had told her about the man.

"Raymond," Lucy began, drawing herself up slightly. "The money I keep in the sugar canister is missing. Did—did you take it?"

"How should I know where it is?" Raymond asked in an irritating whine. "You're the one who put it there."

"I know I put it in there," Lucy said, glancing down. "I don't know what could have happened to it unless you—"

"Did you get the egg money?" Raymond asked.

"Yes," Lucy replied. She looked up at him again, and drew back a little.

"Give it here," he told her.

She took a step backward. "But I'm saving this money to make myself a new dress for the Founders Day Festival. I explained that to you, and you said—"

"You don't need a new dress for some festival," Raymond told her. "Give me that egg money."

When Lucy hesitated, Raymond took her hand, pried open her fingers and picked up the coins. "Go on home now. You need to get supper started. I'll be there after a while."

With that, Raymond turned and left the store.

Anger stirred in Maggie and, for a moment, she considered going after Raymond Hubbard, demanding Lucy's money back. But when she saw Lucy, saw the hurt and humiliation in her face, Maggie did nothing. After a moment, Lucy left the store.

When the last customer left for the day and Mr. Townsend told her she could leave, Maggie bolted from the store, glad to be out of the place. But she came up short on the boardwalk, surprised to see Spence waiting.

He leaned his shoulder against one of the roof's support columns, one ankle crossed over the other, gazing down the street, a thoughtful expression on his face. Maggie's heart fluttered at the sight, though she didn't want it to.

"You look very deep in thought," she called.

Spence's gaze swung to her and he straightened away from the column.

She walked up at him. "Weren't you afraid that I'd managed to buy a pistol somewhere today after all, and come out of the store, guns blazing?"

"No, I didn't consider that." He grinned. "But maybe I should have."

"What are you doing here?"

"Walking you home."

Maggie's heart fluttered a little harder. She'd never been walked home before. "Why?" she couldn't help but ask.

"I want to have another look around the cottage, make sure everything is all right there." Spence's grin widened a little. "Can't have the town's only university graduate too scared to sleep at night."

"Shh!" Maggie waved her arms. "That's supposed to be a secret. You promised you wouldn't tell."

"That's not something to hide. You ought to be proud of it."

"Well, I'm not," she told him, glancing around to see if anyone was close enough to overhear them. To her relief, there wasn't.

They walked to the cottage, and the place seemed

as dreary as ever to Maggie. Spence took the key she offered, opened the door and led the way inside.

"Wait here," he said, then searched through the parlor and bedroom. When he came out, he said, "I'd ask you if anything seemed out of place, but I can see it's all exactly the same as it was when you moved in here."

Maggie glanced around at the shrouded furniture, the dust and grime, uncomfortable under Spence's obvious disappointment with her.

"I guess they don't teach scrubbing floors and polishing windows at that university you attended," Spence ventured.

She gave him a weak smile. "No, they didn't. But if you'd like to learn about the pyramids along the Nile, just ask."

Spence opened the back door and went outside. Maggie went to the doorway and shielded her eyes against the setting sun as he investigated all the buildings, then studied the ground around them. After a while, he came back to the house.

"Looks like somebody's been out there," he said, stepping inside. "I found fresh tracks."

"Since this morning?" Maggie gasped. "Who could it be?"

"Probably Dex. I told him and Ian to keep an eye on the place."

"So it's no one causing trouble?"

Spence pointed toward the street. "The old tracks I saw probably belonged to Mrs. Frazier's nephew. That's her house. I wouldn't put it past the boy to snoop around here."

"But you don't think the footprints you just found are his?"

Spence shook his head. "Ian caught the boy red-handed stealing apples from the Pink Blossom store-room. I told Mrs. Frazier the boy could either go out to her husband's ranch, or I'd put him in jail."

"For stealing apples?"

"He's been trouble ever since he got to Marlow."

Maggie felt a little better. "Well, thank you. I'll sleep better tonight, I'm sure."

She expected that Spence would leave then. Surely, he had important things to attend to, and his work here was done. There was no reason to stay.

But he didn't leave. Instead, he turned around and looked at the interior of the cottage again. Maggie felt uncomfortable under his scrutiny, sure she knew what he was thinking.

"I've never actually fixed up a house before," she said, and gestured to the kitchen area. "Or cleaned, or cooked, or...anything."

"I guess going to school took up most of your time," Spence said.

"Well, not entirely," Maggie said, though not anxious to admit yet another shortcoming. "You see, my father always employed cooks and maids who took care of everything. None of them wanted me underfoot, so I never learned to do any of these things."

"But you're a woman," he said.

A rush of heat swept her from head to toe. "Thank you for noticing, but what's that got to do with anything?"

"Women just *know* how to do these things," he said.

"Well, I don't."

"These things ought to come natural to you,"

Spence insisted. "You don't have to learn everything from a schoolbook, Maggie."

"I am trying," she told him, though in truth, she hadn't the slightest idea of where to start.

Spence looked over at the kitchen. "What are you doing about supper?"

"Mr. Townsend gave me some things yesterday, and I planned to…" Maggie words trailed off as Spence walked over and eyed the meager supplies piled on her sideboard.

"I'll give you a hand with supper," Spence said, and she was relieved he hadn't questioned her—embarrassed her—further.

He took off his hat and rummaged through her supplies, clattering through the cabinets finding pots and pans.

"Come over here. I'll show you what I'm doing," he said.

Maggie stood at his side as he lit the cookstove and got their meal going. She pulled the shrouds off the table and four chairs, then found a rag and wiped down the furniture. When everything was ready, they sat down together and ate.

"I'll send somebody over here to fix the pump and repair the cabinet," Spence said.

He'd seen that the pump was leaking and some of the wood around it had rotted; Maggie hadn't noticed.

"You were right about Lucy Hubbard's husband," Maggie said, as she sipped the coffee Spence had made. "I saw him in the store today. He took her egg money away from her, then told her she couldn't have a new dress."

Spence paused, clutching the fork in his hand. He

didn't say anything, but Maggie knew him well enough now to read his expression and know that he wasn't happy about what he'd just heard.

"It made me mad," Maggie went on. "I wanted to go after that awful man and demand her money back."

"It's best not to get in between a man and his wife."

"I suppose you're right," Maggie agreed. "But it made me angry, just the same. I don't know Ian Caldwell very well, but he's bound to be a better husband than that awful Raymond Hubbard."

"Even if he hasn't touched your love goddess?" Spence asked.

"Too bad the goddess can't make people *nice*."

"If it could, I'd be taking it door-to-door myself."

When they finished the meal, they washed the dishes and put everything away. Spence got his hat and opened the back door.

"Thank you for everything," Maggie said, standing next to him.

Spence didn't answer. He lingered, gazing down at Maggie in a way that made her heart beat faster, made her want to lean closer to him, made her wish that he would—

He kissed her. Spence slid his arms around her and covered her lips with his. Maggie rose on her toes. Her heart banged in her chest as he moved his mouth over hers.

When he finally lifted his head, his breathing was labored, hot puffs against her cheek. She wondered if he would kiss her again, hoped that he would. He didn't disappoint. He leaned in again and took her lips once more, this time gently and only for a moment.

"I'll be back later to check on you," he whispered.

He lingered another moment, then went outside. Maggie hung on to the door, afraid her knees wouldn't hold her up. He turned, nodded, then left.

She swayed back into the room closing the door behind her, her heart still pumping wildly, her thoughts in chaos.

So she was surprised when a knock sounded on the back door again so soon. Spence. He'd come back. Maggie jerked open the door.

A strange man stood on her back porch. He grabbed her.

Chapter Seventeen

Spence paused at the corner of West Street and Main, glad for the evening breeze that swirled around him. He needed to cool off.

Yet despite himself, he glanced back at Maggie's cottage. The familiar heat flared in him again. He'd kissed her just now standing at her back door—kissed her twice, in fact. Yet it hadn't been enough. He wanted to kiss her again. He wanted to linger, to stay there with her and…

And what? The notion startled him a little, yet didn't diminish the craving that still claimed him. Spence drew in a breath and let it out slowly. Maggie was a respectable woman, a lady, not the kind of female to be trifled with. Spence had long ago learned the difference. Yet he knew what he wanted to do with Maggie.

For a moment, he was tempted to go back to her house, knock on her door, slip inside. He hadn't had those feelings for a woman in a long time. Not since—

Not since Ellen, Spence realized. The hurtful

memories filled his mind, as always, and he let them come. He deserved them.

But this time another vision crept into his thoughts. Maggie. Nothing hurtful about thinking of her, although his thoughts were far from pure.

What man wouldn't do just the same? Even where Maggie was concerned.

True, she was a little different from most of the women he'd known. She was book smart, with not quite as much common sense as she needed, especially for dealing with life here in Colorado. She'd traveled the world, yet wasn't particularly worldly about life…about men. Of course, after she'd explained how she was raised, Spence understood.

He understood, too, how a smart woman like Maggie might intimidate other men, how her education could scare them off. He was neither intimidated nor scared.

But it wasn't Maggie's brain he was interested in at the moment.

All the more reason to move along, go about his business, Spence decided. He'd left her tucked inside the cottage, safe and sound, only moments ago. She was fine. Even Maggie couldn't find trouble in so short a time.

Turning away, Spence headed east on Main Street.

At this hour of the day, just after sunset and before darkness fell, Spence walked through town. He kept an eye on the stores as they closed for business. He knew which shopkeepers took their day's receipts to the bank, which slept with them under their pillow at night. Either way, he liked to make sure they made it safely to their destination. After dark, Spence made rounds again, rattling doorknobs, checking alleys, this time with his street-sweeper, a sawed-off shotgun.

Spence had known since he was a boy that he wanted to be a sheriff. His first job had been in his hometown, cleaning Harmon's Dry Goods Store after school. Until, that is, two gunmen had burst into the store one evening, robbed the place, and shot Mr. Harmon to death. All that blood. Mrs. Harmon screaming.

But seeing the old man gunned down right before his eyes hadn't scared Spence. It made him mad. Madder than he'd ever been. The injustice. The arrogance of the outlaws. If he'd had a gun in his hand that day instead of a broom, he'd have shot those men on the spot—and not given it another thought.

Afterward, the store had closed, Mrs. Harmon left town. Spence lost his job. Yet he had found his calling.

He still thought of Mr. Harmon occasionally when he passed by Townsend Dry Goods or Norman Kirby's store. Up until now, that is. Now the stores reminded him of Maggie.

A lot of people in town believed they owed Spence a favor or two for getting them out of a jam, professionally or personally. He didn't see it that way; to him, he was only doing his job. Hank Townsend was one of those people.

Back before Hank's son and daughter-in-law had moved to Texas, Spence had been making his evening rounds just as two drunk cowboys decided to take a liking to the young woman as she was headed for choir practice. Spence had broken it up before anything happened. He never felt he'd done more than what any other decent man would have done—

let alone a town sheriff—but Hank insisted he owed
Spence a special favor.

Spence hadn't had to remind Hank of the incident
when he asked Hank to give Maggie a job, but he
could tell the shopkeeper wasn't all that happy about
repaying him with *this* particular favor.

Spence's footsteps slowed on the boardwalk as
Maggie came full into his mind again. He stopped,
looked back, debated returning to her place. He felt
the pull to go to her and was tempted to give in.
Instead he determinedly kept to his evening rounds,
mindful of his duty.

As he approached the Marlow Bake Shop, Spence
saw Seth Grissom leaving the store, a cookie in each
hand. His conversation with Maggie earlier in the
day came back to him, and he wondered now if what
she'd told him about Griss being sweet on Emily
might be true. Spence realized now that he often saw
Griss going and coming from Emily's shop. He'd
thought the man just liked baked goods, but now he
considered that there may be something to what
Maggie had said.

Emily had moved to Marlow last fall and opened
the business with the help of her brother Jack, one
of the few honest saloon owners Spence knew. She'd
come from New York, a fine, well-groomed, genteel
lady, the kind Marlow saw few of; somehow, she'd
fit in right away. It was as if—

Spence came up short as a thought came to him.
He mulled it over for a moment, then decided a visit
to Emily Delaney—a private visit—was definitely in
order.

"Evening, Sheriff."

Spence looked up, saw that Seth Grissom had

stopped on the boardwalk up ahead and was waiting
for him. In the closing light of day, Spence realized
that perhaps Maggie was also right about Griss. A
woman might find his appearance more than a little
frightening.

"How's things going, Griss?" Spence asked, stopping beside him.

"Tolerable, I suppose," Griss said, and popped
the last cookie into his mouth.

"I couldn't help but notice that you're in and out
of Miss Delaney's bakery a lot," Spence noted. "Her
cookies are something special."

Griss gulped hard. "That they are."

They headed off down the boardwalk together.

"Have you got time for a side job?" Spence
asked. Griss was the best carpenter in town. He'd
been busy for months with new stores and businesses
going up, and was working now on the office of a
new attorney who'd moved to Marlow. Everybody
was getting ready for the railroad to come through,
despite its many delays.

"Sure thing, Sheriff," Griss said, "if it's important to you."

"I need you to repair a leaky pump and replace
the rotted boards around it," Spence told him.

"Over at the jail?"

"No, at the cottage where Hank Townsend's son
used to live," Spence explained. "Hank's letting
Miss Peyton live there now."

Griss stopped, causing Spence to do the same.

"You keeping company with Miss Peyton?" Griss
asked, narrowing an eye at him.

"No," Spence said quickly. The words sounded
like a lie, even to his own ears. "Well, not exactly."

"And I'm just *crazy* about cookies." Griss
grunted and hitched up his trousers. "I swear, if I
don't get up nerve enough to talk to Miss Emily
pretty soon, I'm going to have to get my pants let
out."

"Well, hell, Griss," Spence said. "If you like the
woman, you ought to start calling on her."

"I'm working up to it." Griss shifted his big
frame, and nodded down the street. "'Course, that's
more than I can say for some people."

They'd reached the corner, and Spence followed
Griss's gaze down East Street to where Ian Caldwell
stood in the shadows outside Norman's General
Store. But his deputy wasn't concerned about some
problem in the shop. His attention was riveted on the
little cabin at the end of the street. Lucy Hubbard's
place.

Spence's chest ached a little at the sight. He'd
known for months that Ian was crazy about Lucy,
known too that the two of them would be married
by now, if circumstances would allow. He wondered
how Ian could bear to stay in Marlow and see Lucy
every day, knowing that she went home to her husband at night. Yet, difficult as it was, perhaps it was
better than never seeing her again.

Maggie sprang into Spence's mind, and once more
he was tempted to go back to her cottage.

"'Course, your deputy would make his intentions
known, if he could," Griss observed.

"He sure would," Spence agreed, knowing Ian
would do just that, given half a chance.

"You've got to admire a woman who'll stand by
her vows," Griss mused. "Especially when things
turn out so bad, like they have for Miss Lucy. Every-

body knows what that husband of hers is like. He
ought to be shot.''

"Yep, he ought to be," Spence agreed. "No
woman deserves a husband like that.''

They lapsed into silence. Spence's mind drifted to
Maggie once more, and he suspected Griss's
thoughts had turned to Emily.

Whatever thoughts Ian might have been having
about Lucy changed abruptly, apparently, because he
turned away and headed toward the corner where
Spence and Griss stood. As he approached, he saw
Spence.

"I was just…ah…" Ian gestured behind him. "I
was just doing rounds.''

None of the men spoke for a few moments, then
Griss said, "How about we head over to the Lucky
Streak? I could use a beer.''

"Sounds good," Ian agreed, and looked as though
he would appreciate a distraction from his own
thoughts.

Spence usually went to the saloons in town just to
make sure everything was under control, or to break
up a fight. He seldom drank. Tonight, though, he
decided to make an exception.

"Let's go," he said, and the men started walking.

When they reached the corner at West Street,
Spence stopped. He glanced down the street at Maggie's little cottage. A lamp burned inside, making the
windows glow. He'd been by this place dozens of
time, when Hank's son lived there and since he
moved away. Never before had he felt the tug to
walk down there as he had tonight. Was it Maggie?

Or something else?

"Are you coming?" Ian called.

Spence glanced at the two men and saw that they had gotten ahead of him on the boardwalk. He paused, unsure of what to do—which wasn't like him.

Irritated with himself, Spence said, "Yeah, I'm coming."

He turned his back on Maggie's cottage and kept walking.

Chapter Eighteen

In an easy motion, the man slammed the back door closed and pushed Maggie against the kitchen wall, pinning her there with the weight of his body. A few horrifying seconds passed before she pulled in a deep breath and opened her mouth to scream.

"No, ma'am...please don't...please don't scream...I just...I just need your help."

His voice was a whimper against Maggie's ear, and she realized that he wasn't so much holding her against the wall as he was using her to keep himself upright.

Maggie eased her head away from him, stunned to see that his left eye was horribly bruised, swollen half shut. More bruises covered the side of his face. His lip was puffy. He'd been beaten, and yet he looked familiar.

"You're that boy," she realized. Maggie squirmed away from him. "That boy from the stagecoach holdup."

He leaned heavily against the wall, struggling to remain on his feet, and protecting his left side with his arm curled against it.

"Yes, ma'am, that's right. Henry, Henry Donovan," he said, the words spoken with considerable effort.

The young man was no threat to her—he wasn't even armed. Her concern turned from herself to him.

"Good gracious, Henry, what happened to you?"

He swallowed hard and swayed, then shifted his weight, struggling to keep his balance. "If I could sit down…for just a minute…"

Unsure of the extent of his injuries, Maggie cautiously took his right arm and assisted him into the kitchen chair. He sat down heavily, his head rolling back. Dried blood crusted in spatters across the front of his shirt. His clothing was dirty and torn.

She hurried to the pump and got him a glass of water. He took it, wincing when he gulped it down.

"I'll get the doctor," Maggie said. "Stay here."

"No," Henry said, reaching out a dirty hand to her. "No, please. No doctor. He'll tell the sheriff…."

Of course he would. And regardless of what the boy had been through, what injuries he'd suffered, he was still a stagecoach robber. Spence would take Henry off to jail.

Why shouldn't he? The boy was an outlaw. A thief. He—along with the rest of his gang—had taken Maggie's own money, left her tied up and alone in the wilderness with Spence. He deserved to be in jail.

But as Maggie looked at his battered face, she couldn't bring herself to turn him in. Not until she found out why he was here.

She sank into the chair beside him. "Tell me what happened."

Henry grimaced, the effort of recalling his recent ordeal seemingly almost as painful as his injuries.

"We were riding over toward Keaton," Henry began.

"You and the other gang members?" she asked, startled to realize that perhaps Henry had sustained his injuries during the commission of another crime. Had some innocent bystander, some victim, been injured far worse? Left to die?

"I'd better get the sheriff," Maggie said, easing out of her chair.

"No, ma'am, please," Henry said. "Don't do that."

She sat in the chair again. "No guarantees."

He nodded with some effort. "Like I said, we were riding over toward Keaton and I told Uncle Mack that—"

"Your uncle is a member of the gang?" Maggie asked, her voice rising slightly.

"Yes, ma'am. He's the leader."

She leaned toward him. "Your *uncle* turned you to a life of crime?"

"After my ma died I didn't have no other place to go," Henry said. "Anyway, I told Uncle Mack that I didn't want no part of being in a gang anymore. I'd thought it over and I'd decided. But when I told him, he…he got mad."

Maggie eased back in her chair a little. "Your uncle did this to you?"

"Yes, ma'am. Like I said, he was pretty mad."

"Why did you come here?"

"Marlow was the closest town I could get to on foot," Henry said.

Maggie realized then that it was Henry's footprints Spence had seen outside her cottage. He'd been there yesterday, watching her.

"Why did you come here? To my place, I mean?"
she asked.

"I needed to hide. This place is on the edge of
town. Then I saw you. I remembered that you were
nice to me at the stagecoach robbery, asking about
my ma and all. I thought maybe…" A new weariness
showed on his battered young face. "You aren't going to hand me over to the law, are you?"

Maggie didn't know what to do. Henry was an
outlaw, no question about that. But he was also
young, with painful injuries and a difficult past.

"Let's get you cleaned up first," Maggie decided,
rising from the chair. "We'll worry about everything
else later."

She pumped the washbasin full of water from the
leaky pump and brought it over to the table. As
gently as she could, she cleaned Henry's wounds and
had him wash his hands. He didn't look much better,
and the effort seemed to take what was left of his
strength.

"Hungry?" she asked.

He barely managed a nod.

Maggie gave him what was left of the supper she'd
shared with Spence, all the while wondering what
Spence would think if he knew the meal he'd prepared for the two of them was now feeding an outlaw.

Maggie paused as she set the plate in front of
Henry. She didn't have to wonder what Spence
would think. She already knew.

Henry wolfed down the food while she contemplated what she should do. Turning the boy out into
the street was unthinkable, given his condition.

Handing him over to Spence didn't seem quite right, either.

"You can stay here for the night," Maggie said, taking away the dirty dishes. Tomorrow, she'd go to the jail and, if she explained Henry's injuries and his troubled family background, Spence would surely be more lenient on the boy.

"I don't want to get you into no trouble," Henry said.

"I won't get into trouble," she replied, hoping that was really true.

Spence had already accused her of trying to steal the love goddess and threatened to put her in jail. Of course, that was before he'd kissed her. Surely that counted for something.

"You can sleep on the settee," Maggie said, gesturing to the shrouded furniture. "I'll get you a blanket."

She went into the bedroom and pulled another blanket from the chest. When she returned, Henry was already on the settee, sleeping.

Clutching the blanket in her arms, Maggie gazed down at him. Battered, bruised, dirty. His life on the downward slide. Yet there was an innocence about him as he slept, making her believe that inside him somewhere was a kernel of goodness, the possibility that his life could be put back on track again.

He'd make an interesting entry in her journal, Maggie thought as she spread the blanket over him. Her father would be fascinated.

Her father. Going home. Only a few days ago, leaving this town had been the most important thing to her. But, somehow, things seemed a little different now. She wasn't sure why. Perhaps—

A knock sounded on her front door, bringing Maggie up short as she headed for her bedroom. Who would be coming to call this late at night? When she'd opened her back door a little while ago, an outlaw had fallen into her arms. She decided to be a little more cautious this time.

Slowly, she opened the door a crack and peeked out with one eye. Spence. Her mind raced. What had she gotten herself into? She had a known outlaw sleeping on her settee and the sheriff on her doorstep. What should she do now?

She slammed the door.

"Maggie?" Spence's voice carried surprise, but also concern. "Maggie, are you all right?"

"I'm fine," she called, trying to sound light and airy.

He must have heard the tremor in her voice—mistaking her guilt for peril, obviously—because he barked, "Open the door."

Maggie cringed. Now what should she do? If she didn't open the door, he might come crashing inside on his own. But if she did open it, he would recognize Henry and—

"Open the door."

He hadn't shouted or even raised his voice, but the command in his words couldn't be denied. Maggie eased the door open a few inches and looked up at him, stealing herself against his menacing scowl.

"What's going on in there?" he demanded.

How did he *know?* It was as if this man could read her every thought, her every emotion.

"Nothing," she said sweetly, trying to sound as if there wasn't a thing to be concerned about. "But it's late and—"

Spence shoved the door open and stepped into the room, his face set in determined lines. His gaze swept the room and landed on Henry just as the boy lurched from the settee and ran toward for the back door. Spence went after him.

"No!" Maggie shouted.

Spence caught him in three quick strides, grabbed the back of his shirt, shoved him hard face first against the wall and held him there.

"Don't!" Maggie laid her hand on Spence's arm. She couldn't restrain him, couldn't pull him off Henry; he was too strong, too powerful. "Please, Spence. Don't hurt him."

Spence looked down at her, his gaze burning hot.

"Please," she said again. "He's already injured."

Spence turned Henry around and shoved him against the wall again, holding him in place by his shirt collar. He gave the boy's bruises nothing more than a cursory glance, then swung his gaze to Maggie once more.

"Did he hurt you?" Spence demanded.

The venom in his voice startled Maggie, robbing her of a reply for a moment.

"Did he hurt you?"

"Don't shout at me!" she told him, anger suddenly overtaking her.

"Then answer my question!"

"I'm fine!" she answered.

He glared hard at her. She felt his hot breath, sensed his power, his strength, barely contained.

And all she could think was how handsome he was.

Maggie almost gasped aloud as she stepped back.

How in the world could she have had such a thought?
And at a time like this? What was wrong with her?

Spence yanked Henry away from the wall and
pulled him toward the front door, one hand on the
boy's collar, the other secure around his arm.

"What—what are you doing?" she asked, coming
out of her stupor and hurrying after them. "Where
are you taking him?"

"To the jail," Spence said, not bothering to look
back.

"But he's hurt—"

Spence pushed Henry out the door ahead of him,
then finally turned to Maggie.

"Lock this door," he barked. "Lock it now and
don't open it again tonight—for anybody."

"But—"

He slammed the door shut, leaving her staring at
it, alone in the silent cottage.

Chapter Nineteen

Would this morning ever end?

Maggie dragged the broom down the canned goods aisle of Townsend Dry Goods, each moment crawling by with excruciating slowness. Already, she'd swept the entire store, the boardwalk, dusted the shelves, straightened and squared off everything in sight. But no matter how hard she tried, the morning continued to creep by. It seemed that her noon break from the store would never arrive.

She suspected Hank Townsend was as anxious for her to be out of the store as anyone. After so many days in his employment, Maggie had yet to make a single sale. She hadn't pleased one customer. In fact, she'd contributed nothing to the success of the business.

And worse, just this morning she knocked over a display of shovels by the front door when those dreadful twin boys had charged into the store, causing her to jump out of their paths; why they weren't in school, she didn't know. Hank hadn't said anything, but he glared at her. She knew what he was thinking. Only yesterday, she made a little girl cry when she'd smiled at her. The child's mother had unloaded the many items she'd gathered in her basket and left the store in a huff without spending a cent.

Leaning on the broom, Maggie gazed longingly out the store's open front door at the people passing by. How she wished to be among them, free to do as she chose rather than being confined in this store where she was constantly reminded of her shortcomings—and displayed them throughout the day for her employer and all the town to see.

She drew in a deep breath and turned away from the door, her spirits sinking further. She should have known she couldn't do this job. Desperate as she'd been at the time, she should have refused the offer. Why had she tried? She couldn't possibly fit in here.

"Good morning, Maggie."

She turned at the sound of the familiar voice and saw Lucy Hubbard enter the store, her market basket hooked over her arm. Lucy smiled pleasantly, but it seemed to be with effort. Maggie thought she looked tired and wondered if she'd been up late last night preparing whatever it was she hoped to sell to Hank today.

"More soap?" Maggie asked.

Lucy nodded, then pulled back the cloth, displaying small, colorfully wrapped packages.

"They're very popular," Maggie said. "Most all the women who come in pick them up, and comment on their scent."

Lucy smiled modestly. "They do sell quickly. I'm grateful for that."

Maggie stepped aside as Lucy went to the counter to talk with Hank, then returned to her sweeping. A few minutes later as Lucy left the store, she made a point to speak to Maggie.

"I guess I'll see you at church services on Sunday?" Lucy asked.

Maggie's stomach twisted into a familiar knot. Church. Just the sort of social gathering she dreaded. She was even more uncomfortable there than here at the store.

All those people—friends and neighbors—standing in tight groups, chatting, laughing, enjoying the fellowship. What would they talk about this week? Hank Townsend's new incompetent employee?

Probably.

Maggie envisioned herself standing alone at the edge of the churchyard, once more unable to fit in. She supposed she should be used to that situation by now, but she wasn't.

Maggie managed a small smile and said, "Yes, I'll be there."

"Good," Lucy answered. "Have you met Mrs. Frazier yet?"

"I don't think so."

"If you'd met Mrs. Frazier, you'd have remembered," Lucy said with a gentle laugh. "She runs most of the church and civic events here in Marlow. I'm sure she'll want you to join the ladies auxiliary group."

Maggie doubted it, but managed another smile. "That sounds as if it's a very worthwhile organization."

"We're always busy," Lucy agreed. "Mrs. Frazier keeps us hopping. There's so much in town that needs to be done. Well, I'd better go. I'll see you on Sunday."

Maggie watched with longing as Lucy left the store, wishing that she, too, could simply walk out.

"You can leave now," Hank called from behind the counter.

Maggie's spirits soared, not expecting him to send her on her noon break so early. She dashed behind the counter and stowed the broom, then pinned on her hat and grabbed her market basket.

"I'll be back soon," she said.

"Don't rush," Hank grumbled.

Not even her employer's disparaging remark dampened Maggie's enthusiasm or slowed her pace as she left the store and headed down the boardwalk.

The sun had never seemed to bright, the breeze so gentle, the air so fresh. Not even along the Nile, or in the mountains of South America, or at the banks of the Thames—anyplace she'd ever visited.

Maggie drew in a deep breath, basking in the freedom from her enforced bondage at the dry-goods store.

Her first stop would be at Marlow's Bake Shop; she'd decided that this morning as she left her cottage. Now she stopped quickly on the boardwalk as Seth Grissom exited the bakery. She considered abandoning her plan in order to avoid him, but to her relief, the mountain man ambled away in the opposite direction.

With quick, light steps Maggie went into the bakery. It smelled of fresh bread, cookies and pies. Delicious.

Emily stood behind the counter, looking a little flustered, a little lost in thought.

"Oh. Sorry." She smoothed down her apron, giving Maggie her full attention. "What can I get for you?"

Maggie slid her hand into the small pocket of her skirt and threaded her fingers through her coins. She'd counted them carefully this morning before leaving the house as she'd made her plan for the day, and knew exactly how much she could afford to spend.

"Four oatmeal cookies, please," Maggie said and laid the money on the counter.

As bad an employee as she was, and as much as she disliked being confined in the dry-goods store, it was some consolation that at least she could eat now.

"There you go," Emily said as she wrapped the cookies and handed them over. "Anything else?"

Maggie hesitated, then said, "Two more, please?"

"Sure," Emily said, going into the glass display jar once more. "The oatmeals are the best, if I do say so myself."

"Mr. Grissom seems to like them," Maggie said.

Emily's cheeks turned pink. "Yes, I suppose so."

Maggie paid for the extra cookies, tucked them inside her basket and headed for the door. To her surprise, Emily walked with her out onto the boardwalk. Maggie wondered if she was just being friendly, or perhaps hoped to catch a glimpse of Seth Grissom on the street.

The mountain man was nowhere to be seen, but they did spot Lucy Hubbard and her husband standing at the entrance to the alley a few feet away. Lucy looked upset.

"Raymond, you promised me you would stop—"

"I didn't do nothing," he told her, his voice a whiny plea on the breeze.

She drew in a breath. "This morning I found a whiskey bottle in the bushes behind the house. You promised me you'd stop—"

"Well what makes you think it was my bottle?" he wanted to know.

"If it wasn't yours, then how did it get there?"

"How should I know?" he asked. "Probably it was somebody trespassing on my property. I'm going to go ask the sheriff what kind of town he's running here."

"But Raymond—"

"I'll be home later," he told her and walked away.

Lucy lingered in the alley for a moment, her shoulders slumping, then finally walked away.

Maggie and Emily exchanged an uncomfortable glance. They hadn't meant to eavesdrop, but Lucy and her husband couldn't have expected privacy on a public street.

"Well, thanks for the cookies," Maggie said, and went on her way. Looking up ahead, she caught sight of Raymond as he walked past the sheriff's office. He hadn't intended to go there at all. More than likely, he was headed for the saloon.

Irritated, Maggie pushed the man from her mind. She had only a short time before she had to return to the store and couldn't waste a moment. She headed for the jail.

"Here comes trouble."

Spence's head snapped up from the new packet of Wanted posters he was looking over, his attention riveted on Ian as he looked out the jailhouse window. Despite his words, Ian didn't look all that concerned about what he'd just spotted outside on the street. Still, Spence got to this feet and walked over.

Main Street was crowded with pedestrians, wagons and horses, but Spence knew immediately what Ian meant.

Maggie. Headed straight for the jail.

"What'd you do?" Ian asked in a tone that told Spence here was a man used to dealing with women.

"Nothing," Spence declared.

"You must have done something," Ian insisted, "judging by the look on her face."

Spence couldn't disagree with his deputy. Even a one-eyed man could see that Maggie wasn't happy. Spence knew why, but he wasn't inclined to share it with Ian.

Last night when he'd stood at the corner, debating on whether to go to the saloon for a beer or check on Maggie again, he hadn't been able to fight off the lure of her cottage. Finding that outlaw inside with her had made him so mad he'd shouted at her, treated her badly. But she'd let the kid into her home, she had him sleeping on her settee. It was just about the craziest, most reckless thing he'd ever witnessed.

"You went to her place last night." Ian's words were more an accusation than a reminder.

"To check on her, make sure she was all right," Spence told him. He hadn't mentioned to either of his deputies that the young outlaw now confined to one of their cells had been caught inside Maggie's house. News like that would do her reputation no good at all.

Ian glanced up at him. "So you were just doing your duty with her last night?"

"Yeah," Spence insisted. "Just checking on one of the townsfolk."

Ian snorted as if he doubted it, then took his hat from the peg beside the door. "Then, Sheriff, I'll leave you to handle this citizen alone."

Chapter Twenty

Maggie nodded to Deputy Caldwell as he exited the sheriff's office, which wasn't easy since she'd pushed her chin upward in what she hoped would convey her anger and disdain as she prepared to enter the jailhouse. The nerve of Spence, yelling at her last night, refusing to listen to a single word she had to say. She'd hardly slept at all for thinking about him.

And not about how handsome he was, either.

Irritated, Maggie forced that thought from her mind, marched into the sheriff's office and pushed the door closed.

"I'm here to see the prisoner," she announced, drawing herself up, keeping her chin even higher.

Across the room, Spence stood beside his desk, tall, broad shouldered, freshly shaved and smelling good, even from this distance. Maggie's heart fluttered, warming her from head to toe.

Spence just looked at her for a moment, then raised one eyebrow. "I figured you'd come to turn yourself in."

"*What?*" The warmth spreading through Maggie

turned to ice. "Turn myself in? What are you talking about?"

He nodded slowly. "Thanks for saving me a trip over to Hank's store."

Maggie gasped, horrified at the very thought. She glanced at the door, considered whether to make a run for it.

"I haven't done anything," she told him.

Spence came closer, planting himself in front of her. "How about harboring a fugitive?"

"You don't know that I didn't intend to come and get you as soon as he fell asleep," Maggie countered.

"Then what about aiding and abetting a criminal?"

"Maybe I was simply offering him comfort so he'd stay put until I could come and get you?" Maggie proposed. "You don't know that wasn't my plan."

"Okay." Spence leaned down. "Then how about stupidity?"

Maggie mentally cringed. He was right, of course. Letting Henry stay at her house wasn't the smartest thing she could have done, regardless of the circumstances.

Still, she wouldn't let him get the upper hand. She pushed her chin up again. "Is that a crime?"

"If so, you'd be behind bars right now."

"There were mitigating circumstances," she insisted. "He was hurt and—"

"It was foolish of you, Maggie," he said, cutting her off, sounding angry now. "Yeah, he's just a kid. But he helped rob the stagecoach. The driver was killed."

"Yes, I know, but—"

"Have you forgotten what happened out there that day?" Spence challenged.

The vision of her hand shoved deep into his trouser pocket flamed in Maggie's mind. Heat swamped her. Her cheeks tingled. The same mental image must have leaped from her into Spence's mind because he flushed, too. His nose flared a little and his chest expanded. She nearly flung herself into his arms. He looked as if he hoped she would.

He must have come to his senses the same instant as she, because as Maggie pushed away the tantalizing thought, he backed up a step. She shifted her basket to the other arm, stalling until she composed herself again.

"I'd like to see Henry now," she said, trying to sound aloof but managing only a breathy whisper.

Spence shook his head. "Jail is no place for a woman."

"Why not? Is there something going on here you don't want me to know about?"

Spence heaved a sigh of resignation. "All right. Go on back there if you want. But first, show me what's in that basket."

She huffed to let him know she considered his suspicion of her ridiculous, then pulled back the cloth and threw him a sour look. "I left my file and gun in my other basket."

"A book, huh?" Spence asked, peering inside. He drew a little closer. "Are those cookies?"

"Yes, I thought Henry would appreciate them." Maggie withdrew two of them. "I bought these for you."

Spence's brows pulled together.

"I thought they might sweeten your disposition,"

Maggie told him, then pulled them away. "But I can see now that my intentions were misguided."

Spence snatched the cookies from her hand. "I'll think about it."

Then he grinned, and Maggie started to melt all over again. Oh, those dimples…

He was all business again as he put the cookies on his desk, and walked her to the doorway that led to the cells.

"Wait here," he told her.

Maggie did as he asked while he went down the narrow, dim hall to the last cell. She could see Henry inside, lying on a cot that was built into the cell's rear wall.

"Somebody's here to see you." Spence's voice held not a ounce of kindness or tolerance.

Henry raised his head, his gaze darted to Maggie and he sat up quickly.

"You stay back there on that cot," Spence told him. "Don't even get up."

Spence strode back down the hallway and fetched a cane-bottom chair from beside the potbellied stove. He placed it outside Henry's cell, against the far wall, a good arm's length from the bars.

"You can sit here. Don't move any closer," Spence said to Maggie. He turned to Henry. "Watch your mouth, boy."

Spence kept a watchful eye on Maggie as she settled into the chair, then threw a look at Henry before leaving them alone; Maggie knew he wouldn't be far away.

"How are you feeling?" she asked Henry.

He looked smaller, more frail than he had last

night, the cell—and the circumstances—dwarfing him.

"'Bout the same, I reckon," he replied.

"I'm going to ask the doctor to come by and check your injuries as soon as I leave here," Maggie promised.

"Doctor's been here," Henry said. "Last night. Sheriff brought him."

Maggie glanced down the hallway toward the office, a little surprised at Spence's kindness in view of how he'd treated the boy at her home last night.

"Doc said nothing was broken," Henry said. He uttered a short laugh. "Said I'll live."

"I'm sure you'll feel better soon."

Henry shifted on the cot. "I appreciate what you did for me last night. I don't rightly recall the last time anybody done something nice like that."

"I can see that you've had your share of difficulties."

"Sorry about the stagecoach robbery and all," he said. "I figured that what Sheriff Harding was saying that day about you being crazy in the head, wasn't true. You seemed like a nice lady to me."

"Thank you, Henry."

"Well, maybe you seemed a little crazy," Henry amended, "but not crazy enough for the asylum."

Maggie laughed gently. "Thank you again."

"Sorry about taking your handbag," Henry said. He gestured toward her. "You didn't get you a new one yet?"

"No, not yet," she said, a little surprised that he'd noticed. She'd wanted to buy herself a new handbag, but decided she should save as much of her salary as possible to buy her father's artifact from Professor Canfield.

"I brought you a book," she said, pulling the leather-bound volume from her basket. "I thought it would help you pass the time."

"You got a book with pictures?" he asked. "I don't read so good."

"Oh. Well, if you'd like I could read it to you."

"Yes, ma'am. That'd be nice."

She opened the book. "I hope you like Mark Twain."

"Can't say that I know him."

"He's the author," she said. "He wrote the book."

"Oh…"

"It's called *The Adventures of Tom Sawyer*," she explained. "It takes place on the Mississippi River."

"Is that down around Texas?"

"Not exactly," she said, then opened the book and began to read.

Henry proved a rapt audience and Maggie enjoyed reading to him. She wasn't sure he understood all the words, but he never stopped her to ask for an explanation. She supposed that having someone close, hearing another human voice might be enough for him, given the circumstances.

When she realized that it was time—past time, really—to get back to the dry-goods store, she tucked the book inside her basket and laid the cookies on the chair.

"Thank you for coming, Miss Maggie," Henry said, rising to his feet with some effort. "I appreciate it, I really do. And I'm sorry…about everything."

"Be good, Henry," Maggie said and went into the

office. Spence waited beside the doorway; she suspected he'd remained there the whole time and overheard their conversation.

"What's going to happen to Henry?" she asked.

"That's up to the circuit judge," Spence said. "He'll be around soon."

"But don't you have some say in the matter? I mean, if you told him Henry was really a good boy—"

"He's not a good boy, Maggie."

"He's had a very difficult life. His mother died, then he fell under the influence of his outlaw uncle."

Spence's expression hardened. "Would you like to explain that to the family of the driver who was killed?"

"You don't know that Henry was the one who shot him."

"You don't know that he wasn't," Spence countered.

Maggie heaved a sigh of resignation. She'd seen that determined look on Spence's face before. He wouldn't change his mind—not now, anyway.

"Is it all right if I come back and see him again?" she asked. When Spence didn't answer right away, she added, "I'll bring cookies. You seem to enjoy them."

She reached up and brushed away crumbs that had gathered on the front of his shirt. Yet her hand lingered, held in place by the warmth that seeped through the fabric. She imagined his heart beat harder beneath her palm.

Embarrassed, she pulled her hand away. Good gracious, what was she doing? But Spence caught her hand and pressed it to his chest again. His fingers remained over hers, his grip strong yet gentle as he held her captive.

Not that she wanted to leave. Answering some voiceless call, Maggie moved closer. He leaned down and slid his other hand to the back of her neck, and kissed her.

Gently he moved his lips over hers while his fingers toyed with the loose strands of her hair and strummed her flesh. Maggie swayed against him, their bodies touching, causing her to tingle with exquisite delight.

When Spence lifted his head, they gazed into each other's eyes for a moment, then he released her and stepped back.

"I'd better get to work," Maggie said softly.

"I can't leave a prisoner alone."

"I understand," Maggie said, though she was disappointed.

Spence walked her to the door, stepped out onto the boardwalk and watched as she crossed the street. At the entrance to the Townsend Dry Goods store, she paused, looked back for a moment, then hurried inside.

Even then, Spence didn't go back into the jailhouse. He knew there was no way in hell he'd get any work done now. Not with this craving that clawed at him. Not when all he could think of was finding another reason to see Maggie.

Spence dragged in a slow breath. Time to pay a late-night visit to Emily Delaney.

Chapter Twenty-One

She'd stood it as long as she could. Really, she had. And she'd tried. She'd certainly tried.

Maggie placated her somewhat guilty conscience as she left the Townsend Dry Goods store earlier than the designated closing time. She'd told Hank that she had an important errand to run when, in truth, she simply couldn't bear to be inside the store another second.

For a moment she considered that she should have gone ahead and sought work at the local undertakers, one of the few places in town she hadn't inquired with; at least there the customers wouldn't complain about her.

With the late-afternoon sun slipping westward, Maggie went about her "important errand." Hank Townsend probably wouldn't agree, but it was important to Maggie.

The only reason she was in this town, enduring a dreadful job and living in a quiet, lonely house was that Professor Canfield hadn't yet returned to Marlow. At least, as far as she knew. It had occurred to Maggie earlier in the day that the man might have come back and she hadn't known it. After all, he hardly knew she was looking for him. And since she'd never laid eyes on him, he might have walked right past her and she'd not have known it. So she'd decided to pay another call on his place of business and leave a message for him. It was the sensible thing to do. And it got her out of work.

When she arrived at Professor Canfield's Oddities of the World Museum, she wasn't surprised to find the door still locked. Just to be sure, though, she knocked, then cupped her hands and peered through the window. No sign of life.

A wave of longing washed through Maggie. A museum. The eclectic exhibits. They made her think of her father. She'd been at his side as they'd toured museums and discussed exhibits all over the world.

She wondered if Professor Canfield knew the details of the exhibits his own little museum housed as well as she did. He could probably explain the two-headed rattlesnake and the wax figurines of infamous outlaws. But what about the dinosaur bones? The Egyptian mummy on display? The area where the silver cross was alleged to have been recovered from Noah's Ark? How she wished he'd return, simply so they could talk about his collection.

She was sure he'd keep the knowledge of her education a secret from the townsfolk. Already, it was difficult enough for her to fit in here in Marlow. If everyone knew the truth about her...

With one last glance through the window, Maggie withdrew from her pocket the note she'd written earlier today and slid it under the front door.

Her heart a little heavy, Maggie headed for the cottage that was her home now. She didn't really want to be alone, but the few women she knew in town—Emily Delaney and Lucy Hubbard—would both be very busy working and not likely have time to sit and chat.

Not that Maggie knew what to chat with them about.

Spence floated into her mind and her spirits lifted. She considered going by the jail, but knew he'd be busy, too. He had an entire town to watch over.

That left her with an evening devoted to reading and writing in her journals. And, really, that wasn't so bad.

Inside her cottage, Maggie unpinned her hat and tossed it on the table. She sorted through the supplies still piled haphazardly on her kitchen counter, trying to decide what to eat for supper, when the head of a shaggy beast appeared at her kitchen window.

Maggie screamed. The creature jumped back, then reappeared looking at her quizzically. She heaved a sigh of relief. The beast was Seth Grissom. She opened the back door as he ambled toward her, feeling a bit embarrassed by her outburst.

"Didn't mean to scare you, Miss Maggie," Seth mumbled, turning his hat over in his hands. "I was just looking to see if you were home yet."

"You didn't frighten me," Maggie insisted. "I was just…just startled, that's all."

"Sheriff asked me to come by and see to your leaking pump."

Vaguely she recalled Spence saying he'd arrange for the repair. "Please, come in," she said, stepping back from the door.

Seth stepped inside carrying a tool box, his sheer size seeming to shrink the already tiny cottage.

"It's right here," Maggie said, then realized how silly she sounded. He lumbered over to the pump. "Can I get you anything?" she asked, which was even sillier since there was little in the cottage in the way of refreshment—and she wouldn't have known how to prepare anything he might have asked for.

Seth placed his tool box on the counter. "I'll take care of this and be on my way."

"Fine." Maggie gave him a nervous smile.

She went into the bedroom intending to read, then spotted her journals atop the chest. Since leaving New York she'd filled page after page with the sights and sounds of her journey west. And the people, of course. That's what was of most interest to her—and would be to her father once she returned to New York with his love goddess.

But what if she could tell her father that she'd actually witnessed the powers of the love goddess firsthand? What would a detailed account mean to him? Surely, it would go a long way toward him forgiving her for losing the priceless artifact in the first place.

Maggie thought it over for a few minutes, then selected the journal that she intended to present to her father. Since arriving in Marlow she'd started a second journal in which she recorded her personal thoughts that her father—or anyone else, for that matter—would never see.

Back in the kitchen, she eyed Seth Grissom working on the water pump. For a while now, she'd suspected that the ancient love goddess had worked its magic on Seth and Emily. Now was her opportunity to confirm her theory.

She laid her journal aside and sidled up near him, pretending to watch him work.

"Is this a difficult job?" she asked, just for something to say. He was using some sort of tool to disconnect parts of the pump.

"No, ma'am," Seth replied, keeping his attention on the job.

"I stopped by the Oddities of the World Museum today," Maggie said, watching closely for any reaction. "I was disappointed to find it closed."

Intent on his work, Seth didn't reply.

"Have you been there?" she asked.

"Yes, ma'am."

Her excitement built. Now she was getting somewhere.

"I looked through the window at the exhibits," she said. "Did you find them interesting?"

"Yes, ma'am."

"Did you happen to notice the small statue on the shelf near the back when you were there? The one with the big feet and outstretched arms?"

"Yes, ma'am."

Maggie leaned a little closer. "Is it possible that when you saw it, Emily Delaney was there also?"

The wrench slipped. Seth's hand banged against the pump. He grunted and stood upright, clenching his fingers into a fist.

"Oh, dear," Maggie whispered, seeing the blood seeping from his knuckles. "Let me get you something."

Seth waved her off and pulled a handkerchief from his pocket that he pressed against the injury.

"I didn't mean to cause you to hurt yourself," Maggie apologized.

Seth shrugged away her concern. "Guess my feelings for Miss Emily aren't much of a secret. Must seem silly, a man like me interested in a fine lady like her," he said softly.

Maggie's heart went out to him. He spoke Emily's name with reverence. His face—what she could see of it above his unkempt beard and mustache—held a hopeless longing.

"Everyone in town speaks highly of you, Mr. Grissom," Maggie said, overwhelmed with the need to make him feel better.

He just shrugged and grunted.

"It's my belief that Emily has feelings for you, too," Maggie told him.

His gaze swung to her, riveted her with his soft blue eyes. "Do you think so?"

"Yes, I believe it's true."

Seth shook his head. "She never let on to me that I was anything more than a customer. Sometimes…sometimes I think she doesn't even like me coming into her shop."

That was probably because his looks were so frightening, but Maggie couldn't bring herself to say that to him.

"Would you like me to speak to Emily on your behalf?" Maggie offered.

His cheeks reddened. "No, ma'am," he said, and went back to work.

Maggie retired to her bedroom with her journal. She hadn't learned for certain whether or not Seth and Emily had touched the love goddess, so how could she know if they were under its spell? Was the love goddess at work here?

Or did it need a little help?

* * *

"I guess you want this pretty bad?" Emily asked.

Spence didn't answer, letting her have her moment to fret him a little, make him squirm a bit. When he'd gone by her shop earlier and whispered what he wanted, she hadn't seemed surprised. Now, standing at her back door under the cover of darkness, he figured her knowing smile was just something he'd have to put up with—if he was going to get what he'd come for.

"I wouldn't have asked if I didn't want it," Spence said.

"And you're sure about this?" she asked.

"I'm sure."

Emily smiled. "I have to admit, yours is one of the…oddest requests I've ever heard. Are you going to give me the details?"

"Look," Spence said, losing patience. "Can I have it or not?"

She gave him a crooked grin. "Do I seem like the kind of woman who would hold out on a man so obviously in need?"

"Could you just hurry it up? It's getting late."

"Desperate and grouchy? That can mean only one thing." Emily stepped back into the kitchen of the bakery, then reappeared with the magazine he'd come there for. She held it out. "It's for Maggie, isn't it."

Spence shifted, uncomfortable that his intentions were so obvious. "Yeah. It's for her."

"I thought so." Emily passed him the magazine. "Direct from New York. The latest issue. Complete with articles on home decorating, recipes and menu planning. There's even a short story in there, and some advertisements for products for women.''

"Thanks," Spence said, then felt the need to explain. "Maggie's a smart woman. She just needs a little help with certain things.''

"Don't we all," Emily said with an easy smile.

He glanced down at the magazine. "I'd appreciate it if you'd keep this to yourself. She wouldn't want everybody knowing her shortcomings.''

"Of course," Emily said. "As long as you do the same. Mrs. Frazier will be beside herself if she learns I didn't give this issue to her first.''

"Deal." Spence gave her a nod of thanks and left.

Just before he reached the end of the alley, he unbuttoned his shirt and slid the magazine inside. How would it look, the sheriff walking the streets of his own town carrying a magazine full of decorating tips and recipes? And ads for "women's products"? Spence didn't want to think too much about just what those things might be.

He closed the buttons on his shirt. It was dark now and a little late to go calling. For a moment he wondered if he should wait. Maggie might already be in bed, or in her nightgown and it wouldn't be proper for him to be there.

A tremor passed through him with predictable results. Damn. All he had to do was think about her and that happened.

True, it would be wiser to go home. But...

He headed for Maggie's cottage.

Chapter Twenty-Two

Lost in her journal, Maggie jumped when a knock sounded on her back door. She got up from the table and, since she didn't know any more outlaws likely to come calling after dark, opened the door. Spence stood on her back porch.

"Maggie, don't open the door without asking who's there," he said, sounding a little annoyed.

"Did you come all the way over here just to scold me?" she asked, planting her fist on her hip.

"No," he said, looking a little contrite. "I brought you something."

"You did?" Her heart fluttered. "Well, then, please come in."

She stepped back from the door allowing Spence into the cottage. Just as Seth Grissom had done when he'd come to fix the pump, Spence filled the room with his sheer size. But there was something different with Spence. He seemed to exude an energy, a warmth that Seth hadn't, as if the air was somehow charged by his presence.

"I got this for you," he said and presented her

with the magazine he'd held behind his back. "I thought it might…help."

Cautiously, Maggie took it from his hand. When she saw the cover and flipped through the pages, she felt her cheeks flush.

"You're a smart woman, Maggie. I think you could've figured all of this out on your own, sooner or later. Women just know things like this." Spence shrugged as if he didn't understand the concept, yet accepted it. "But if it takes reading some instruction to make you feel better about living here, well, there's nothing wrong with that."

"I don't know," Maggie said, shaking her head as she looked at one of the pages.

"Learning from books is how you fit into your father's world, how you earned his favor," Spence said.

Her gaze came up quickly. "Oh, my…you're right. I never thought of it that way before."

"Learning from a magazine will help you fit in here in Marlow."

Maggie turned back to the magazine. "But I've never done this sort of thing before."

Spence touched her chin, turning her face up. "Forget all those things your father and those other professors told you, Maggie. You're capable of a great deal more than you realize."

"Do you think so?"

"Oh, yeah."

He smiled, and that made Maggie smile, too.

"I, ah, I made some coffee earlier," she said. "Would you like some?"

He didn't hesitate. "Sure."

Maggie hurried to the stove. "It took a while, but

I finally got the fire hot enough so that the water boiled. The water was supposed to boil, wasn't it? Anyway, the coffee tasted a little strong to me, or maybe it was weak. I'm not sure. But—''

''What the hell is this?''

Maggie turned away from the stove and saw Spence at her table, glaring down at the journal she'd left there.

''My name's in here,'' he declared, pointing to the open page. ''You're writing about *me* in your journal?''

She walked closer. ''Yes, I'm writing about you. About us, really.''

''What the hell for?'' he wanted to know.

''Scientific research.''

He looked as though he was certain now that she'd taken leave of her senses. ''What?''

''Scientific research,'' she said again. ''About the love goddess.''

''For chrissake…'' Spence rolled his eyes. ''That thing is nothing but a worthless hunk of rock.''

''It has ancient powers,'' she insisted. ''We both touched it. It's affected our lives.''

''Like hell it has.''

''Isn't it obvious?'' she asked. ''We're attracted to each other. We think about each other. When Henry came into my house and I was frightened, you instinctively knew it and came here. We're connected. You *kissed* me.''

''And you're writing that down?'' he asked, his eyes widening.

''I'm documenting our experiences,'' she said, gesturing to the open journal.

"You're going to have your father read about all of this?"

"Well, no, not everything," she admitted.

Spence studied her for a moment. "You honestly think the only reason I kissed you was because of some statue your father hauled back from South America."

She shrugged. "Why else would you?"

"How about because you're smart? Because you're a good person? Because you're easy on the eye? Maybe I just like you for who you are. Did you ever think about that?"

"We've discussed this before." She dismissed his words with a wave of her hand. "A man like you could have any woman he wants. You wouldn't give me a second thought if not for the effect of the artifact."

"Look, Maggie, no hunk of stone controls my actions," Spence told her. He flung his hand toward the journal. "And I don't like being written about as if I'm some sort of bug in a jar."

"My notes, this study, could be of great public interest and benefit to the scientific community," Maggie insisted.

"Hell…" Spence tossed his hat on the table and raked his fingers through his hair. He jabbed his thumb against his chest. "I control my own actions. Not some supposed ancient artifact."

"How can you be so sure about what you're feeling?" Maggie asked, and it suddenly occurred to her that there was much of Spence's life she knew nothing about. "Have you been in love before? Been married?"

"Married?" He shook his head. "No."

An odd tightness twisted in Maggie's chest. "Have you been...in love?"

She thought—hoped—to hear an outright denial. Instead, Spence's expression clouded as if he'd been swept away to a place only he could see. Then he sat down heavily in the kitchen chair and looked up at her.

"Yeah...I was in love once. Well, close to being in love, I guess."

"Oh..." Maggie hesitated, not sure if she should ask more. Whatever memories filled his mind at the moment were troubling and, really, none of her business. Yet he looked so distressed she couldn't leave him to his own thoughts.

She sank into the chair next to him and covered his outstretched hand with her palm. His gaze swung to her quickly, but he didn't pull away.

"Who was she?" Maggie asked gently.

"I was sheriff of a little cow town down in the panhandle a few years back. I took a fancy to a woman there," Spence said. "Ellen."

"You were courting her?"

"No." Spence shook his head and drew in a breath. "I guess I was working up my nerve to do just that, but in the meantime I watched every move she made when she was in town. She was a pretty thing. Always dressed up. Sweet and honest. Lots of men in town must have felt the same way I did. She'd have made somebody a fine wife, a good mother, or a teacher or...or just about anything."

"What happened?"

Spence was silent for a long time, and Maggie wondered if she'd gone too far, asked too much. Then, finally he spoke.

"I was standing in front of the bank one day, watching her across the street. She had on the prettiest yellow dress I'd ever seen. It seemed to sparkle in the sunlight." Spence withdrew his hand from Maggie's grasp. He didn't want her comfort now. "A fight broke out at the saloon down the street. Two drunk cowboys crashed through the glass window, started shooting."

Maggie's stomach clenched. "Did they…?"

"The feed store owner caught a round in his shoulder." Spence pressed his lips together, then finally said, "Ellen died."

"Oh, Spence…" Even though he'd pulled away from her a moment ago, Maggie grasped his hand again. "You must have been devastated."

"Yeah." His tone turned bitter. "Since it was all my fault."

"Your fault? But you didn't—"

"I wasn't paying attention to my duties," Spence said harshly. "I was watching her, thinking how pretty she looked when I should have been keeping an eye on what was happening around me. I was suppose to protect her, and I got her killed."

Maggie didn't respond. Though she didn't agree that the incident was his fault, Spence carried the burden of blame for what happened. She understood now why he fussed at her for being on the street late at night, for opening her door to strangers, for his reluctance to consider that Henry Donovan might be a decent young man. Spence took his responsibilities seriously. An admirable trait. Yet misplaced, Maggie felt, where Ellen's death was concerned.

Maggie wished she could convince him of just that, but the tormented expression on his face told her it was unlikely. Still, she couldn't sit there and do nothing.

"Sounds like an accident to me," Maggie said softly. "Sounds as if those drunk cowboys were the ones to blame, not you."

"No..."

Maggie tried again. "You say the love goddess doesn't control you. Yet this situation with Ellen has dictated how you've lived your life for years."

Spence's gaze bored into her. He didn't like what she'd said, but couldn't seem to disagree with it, either.

"That statue doesn't have any special powers," he insisted, clinging to the thing he wanted to believe.

"If you're so sure, why won't you take part in my research project?" she asked, nodding to the journal on the table. "If you're convinced I'm wrong, this is your chance to prove it."

He thought for a moment. "I guess it depends on exactly what's involved in a research project."

"Nothing you haven't already done."

"You mean like kissing you?"

Maggie blushed. "I didn't mean that I expected you to—"

Spence rose from the chair, took her hands and pulled her to her feet. He gazed down at her. "I suppose I could manage—as long as it's for the good of mankind."

Maggie laughed gently. But her giggles died as Spence pulled her into his embrace and kissed her.

She went willingly, the familiarity of his touch, his lips beckoning her. Warmth filled her as he worked his mouth over hers, but she didn't linger when he pulled away.

She picked up her pencil and began writing in her journal.

"What the hell are you doing?" Spence asked.

She blinked up at him. "Recording what just happened."

He looked offended. "When I kiss a woman, I don't mean to inspire her to *make notes.*"

"But that's the point of the research. Everything must be documented so that—"

"Come here."

Spence caught her upper arms, yanked her against him and smothered her mouth with his. A little mewl gurgled deep in her throat as he pushed his tongue past her lips, thoroughly acquainting himself with her. Then he released her.

"Oh, my…" Maggie drew in a breath to quiet her pounding heart, then picked up her journal and poised her pencil over the page. "Tell me what you're thinking."

"Huh…?"

"Tell me what you're thinking."

"I, ah…I'm not, uh, I'm not thinking anything."

She gazed up at him. His breath had grown rapid, and he looked slightly befuddled.

"What do you mean you're not thinking anything?" she asked, adjusting the grip on her pencil.

"Ah…well…"

Her brows pulled together. "You're simply empty-headed? Your mind is a complete void? How is that possible?"

"Dammit, woman, I'll show you."

Spence grabbed her journal and pencil and flung

them across the room. Then he wrapped both arms around her, yanked her full against him, and locked his lips over hers.

He kissed her hard, slipping his tongue inside her mouth, bending her backward across the kitchen table. As his lips worked their magic, he splayed his palm across her cheek, then slid his hand downward. At her collar, he slipped his fingers inside, caressing her delicate skin. Then he moved farther down and cupped her breast with his palm.

Maggie moaned. Spence groaned. She opened her mouth to him. He kissed her harder until she collapsed onto the table. He hovered above her, bracing his arm on the table top. When he angled his body against her thigh, Maggie gasped as the hard length of him pressed against her flesh, and pulled her lips from his.

His hot breath puffed against her mouth. His eyes, heavy with desire, burned into her. The warmth he'd ignited deep inside her still smoldered, despite her realization.

"You're…you're having…fond thoughts of me?" she whispered.

A slow grin spread over his face. "Oh, yeah."

Her insids quivered. She'd done that to him? She'd caused it to happen?

"Oh, my…" she whispered. "But I didn't mean to…that is, I didn't realize…"

Spence touched his finger to her lips. "I'm not complaining."

She smiled again. "So you're pleased?"

"Oh, yes." Spence brushed his lips against hers once more. "But unless you want this research project to come to its natural conclusion, we'd better stop now.''

''Oh...?'' Then her eyes widened. ''Oh!''

Spence straightened up and pulled her up with him. Maggie's knees weakened and he caught her, settling her against him with a protective embrace.

It seemed the most natural place to be, locked in the safety of Spence's arms. But as she nestled closer, his desire for her pressed against her thigh.

She gasped and looked up at him. He gave her a resigned grin.

''I'm still having 'fond thoughts of you,''' he said.

Maggie blushed.

''And I'll probably have them for a while.''

''I'm sorry. I didn't realize that—''

''You've got nothing to apologize for.''

He stepped back, releasing her from his embrace, taking away his warmth. Maggie had never felt so chilled in her life. He got his hat and walked to the back door.

She followed, not sure of what to say or do. ''Well, thank you for your...assistance.''

He stopped in the doorway. The cool evening breeze flowed in around him. Spence turned his hat over in his hand. ''I wouldn't be opposed to 'assisting' you again—in the name of science, of course.''

Maggie grinned. ''Your concern for the betterment of mankind is inspiring.''

Spence stepped outside and settled his hat on his head. She wondered—hoped—that he was reluctant to leave.

''I'll see you at church tomorrow,'' he said.

Maggie's shoulders slumped a little. ''Oh, yes, church.''

He frowned. "You're going to church, aren't you?"

"Well, yes." Though she wasn't looking forward to it, she had to go. Decent people went to church.

"What's wrong?"

How did he always *know?* Maggie straightened her shoulders. "I'm not very comfortable in social settings. I hardly know anyone in town, and I won't know anything to talk about."

"Marlow is a good town," Spence said. "You'll make friends."

"But I'm different from the other women. I won't fit in."

"You will."

Something about his comment alarmed her. "You promised you wouldn't tell anyone about my education. You promised, Spence."

"I think you fit in better than you realize," Spence told her. "Lock that door, now. And don't open it just because somebody knocks."

"All right," she promised, wishing he didn't have to leave.

He hesitated for a moment, then touched his fingertip to her chin, rubbing gently. He gazed into her eyes. "You're just fine the way you are, Maggie. Just fine."

He disappeared into the night. Maggie shut the door, then fell back against it.

Oh, if only he were right.

Chapter Twenty-Three

The only thing worse than being a misfit and going to church was being a misfit and arriving *late* for church.

Maggie dashed around the cottage, pinning on her hat as visions of walking into the church after everyone was already seated filled her mind. Heads turning her way. Stares. Whispers. A finger-point or two.

The stuff of nightmares.

If only she'd gotten up earlier. Maggie berated herself for oversleeping. She'd stayed up late into the night—for a good cause—but it would mean nothing if the reverend actually stopped his service to acknowledge her late arrival.

"Oh, dear…" Maggie moaned aloud, yanked open her front door and hurried outside, only to come up short at the sight of Spence lounging on her steps.

He rose, brushed off the seat of his pants and smiled at her. "Good morning."

"What are you doing here?" she blurted out.

"Walking you to church."

She hurried down the steps. "We have to hurry. I

don't want to be late. Should we cut through the alley? It will be faster.''

"Slow down," Spence said, touching her arm as she rushed past. "The church isn't going anywhere."

"Oh, Spence," she said, wringing her hands. "I can't arrive late. I simply *can't*. All those people looking at me, thinking—thinking goodness knows what."

Spence raised an eyebrow. "The only thing they might be thinking is that your hat's on crooked."

"*What?* Oh, goodness…" Maggie clasped both hands down on her hat, then flung them out in surrender. "I can't go. I can't. I'm staying home. I shouldn't even have tried to do this."

Spence shifted, blocking her path. "I saw you stay calm and collected during a stagecoach robbery. You packed up supplies, hiked for miles, faced spending the night out in the open. You had a known outlaw burst into your home. All of that and you didn't even bat an eye. Yet you're crumbling to pieces about going to church?"

"This is *different*," she exclaimed.

Spence caught her flailing arms and pulled her hands against his chest. "Settle down. Take a breath."

Maggie resisted for a moment, then decided his advice couldn't hurt. She drew in a big breath, held it, then let it out slowly.

He gave her fingers a little squeeze. "You're going to be fine."

Somehow hearing Spence say those words, feeling the strength in his hands, made her think maybe it might be true. Maybe…

"Now, straighten your hat and let's go," Spence said.

She repinned her hat, and when he nodded his approval, they headed for the church. Maggie forced herself not to hurry; how would it look if she arrived in a sweat?

"So did you read that magazine I brought you last night?" Spence asked as they walked.

"'A home is but a stage, and its mistress a shining star upon it,'" Maggie announced. She glanced up at him. "That's according to one of the magazine articles."

"A shining star, huh?"

"Yes, and 'the most formidable obstacle which lies in the way of a properly decorated home is the indifference with which the mistress regards the form and fashion of her surroundings.'"

"I'd suspected that," Spence mused.

"There was an entire column on fringe," Maggie reported. "I'm now an expert on fringe."

"Sounds interesting."

"And did you know that 'the sense of pleasure, which in civilized life we derive from the senses, is to a great extent instinctive. One has merely to give oneself over to color and design'?"

Spence looked down at her. "Did you give yourself over to 'color and design' last night?"

Actually, she'd given herself over to *him* last night, and the recollection caused Maggie's heartbeat to quicken a little. She glanced up at Spence and realized, for the first time since she'd found him sitting on her front steps this morning, that he looked terribly handsome.

He wore a crisp white shirt beneath his gold-threaded vest and a string tie. He'd brushed his hat and polished his boots, it seemed, and would have looked like any other man heading for church if not for the badge on his chest that reflected the morning sun and the Colt .45 slung low on his hips.

A hint of a grin showed on his lips and a solitary dimple teased one of his cheeks. Maggie was sure he was thinking about last night, too.

She decided to change the subject.

"Will Henry be at church this morning?" she asked.

"Prisoners don't go to services," he said, the grin and dimple disappearing. "Preacher will go by and see him this afternoon."

They'd reached the edge of the churchyard. Maggie stopped, her gaze taking in the townsfolk gathered outside the church, beneath the trees.

"I always sit on the last pew," Maggie said, "in the seat closest to the door…just in case…"

"That's *my* seat."

She threw him a look. "Not if I get there first."

"Hold on," Spence said, discreetly catching her elbow and holding her in place. "You're not going to duck into the church without speaking to anybody."

"Oh, but Spence…"

Maggie's mouth went dry as she gazed on the churchyard again. So many people. Then, to her horror, several of them turned her way. One woman nudged another and pointed. Two more women put their heads together and whispered. Soon, nearly everyone looked their way.

"Oh, dear… They're looking at me…"

"No, they're not," Spence said and moved a little

closer. "They're looking at me. Wondering why, all of a sudden, I'm escorting a lady to church services."

Spence had made himself the target of the town's gossip to save her from that exact fate? The very idea knotted Maggie's stomach.

"I didn't want you to do that," she rushed to say. "I would never ask anyone to put themselves in so terrible a spot—for me."

"Doesn't bother me," Spence said with a casual shrug. "I don't care what people say."

"You *don't?*" Maggie asked. She couldn't imagine such a thing. Not caring what people said about you?

Then she looked up at his calm expression, his composure, his lack of concern that he was the congregation's center of attention this morning.

"You mean that, don't you," Maggie realized.

"People are always going to talk," he observed. "That doesn't mean you have to listen…or care."

"Oh, Spence. This is the sweetest thing anyone has ever done for me in my entire life," Maggie declared. "I—I could just kiss you right now."

His brows raised a little. "Let's not give them *too* much to talk about."

Maggie giggled softly, then eyed the crowd.

He offered his arm. "Ready?"

She slid her fingers around his elbow and drew in a big breath. "Ready."

But Spence hesitated a moment. When Maggie looked up at him, he whispered, "You're fine, Maggie. You've always been fine. Relax and be yourself. That'll be good enough."

"If you say so," she said as he led her toward the

church. "But when you introduce me to people, try to mention *fringe* in the conversation, will you?"

As they crossed the churchyard, Spence said, "Looks as if that love goddess of yours might be losing some of her powers."

Maggie followed his gaze to where Ian Caldwell and Seth Grissom stood together under the trees, Ian seemingly engrossed in what Seth was saying. On the opposite side of the yard, Emily Delaney and Lucy Hubbard chatted in a tight circle of older women. None of them displayed the least bit of interest in anyone else.

"I don't think she's lost her powers," Maggie said. "I think she might need a little help."

Spence grumbled under his breath as he steered them to the closest group of women. Maggie recognized most of them. They'd come into the dry-goods store. Some had nodded to her, some had smiled; none had let her wait on them.

"Morning, ladies," Spence greeted, touching the brim of his hat. "Have you met Maggie Peyton?"

As one, the women's gazes swung to her and they all smiled in turn as Spence made introductions. Doris Tidwell, Nelly Walker—her husband was the blacksmith—Inez Becker, wife of the senior agent at the express office. Two other women whose names escaped Maggie completely.

Then Spence said, "Miss Peyton is visiting from New York."

Fringe! Maggie almost screamed. He was supposed to talk about *fringe.*

"New York?" Doris asked. "Why, our Emily is from New York, too."

Maggie plastered on a smile and was saved from responding by Nelly Walker.

"Are you all settled in Hank's cottage?" she asked.

Maggie gulped, not sure what to say. Then a line from the magazine she'd read cover-to-cover last night sprang to mind.

"A woman knows no true contentment until she's transformed her house into a home."

All the ladies nodded in unison. "So true," one of them murmured wisely. "You're so right," someone else said.

Maggie braced herself. Good gracious, she was actually having a conversation with other women—about housekeeping. Could this really be happening? Was she actually fitting in?

"Miss Peyton is well traveled, also," Spence said. "She's been to Europe, the Far East. All sorts of places."

Then she got *the look*. The same one she'd seen so many times before.

Two of the women drew back a little. Doris Tidwell's eyes widened to the size of saucers. Inez Becker's mouth sagged open.

Maggie's blood ran cold.

"Services are starting." The words drifted across the yard, drawing everyone toward the church.

Maggie stayed put and tugged on Spence's sleeve, keeping him beside her. "I asked you not to tell anyone—"

"No sense hiding who you are, Maggie," he said. "Beside, you ought to give people a chance, not go making up your mind about them just because of what happened to you in the past."

Maggie seethed for a moment—mostly because she knew he was right. Still, she wouldn't tell him that.

"I hate you," she informed him. "And *I'm* sitting on the last pew, closest to the door."

She strode past him and up the steps into the church. But as she stepped in front of the last pew, Spence was on her heels, crowding her.

She glared up at him. "I can't believe you're being so territorial about a seat."

"It's not that." He leaned down a little. "I just don't want everybody thinking I escorted a woman to services who slipped out during the first hymn."

Her mouth fell open. "I would never—"

"Sit down," he said softly. "People are watching."

Her jaw snapped shut and she sat down quickly, leaving room for Spence at the end of the pew.

The ten-person choir opened the service with "Onward Christian Soldiers," then Reverend O'Donnell took the pulpit, offered prayers to the shut-ins, then welcomed Maggie and the new attorney in town to the church. Halfway through the service, Spence began to fidget, and Maggie thought he might be the one to slip out early. After the collection plate made its rounds, the reverend said a final prayer, then asked Emily Delaney to come forward.

She looked pretty, Maggie thought, in a dress she must have brought with her from the East, and her cheeks were a little flushed as she rose and made an announcement about a pie social planned for the following Sunday. Maggie turned her gaze to Seth Grissom; this was the first time he'd showed interest in anything this morning.

"As you all know," Emily continued, "this pie social is the ladies auxiliary's annual fund-raising event before the Founders Day Festival. Pies will be auctioned off right here at the church, followed by a social. Now, we all know whose pie will fetch the highest bid."

A murmur went through the church and most everyone nodded as Lucy—whose husband was noticeably missing—blushed bright red from the compliment. She made the best pies in town; Maggie had heard it several times.

"But we want all you ladies to bring your best pie and support this fund-raiser," Emily said, "because the name of this year's winner will be listed in a place of honor at the Festival, plus she'll be the final judge at the baking contest."

Oohs and *aahs* rippled through the congregation.

"Are you thinking about baking a pie for the social?" Spence whispered to Maggie.

She considered it for a moment. "Perhaps I should."

Spence gave her a nod of approval, then rose and escorted her toward the door along with the rest of the congregation.

The reverend stood at the foot of the steps, shaking hands and speaking with everyone who passed. He seemed genuinely glad Maggie had attended the service and invited her back next week; she couldn't help smiling in return.

"I'd say that went pretty well," Spence observed as they walked into the churchyard.

Maggie wasn't so sure. She was exhausted, emotionally and mentally. Sitting at the back of the church, seeing nearly everyone in the congregation turn at some time or another throughout the service to sneak a look at her had taken its toll. She was sure the five women whom Spence had told about her travels had already spread the word to everyone who'd been in the church.

"Can we please go?" she asked. "All of the fellowship and goodwill has given me a headache."

Spence eyed her for a moment, then said, "All right. Let's go."

But as they turned, Miss Whitney stopped them. Maggie had met the schoolteacher when she'd made her rounds through Marlow looking for work.

"I was wondering, Miss Peyton, if you'd consider coming by the school sometime," Miss Whitney said. "I'm sure the students would love to hear about your travels."

At first, Maggie didn't know what to say. Someone was actually interested in where she'd been?

Spence gently nudged her. "Oh, yes. Yes, Miss Whitney, I'd love to."

She smiled. "Thank you so much."

Maggie watched the teacher blend in with the congregation leaving the church. "Oh, my…"

"Still want to leave?" Spence asked.

Maggie thought about it for a moment, and decided not to push her luck. "Maybe we'd better."

They'd almost reached the edge of the churchyard when a strident voice called out.

"Miss Peyton! Miss Peyton!"

Maggie and Spence both turned as a tall, robust woman with graying hair, wearing a garnet dress and a matching hat strode toward them.

"Damnation," Spence muttered. "It's Mrs. Frazier."

Maggie glanced up. Spence seemed none too happy about seeing the woman. Maggie resisted the urge to run.

"Miss Peyton." Mrs. Frazier planted herself in front of them, her face drawn in lines of sheer determination. "I simply will not allow you to leave this church until you hear me out."

Chapter Twenty-Four

Maggie couldn't remember when she'd felt so joyously tired. Not hiking the Andes or trekking through desert sands or struggling to keep up with her father's long strides through miles of ancient ruins had left her with such a good feeling of exhaustion.

Keeping house was extremely tiring. Yet she'd enjoyed it.

The streets of Marlow were quieter than usual, but that was to be expected, she'd learned this morning when she'd reported for work and Hank had sent her packing with a scowl and a disgusted shake of his head. It was Monday, he'd informed her. The shops in Marlow—and everywhere else, for that matter— did little business that day.

Despite his rebuke, Maggie had left with a smile, glad to have another day off.

She'd spent it working in her cottage. After studying the many articles contained in the magazine Spence had given her, she was pleased with the results she'd achieved so far. The place was shaping up nicely...or it seemed that way.

Outside the jail, Maggie paused to pat the back of her hair and tuck an errant strand into place. She caught her reflection in the glass window, made sure her hat was straight, then opened the door and stepped inside.

Spence sat reared back in his chair studying the Wanted posters strewn across his desk. He glanced up, saw Maggie and pushed to his feet.

She'd missed him. The thought raced through Maggie's mind. Not even a full day had passed since he'd asked her to have supper with him at the Pink Blossom after services yesterday, yet it seemed as if a long time—a very long time—had passed.

He came around the desk to meet her. "Afternoon, Miss Peyton."

She paused, a little put off by his formality, then realized that his deputy stood on the other side of the room pouring coffee at the potbellied stove in the corner.

"Good afternoon, Sheriff," she answered.

"Dex," Spence called. "How about heading over to Norman Kirby's place and make sure he's not having any problems over there."

Dex paused, a steaming cup halfway to his mouth, and fished a small tablet from his shirt pocket. "Can't do that, Sheriff. In seven minutes I've got to get over to the Pink Blossom and pick up supper for the prisoner, then ten minutes after I get back I need to get those Wanted posters hung up, and then I've got to—"

"Dex."

Spence didn't shout, didn't raise his voice, but the deputy jumped just the same. His gaze shifted from Spence to Maggie, then back to Spence again.

"Oh. Well, uh, guess I'll head on over to Norm Kirby's place and check on things. Won't matter if the prisoner's meal's late...much...I reckon. Afternoon, Miss Peyton." He left his coffee cup beside the stove and nodded respectfully to Maggie as he left the jailhouse.

The office was silent for a moment in the wake of the slammed door. Yet that seemed to be all right with Spence, Maggie thought as he just looked at her. She didn't mind it, either.

"Did you know that Monday was wash day?" Maggie finally asked.

Spence settled onto the edge of his desk. "I'd heard that."

"I like wash day," she said and gave him a little smile.

His brows rose. "You do?"

"Oh, yes," she said, and her smile widened. "It seems women don't shop on wash day, which means I didn't have to go to work."

"Did you do your washing?"

"Well, no." She shrugged. "Wash day wasn't covered in the magazine you gave me."

"You're still reading that magazine?" Spence asked and seemed pleased.

Maggie cleared her throat. "'It is a great pity that ladies who devote much of their time to the execution of small-mindedness do not exercise more discrimination in their choices of fabric and color.'"

"What does that mean?"

"I'm not sure. I'm hoping the author will expand on it in an upcoming issue," Maggie said. "In the meantime, I'm rereading the articles titled 'The Little

Courtesies of Daily Life' and 'The Ceremonial Aspect of Teas and Luncheons.'"

"Is that for Mrs. Frazier's meeting this week?" he asked.

"Yes. I want to be prepared just in case I can't work 'fringe' into the conversation." Maggie shook her head. "I still can't believe she invited me—me—to the ladies auxiliary meeting. *Everyone* will be there. When she stopped us leaving church yesterday, that's the last thing I expected."

"You'll do fine," Spence told her. He nodded toward the doorway that led to the cells. "I guess you're here to see Henry."

"How's he doing?"

"All right."

"He hasn't been any trouble at all, has he?"

Spence's expression soured just a little so she knew her assumption had been right.

"You just don't want to believe he's really a decent young man, do you?" she asked.

"I can't, Maggie. Not until I see some proof of it. Something more than behaving himself behind bars." Spence nodded toward the market basket she carried. "Got something in there for me?"

"A lawman who expects bribes." Maggie *tsked*. "What is this world coming to?"

He wiggled his fingers. "Hand them over."

She reached beneath the cloth and presented him with two wrapped oatmeal cookies fresh from the Marlow Bake Shop.

"What else have you got in there?" Spence asked.

Maggie pulled back the cloth displaying the items she'd loaded into her basket before leaving home.

Spence frowned and picked up the scissors lying beneath the Mark Twain novel.

"You'll have to leave these out here," Spence said, placing them on the edge of his desk along with the cookies.

"Really, Spence," she said. "Do you think he'll use scissors to cut his way through iron bars?"

"No. But he might hurt himself with them."

Maggie's stomach jolted. "Oh…"

Spence went down the hallway ahead of her and placed the same chair she'd previously used outside Henry's cell. She heard him give the boy the same warning as last time before he allowed her to sit down. He lingered a moment, then went back into the office.

"How are you doing, Henry?" Maggie asked, placing her basket on the floor beside her.

"'Bout as good as usual," he said.

As before, Henry sat on the bunk at the rear of the cell. The light was dim, but Maggie thought he looked thinner, more pale and drawn than before, even though his bruises had started to fade.

"Are you being treated well?" she asked.

"Yes, ma'am."

Maggie's heart went out to him. So young. So many problems. No one to help him.

"Henry," she said, scooting to the edge of her chair. "Did you shoot the stagecoach driver at the holdup? Was it you, or one of the other men?"

He drew back a little, then turned his head away.

"I know you were expected to act the same as the other gang members. But was it you who killed the driver?" Maggie asked. "It's important, Henry, that you tell me."

But he clamped his lips together and refused, still, to look at her. Maggie clenched her hands into fists, willing the boy to tell her the truth. If only he'd say that it wasn't him, she could convince Spence to put in a good word when the circuit judge arrived. Surely, the court would be more lenient on him.

But Henry said nothing. He wouldn't even look at her. Maggie gave up.

"Would you like to hear more about Tom Sawyer?" she asked, taking the novel from her basket.

Henry turned to her now. "Yes, ma'am," he said softly.

Maggie opened the book and began to read. When she'd finished two chapters, she put the novel away and rose from her chair.

"I brought cookies again," she said and laid them on the seat. She glanced down the hallway to where she was certain Spence waited just out of sight. "Did the sheriff give you the last cookies I brought?"

"Yes, ma'am," Henry said. "That was mighty kind. Thank you."

"Be good, Henry," she said, and gathered her things and went into the office where she found Spence waiting.

"Spence—"

"Don't start." He put up his hand.

"But—"

"Look, Maggie, you can't get too close to somebody like Henry."

"He's a good boy. I just know it."

"No, he's not," Spence said patiently. "I heard you ask him if he shot the stagecoach driver. He didn't answer you, did he. Why do you think that is?"

Deflated, yet trying to work up some annoyance at Spence for being right, Maggie turned her head away. He caught her chin and eased her back.

"It's because he did it," Spence said softly.

She fought back a wave of hopelessness over the situation, the sheer waste of the life of a young boy.

"How can you be so coldhearted?" she asked Spence, not unkindly.

"All I have to do is think about that driver."

She knew he was right. She admired his emotional strength, his sureness in the decision he'd made and in the world he lived in. Yet Maggie was torn by her own feelings.

Spence seemed to read her thoughts. He pulled her against his chest, locked his arms around her and just held her. She tensed, thinking she should pull away.

"It's okay, Maggie," he whispered against her hair. "I understand."

She relaxed against him then, against the hard wall of his chest, listening to his heart beating, soaking up the security of his big arms encircling her.

The last time she'd come to visit Henry, Spence had kissed her. Now, finding herself locked in his protective arms was just as exciting.

When she finally moved away, he smiled down at her.

"How about having supper with me tonight?" he asked.

Maggie was sorely tempted, but shook her head. "Thanks, but I can't. I only have this one day off and there's still so much to do."

Spence nodded. "Then how about if I come by your place later and see what you've done?"

Greater temptation gripped her, but again Maggie

shook her head. "I want to wait until it's finished, so you can see everything I've done."

He looked a little disappointed—or was it her imagination?

"How about tomorrow night?" she offered. "I'll make supper for you."

"Supper, too?"

Maggie straightened her shoulders. "'The hostess who has charm, personality and wit will find it a simple matter to entertain successfully, employing no greater strategy than that of inviting guests who are pleasant and congenial.'"

Spence spread his hands expansively. "I'm pleasant. And I'm sure as hell congenial."

"Then the evening is destined for success," Maggie declared.

She moved to the door. Spence got her scissors from his desk and slipped them in her basket, then opened the door for her.

"I'll see you tomorrow night?" she asked.

"You bet."

Maggie smiled and left.

Spence stepped out onto the boardwalk, watching her as she headed toward East Street.

Maggie was a woman to be admired, that's for sure. Compassionate, concerned for an outlaw like Henry. Brave to have traveled all this way so as not to disappoint her father. And smart, Lord she was smart.

She'd read a single magazine word for word, memorized most of it, and taken it to heart. Spence was anxious to go to her place, see how she'd fixed it up.

He watched the sway of her bustle as she crossed

Main Street. Yes, he was anxious to go to her place, but whether or not she'd hung curtains wasn't his primary concern.

Maybe a little more "research?" Spence's gut tightened and heat swelled inside him.

When she disappeared around the corner, a knot of disappointment jerked in Spence's stomach, bringing reality back.

Better get his mind on business.

Spence scanned Main Street in both directions, saw nothing that looked as if it might lead to trouble, then stepped back into the jailhouse.

He wondered then why Maggie was going to East Street instead of in the direction of home. She hadn't mentioned any more errands. A little wave of anxiety washed through him. He hoped Dex would get back soon so he could go check on her.

Spence went down the hallway to the cell and found the cookies Maggie had left on the chair. He held them out for Henry. The boy got off the cot and came forward, but he curled his hands around the bars and looked hard at Spence.

"I saw what you did," he said.

The boy sounded a little menacing—looked that way, too, with his bruised face and swollen eye.

"Yeah? What do you think you saw?"

"I saw you kiss Miss Maggie. Twice. At her house when I was hiding out back, and again here, last time she came to see me."

A protective, territorial anger sprang up inside Spence. The urge to tell the boy to shut his mouth and mind his own business overcame him, but Henry spoke first.

"She's a nice lady," he said. "You'd better do right by her."

Apparently, Henry felt a little protective and territorial, too. Spence couldn't blame him. Maggie was probably the only person who'd been nice to the boy in a long, long time.

Spence reached through the bars and slid the cookies into Henry's shirt pocket. "Your supper will be here soon."

He picked up the chair and headed toward the office.

"And you ought to go buy her a new handbag," Henry called. "She's a lady. It ain't right for a lady not to have a handbag."

Spence didn't answer, just placed the chair beside the stove and went back to his desk.

A boy who had concern about Maggie's reputation couldn't be all bad. Nor could a boy who realized she needed a new handbag when Spence himself hadn't thought of it.

He dropped into his desk chair. He'd had lots of prisoners in his jail cells over the years, and Spence had heard most of them cry and whimper at night and call for their mamas. But Henry seemed more pitiful than the others. Maggie was right, much as he didn't want to think about it. Henry was young, thrown into a bad situation, his life already ruined and he hadn't even started shaving every day yet.

Spence leaned back his chair and folded his arms across his chest. If only that driver hadn't been killed. If only Henry had denied shooting him when Maggie asked.

He looked at the door again and thoughts of her

filled his head. Then concern chased away Henry's dismal future.

Where the hell could Maggie have been going?

"What are you doing here?" Seth asked, then added, "if you don't mind my asking."

Maggie leaned her head back to gaze up at the big man. He stood in the rear doorway of his workshop, his shoulders almost touching both sides of the casing.

"I'd like to talk with you about something," she explained. "Something rather important."

Seth leaned out and glanced up and down the alley in both directions. "Pardon my saying so, Miss Maggie, but it's not quite proper for you to coming calling all alone, so close to dark."

She reached beneath the cloth that covered her market basket, pulled out the scissors and snipped the blades together.

"Believe me, Mr. Grissom, you'll thank me for this later," she told him. "And so will Emily."

Chapter Twenty-Five

Activity on the streets of Marlow on Tuesday more than made up for the quiet of wash day, Maggie realized as she pulled herself away from the window of the dry-goods store and started straightening shelves again. They'd been open for business only an hour and already the store was crowded.

To Maggie's surprise, several women had actually taken a moment to speak with her. They hadn't wanted assistance with their purchases, but they'd told her it had been nice to see her in church on Sunday. Two women had even mentioned her invitation to Mrs. Frazier's meeting this week.

Yet to her dismay, several women had mentioned next Sunday's social and inquired about what kind of pie Maggie intended to put up for bid.

When Emily had announced the pie auction on Sunday, Maggie had been caught up in the excitement of the social. She'd never been to anything like it before, and thought that joining in would be a wonderful new experience. She'd be just like all the other women in town.

Then reality had set in. Maggie had never baked a thing in her life.

She wasn't sure which would be worse: being the only woman in town who didn't enter, or entering a pie so awful that no one would bid on it. Humiliation loomed, either way.

Her confidence sagged further when Marlow's premier baker stepped into the store.

"Good morning," Lucy greeted her.

Maggie thought her smile seemed wider this morning, her step a little livelier.

"More soaps?" she asked, gesturing to Lucy's basket.

"I'm not selling today," Lucy declared. "I'm buying."

That was unusual.

"Are you looking for something special?" Maggie asked.

"I'd kept a little money tucked away for a rainy day," Lucy explained.

Money she kept secret from that worthless husband of hers, Maggie thought. Not that she blamed Lucy, of course.

"But I've decided to spend it," Lucy said with a smile. "I'm spending every last cent of it on fresh spices for the pie I'm making for the social on Sunday."

"You're sure to win," Maggie said. "Everyone in town says you make the best pies."

"But I really want to give this pie my very best effort. Can you imagine? The winner's name in a place of honor at the Founders Day Festival. And the opportunity to be the final judge for the baked goods competition.'' Lucy smiled. ''I'd be so honored...if that was me.''

Lucy seemed almost giddy at the possibility. Maggie hoped hers would prove to be the winning pie. Lucy deserved the happiness that would come with the honor; she had so little of it elsewhere in her life.

By the afternoon, shoppers filled the store. Women, mostly, with their children just released from school. To Maggie's dismay, Mrs. Fishburn walked in along with her twin boys. Maggie hurried to the other side of the store.

But the boys found her. Maggie braced herself. Who knew what sort of havoc the two little darlings planned to wreak today?

Yet to her surprise, they simply stared at her, two identical faces with questioning expressions. Maggie's mind spun. What were they up to now? Then Jack—or was it Jake?—spoke.

''Are you Miss Peyton?'' he asked.

''Yes,'' she replied cautiously. ''Which one are you?''

''Jake,'' he said and pointed to his brother. ''He's Jack.''

''Teacher says you're coming to our school,'' Jack said. ''She said you're gonna talk about all the places you've been. Is that true?''

Maggie relaxed a bit. ''Yes.''

''Teacher says you've been all over the entire world,'' Jake said, holding up his arms to form a big circle. ''Is that true?''

Maggie glanced around at the other shoppers squeezing past them in the aisle.

''Yes, that's true.''

''Told ya'.'' Jake socked his brother in the arm.

"Uh-uh," Jack insisted, giving his brother a shove. "Ain't nobody been around the whole entire world."

"But it's true," Maggie said, anxious to quiet the boys before Hank came over to see what the commotion was all about.

Jack squinted his eyes at Maggie. "You're making it up."

Maggie glanced across the store and saw Hank assisting a customer at the counter, so she shepherded the boys into a corner away from the other shoppers. She grabbed the footstool she used to reach the high shelves, and sat down. The boys dropped in front of her.

"I'll tell you about some of the places I've been," Maggie said. "I've been to a place where there are no trees or grass, only sand. I've been to a place where people ride camels and elephants instead of horses."

"There ain't no such place," Jack insisted, crossing his arms in front of him.

"Oh, but there is," Maggie told him. "I can show you pictures in books, and maps."

"See?" Jake sneered at his brother.

"Another place I visited has no roads, just water. People travel by boat," Maggie said.

"Tell us about that place," Jake said.

Maggie told the boys about the journey she, her father and his research team had taken to Venice, Italy. The canals, the gondolas, the houses and buildings, the history of the city and the country. Halfway through, a little girl and another boy joined them, all sitting on the floor in front of her, wide-eyed and silent.

When she finished, the children didn't move, and Maggie noticed that the store seemed oddly quiet. A shiver raced up her spine. She turned on the stool and saw a dozen adults staring down at her.

Her cheeks heated. Oh, goodness, they'd all been listening.

"Is that true?" a woman asked.

Everyone else seemed to lean a little closer, waiting for Maggie's answer.

"Well...yes," she said.

"How do you know all those things? Did you go to school, or something?" someone else asked.

Maggie gulped. "I learned most of it at...the university. I...I have a university degree."

Everyone stared for another moment, then walked away without saying a word.

Maggie flipped frantically through the pages of the magazine.

"It is possible to be a successful hostess," she read aloud in the silence of her home, "even in the most humble of abodes with the most modest furnishings. After all, hospitality is of the heart rather than the pocketbook."

No mention of the meal.

Maggie tossed the magazine aside and looked at the pots and pans boiling and sizzling on her stove. Her first real meal. Spence would be here any minute.

Her foods didn't resemble those she'd eaten at the Pink Blossom—or anywhere else for that matter. Perhaps she would be wiser to meet him on the porch and send him on his way. For his own sake.

A knock sounded then. Maggie's heart rose in her

throat as she pulled off her apron and dashed to the front door. She yanked it open. Spence stood on her porch in the fading light of the evening sun.

She could never send him away.

"Supper smells good," he said as he stepped inside and dropped his hat on a little table beside the settee.

Maggie considered cautioning him about the meal, but her words died on her lips as he held out a box wrapped in pink paper, tied with silk ribbon.

"What's this?" she asked, stunned.

"I believe it's called a hostess gift," he reported, then hastened to add, "I didn't read that in one of those women's magazines. Mrs. DuBois told me."

Maggie's gaze swung from the frilly package to Spence's face, unsure of exactly what aspect of his unexpected gift she found so surprising.

"You went to the dress shop? For me? And carried this wrapped gift all the way through town to my house? For everyone to see?"

"Further proof that I am truly fearless," he declared, and hung his thumbs on his gun belt.

"I guess you are," Maggie said with a giggle.

"Go on," he said. "Open it."

She perched on the edge of the settee and opened the package, careful to save the ribbon and paper. She eased off the lid and found a new handbag nestled inside.

"Oh, my..." Maggie gasped softly as she lifted out the ivory, beaded bag. "It's lovely. Just lovely. Did you pick this out yourself?"

He shrugged modestly. "I did. But I let Mrs. DuBois have the last say."

Maggie rose to her feet. "Thank you, Spence. Thank you so much. It's very thoughtful of you."

"I can't take all the credit for it. Henry noticed you still didn't have a handbag," Spence admitted. "But I'm the one who picked it out and brought it over here."

"Thank you again." Maggie put the bag back in its box and waved her hand expansively about the cottage. "Notice anything different?"

Spence's gaze bounced around the room. Maggie smiled with pride as he took in the freshly washed curtains, the scrubbed floors, the polished windows, the furniture she'd beaten the dust from, as well as the fresh flowers she'd picked from the back of the house and set in vases around the room. And, of course, her pride and joy, two shelves of the books she'd brought with her from New York.

"Looks good, real good. Looks like a home," Spence said, nodding his approval. "You're cooking, too?"

"'The successful hostess is not she who provides the richest, most sumptuous meal,'" Maggie recited, "'but she who makes her guests feel comfortable and happy.' I hope you'll remember that when we eat."

Spence chuckled. "Need a hand with anything?"

"I want to do this myself," she told him, squaring her shoulders, then heading for the kitchen.

He followed and leaned his hip against the sideboard, watching her at the stove.

"You can sit on the settee, if you like," Maggie suggested. "You'll be more comfortable."

Spence grinned. "I like the view from here."

Maggie flushed. "Oh…"

"I heard about your university degree this afternoon,'' Spence told her. ''Dex got word of it over at the Pink Blossom and passed it along. I figure the whole town knows by now.''

Maggie sighed heavily. After the news had been forced out of her at the store today, her first inclination had been to run to the jail, to Spence, and tell him, sure that he would make her feel better about it, somehow.

''You know,'' Spence said, ''there are worse things people could say about you than that you have a university degree.''

''Yes. I know,'' Maggie said, finding a little comfort in his encouragement. ''I just hope this won't cause the women in town to stop speaking to me, or Mrs. Frazier to revoke her invitation.''

''Everything will be fine, Maggie,'' Spence said.

He smiled down at her and she basked in the joy of it. He always knew how to make her feel better.

Maggie eyed the chicken frying in the pan. ''Supper's ready...I think. Hungry?''

''You bet.''

She put the chicken on a platter, then stirred up the gravy as she spooned the mashed potatoes and carrots into bowls. She placed everything on the table she'd set earlier, as a good hostess should. Spence held a chair for her and they sat down.

''The chicken seems a little dry,'' Maggie said, swallowing. ''I guess I cooked it too long.''

''Tastes fine to me,'' Spence said, taking another bite.

She dug her fork into the potatoes. ''Do you think the potatoes are a little thin?''

''I like them that way.''

''The gravy has lumps.''

"It's better with a little fight to it," Spence told her and kept eating.

Maggie ate, a little disappointed that the meal hadn't turned out as well as she'd hoped. In fact, it was borderline inedible. But Spence didn't seem to mind. He cleaned his plate, then took seconds and finished those.

"There's pie," Maggie said, as she rose and took away their empty dishes. "Would you like some?"

"Uh...sure," he said, after only a few seconds hesitation.

"I bought it from Emily's bakery this afternoon," Maggie said. "Truthfully, I was tempted to keep it until Sunday and take it to the social, pass it off as my own."

Spence got up from his chair and followed her to the sideboard. "The things that go through that head of yours," he mused.

"Oh, that reminds me. I have something for you."

Maggie opened the lower cupboard, pulled out a pistol and wheeled around. Spence caught her wrist in mid-arc.

"What the hell are you doing?" he demanded.

She released the gun into his hand. "Don't worry. It won't fire."

Spence glared at her, evidently annoyed that she'd startled him, then examined the pistol. "I haven't seen one of these old things in years. Looks like whoever owned it didn't care if it fired or not, from the condition it's in. Hasn't been cleaned in months, probably."

"The firing pin is missing," Maggie pointed out.

Spence checked, then nodded. "You're right. Where did you find it?"

"In the woodshed. I discovered it when I went for more firewood this afternoon," Maggie said. "It belongs to Henry Donovan."

Spence's brows drew together. "You don't know that."

"But I do."

"This pistol could have been lying around out there for a long time. It probably belonged to Hank's son when he lived here."

"It's Henry's. I'll show you."

Maggie bent down to the lower cupboard. Spence pulled her back and opened the door himself.

"See the gun belt?" Maggie asked.

He pulled it out and straightened, turning it over in his hands until he saw Henry's name carved into the leather.

"Henry couldn't have killed the stagecoach driver," Maggie said softly. "His gun won't fire."

"*If* this is the gun he had at the holdup," Spence pointed out.

"Do you suppose he had a gun that worked, then gave it up for this one that won't fire?" Maggie proposed. "It seems doubtful to me."

"There could be a dozen reasons why the boy left this gun in your woodshed," Spence said.

Maggie let a quiet moment pass before she spoke again. "It's because of what happened to Ellen, isn't it?"

Spence recoiled, as if she'd punched him.

"You won't consider that Henry might be a decent person because you fear a lapse in judgement could result in another death," Maggie said softly. "Like with Ellen."

"I swore an oath to uphold the law and protect

the citizens of this town,'' Spence said, his expression hard. ''My duty comes first.''

''You think her death was your fault.'' Maggie shook her head. ''It was an accident, Spence. You couldn't have prevented it.''

''Yes, I could.''

Maggie decided it was better not to push further. Spence had assumed responsibility for what happened to Ellen and he'd lived with it for a long time. He'd need time to change his thinking.

''Ready for some pie now?'' she asked.

Spence shoved the old pistol into the holster. ''No. No, thanks.''

''Did my bringing up Ellen upset you?'' she asked.

''No,'' Spence told her, though she didn't think he was telling the truth.

''Then it must be my supper. Did it upset your stomach?''

''Your supper was fine,'' Spence told her, drawing in a cleansing breath. ''How about if I come back tomorrow night for the pie?''

Maggie's pulse quickened. ''I'd like that.''

She walked with him to the door. ''My supper really was awful, wasn't it.''

''It tasted fine to me.''

''You're sticking by that story?''

''Till my dying day.'' Spence settled his hat on his head.

''You're so sweet.''

''Keep that to yourself. I've got a reputation to uphold around here.''

He gazed into her eyes and Maggie let herself get lost in them for a moment.

"Thank you for my handbag," she said softly. "It's lovely."

Spence slid his hand around her shoulder and kissed her gently on the mouth. Maggie sighed and rose on her toes. He deepened their kiss and pulled her close, blending their mouths together.

When he released her, Maggie wished he'd take her in his arms once more. Spence's expression made her think he considered doing just that.

"Are you going to write about this in your journal?" Spence asked.

"My research project is ongoing," she pointed out.

Spence shook is head. "Good night," he whispered, and disappeared out the door.

Maggie went to the window, watching him walk away. Spence Harding. Tall, strong, brave, fearless. He'd brought her a handbag, and eaten what had to have been the worst meal ever prepared—eaten every bite of it without a word of complaint, *and* had seconds.

She pressed her palm to the windowpane, part of her tearing away as Spence disappeared into the night. A painful hurt, but somehow, a wondrous one. He made her heart beat faster when she simply caught a glimpse of him on the street, or heard his voice—even when she merely thought about him.

Was this the work of the love goddess? Or was it her true feeling?

Maggie wasn't sure. But either way, she wished with all her heart that it would go on and on forever.

Chapter Twenty-Six

"I guess we've got this end of town covered," Ian said.

Spence folded his arms across his chest and stole a glance at his deputy standing next to him. Spence had been milling around here at the corner of Main and West for a while when he'd noticed Ian across the street doing the same, and waved him over.

High noon and the streets and boardwalks were full. People went about their business. A quiet day, same as always.

Yet with two of Marlow's three lawmen loitering at the same corner, a passerby might think a major crime was about to happen, rather than that they were waiting for the ladies auxiliary meeting to break up.

Spence had told both his deputies that he never wanted to see them both in the same place at the same time, unless it was on official business. But Spence didn't have the heart to tell Ian to leave, and he sure as hell wasn't going anywhere.

"You reckon we ought to at least act like we're doing something important here?" Ian asked. "In case the mayor walks by?"

"We're doing something important," Spence insisted. "I came by to tell you something."

Ian's brows rose. "Yeah? What?"

"Give me a minute to think...."

The chatter of voices caught his ear. Spence swung toward West Street and Mrs. Frazier's house. A dozen women flowed down the front steps, heading his way.

Spence's stomach clenched. Maggie. Where was Maggie? Had things gone all right for her at the meeting?

He'd worried about her so much he'd come here to wait for her...just in case. He feared he'd find her hanging back, the last to leave, devastated by whatever had happened at the meeting. Visions of arresting Mrs. Frazier and the rest of the ladies auxiliary for upsetting her swam in his mind.

But to his surprise, he spotted Maggie in the center of the gathering, talking with the other women. When the group reached him on the corner, the ladies greeted him and swarmed past. Maggie stopped.

He looked at her, realizing how anxious he was to hear how her first ladies' meeting had gone. When she smiled, so did he.

But Spence's elation evaporated as he caught sight of Ian standing on the corner, watching Lucy Hubbard walk past. Ian made no effort to hide his feelings for her—Spence doubted he could pull it off, even if he tried. Lucy cast a glance—a single glance—at Ian, not daring to do more, yet it reflected their mutual heartbreak.

Ian stood watch until Lucy and the other ladies melted into the crowd along Main Street. Still, he didn't move.

Spence touched his shoulder. "Why don't you ride out to the Frazier ranch and make sure that nephew of theirs is still behaving himself?"

Ian took one last lingering look at Lucy, then nodded. "Yeah…I think I'll do that."

Spence watched him head toward the blacksmith shop where they stabled their horses.

"It's so sad," Maggie said.

He looked down at her and a bitter rage flared in his belly. He could walk down the street and talk to Maggie anytime it suited him, and nobody could say a word against him. Nobody could stop him. Nobody could find fault with it.

He couldn't live as Ian did—not for a minute. Spence's gut tightened at the very thought of Maggie belonging to another man.

"Let's go," Spence said. He cupped Maggie's elbow and headed down Main Street.

Something about her touch—just her elbow through her dress—calmed him.

"So," he said, "how did the meeting go?"

"Oh, Spence," she declared. "I had such a wonderful time. All the ladies were so nice. Mrs. Frazier's home is lovely. She served tea and pastries."

Spence couldn't help smiling at her excitement.

"Your university degree wasn't the talk of the meeting?" he asked.

"No, actually, it was Seth Grissom."

"I damn near didn't recognize the man when I saw him on the street the other day," Spence said.

"Everyone was surprised that such a good-looking man lurked beneath his beard and all that hair," Maggie said. "The ladies were quite taken with him. Especially Emily."

"Wonder what made him do it?"

"Yes, I...I wonder."

Spence angled a look down at her. He'd seen that expression on her face before. He knew what it meant.

"Something else you want to tell me?" he asked.

"Oh, all right," she confessed. "It was my idea. I told Seth that if he wanted to court Emily he'd have to cut his hair and shave off his beard and mustache. And it worked. Emily's attention kept drifting off during today's meeting. I'm sure she was thinking about Seth."

Spence swept his gaze from one side of Main Street to the other as they walked, watching for trouble and listening to Maggie at the same time. How could he not? Her excitement over the meeting was infectious.

He didn't understand how women could find so much to talk about.

He didn't understand why hearing her talk meant so much to him.

By the time they reached the jail, Maggie's report on the meeting had wound down with a last comment about how excited Lucy Hubbard was over the possibility of receiving the highest bid for her pie on Sunday.

"Lucy deserves something good in her life," Spence agreed.

"Can I visit Henry?" Maggie asked. "I don't have to return to the store for a few minutes yet."

"Henry's not here."

A hint of alarm touched Maggie's face. "Where is he? Did the circuit judge come already?"

"No. He's over at Seth's workshop."

She raised her eyebrows, looking pleased with herself. "Really? Doing what?"

"Seth is building the booths for the Founders Day Festival and he agreed to take the boy on as apprentice for a while."

"So you've changed your mind about him," Maggie concluded, looking even more pleased.

"Now don't go getting all excited, thinking the boy is in the clear on the stagecoach holdup," Spence told her. "I'm just giving him something to do for a few hours a day."

The decision hadn't been an easy one. Spence still believed Henry deserved the law's punishment for his part in the holdup. But after Maggie had shown him the gun she'd found in her woodshed, he was reasonably certain Henry hadn't shot the driver. More than likely he carried the gun for show, to insure that his outlaw uncle wouldn't kick him out of the gang. He'd probably been too embarrassed to admit that to Maggie when she'd asked him about his role in the robbery.

After a near-sleepless night, Spence had talked it over with Seth. The mountain man had taken one look at the scrawny kid, snickered at the notion of his being dangerous, and agreed to give him a chance at his workshop. After a little more discussion, Seth had gone along with Spence's insistence that Henry wear leg irons.

The whole incident seemed worth it now as Maggie smiled up at Spence, so obviously pleased by his decision.

"You won't be sorry," Maggie told him. "Henry is a good boy. I just know it. You'll see. You'll be glad you gave him a chance."

Spence just hoped his decision wouldn't turn out to be a fatal one.

* * *

An air of anticipation filled the church as the Sunday service wound down. Reverend O'Donnell, thankfully brief in his sermon, ended with an invitation for everyone to enjoy the fellowship of the pie social, commencing immediately. The congregation nearly stampeded toward the door. Maggie and Spence, seated in the last pew, were the first outside.

Maggie could hardly contain her excitement as the crowd flowed around her toward the shady side of the church where the social would be held. Upon arrival this morning, all the ladies had placed their market baskets—with pies and picnic lunches tucked inside—on the table until the social began. The reverend's son stood guard.

Several ladies stopped and chatted with Maggie as she waited for Spence. He'd allowed Henry to attend church this morning and the social to follow, on a sworn oath of good behavior. Seated in the pew in front of them during the service, sandwiched between Ian and Dex, Henry didn't seem much of a threat. Jonah Walker, who appreciated any excuse not to sit through church services, had volunteered to keep an eye on things in town.

"This is your big day," Doris Tidwell commented as Lucy joined their little group.

The other ladies nodded in agreement, and it pleased Maggie that everyone in town shared in the excitement of Lucy's impending success at the pie auction.

"Maybe someday we'll learn your secret ingredients," Nelly Walker speculated.

Lucy blushed, unable to hide her pleasure at the compliment. ''I got up before dawn to bake today's pie. I wanted it to be perfect. It hadn't quite cooled yet when I left for church, so Raymond promised to bring it over after the service.''

''We'll tell Reverend O'Donnell to auction yours last,'' Doris said.

''No one will want their pie offered after yours,'' Nelly added, and the ladies nodded in agreement.

The ladies moved on but Maggie remained, waiting for Spence, who was delivering what she suspected was yet another warning to Henry about behaving himself at the social.

Lucy stayed with Maggie, her gaze straying to the edge of the churchyard. ''I thought Raymond would have been here by now. I told him what time the social started.''

''Maybe you should go check on him?'' Maggie suggested, trying to sound kindly.

''Well, I don't know,'' Lucy fretted. ''I told him how important this is to me. He promised he'd be here. He promised.''

''Perhaps he simply lost track of the time.''

Lucy looked relieved. ''That's it. I'm sure you're right. I'll just run home and get the pie myself.''

''I'll tell the reverend not to start without you,'' Maggie called as Lucy hurried away.

''Miss Peyton? Could I talk to you for a moment?'' A young girl stopping beside her took Maggie's attention. Sarah Kirby. She'd waited on Maggie the few times she'd visited her father's general store. Tall, thin, Sarah was blossoming into a young woman, sure to be the apple of some boy's eye very soon.

"Certainly, Sarah," Maggie said. "What is it?"

She twisted her fingers together, glanced around as if to see if anyone was listening, then stepped closer.

"Is it...is it true what everybody says about you?" Sarah asked.

Maggie froze. People were talking about her? Everyone had seemed so friendly, so kind. And all the while they were talking about her?

"About you going to a big university back East," Sarah said. "And going to all those different places."

Maggie's anxiety rose. "Well...yes."

A timid smile tugged at Sarah's lips. "It's true? It's all true?"

"Yes..."

"Oh, Miss Peyton, it's so wonderful." Sarah's smile widened and her face lit up. "I didn't think a woman could ever do something like that. Travel all over the world. And go to a real university."

Maggie smiled along with the young girl, feeling her joy. "Yes, it's possible."

"Did you like it?"

"Yes, I did," Maggie said, and realized that she had, in fact, enjoyed every moment of it.

"I thought I had to stay here in Marlow and get married," Sarah said. She gave Maggie a hopeful smile. "Do you think that I...I could go to a university somewhere? Like you did?"

"Of course," Maggie said. "Why don't you come by some evening and we'll talk about it."

"Some of the other girls are wondering the same thing," Sarah asked. "Could I bring them along, too?"

"Please bring everyone who's interested."

Sarah gave her a grateful smile, and hurried away.

Spence. Where was Spence? Maggie thought she'd burst from the want to tell him what had just happened. But as she spotted him across the churchyard, Mayor Holt stepped into her line of vision.

"Miss Peyton?" The mayor planted himself in front of her and reared back a little, hanging his thumbs in his vest pockets. "Something's come up. I need to talk to you."

Spence gave Henry another few words of caution about his conduct this afternoon, but it hardly seemed necessary. The kid remained docile, quiet. Better behaved than most of the boys his age. If he'd caused even a few seconds' trouble this last week, Spence would never have gone along with Seth's suggestion to let him attend the social.

Spence, Ian, Dex and Seth had agreed to take turns watching the boy. Ian took the first shift, joining the reverend and his family on the blanket they'd already spread out under one of the trees.

As Spence watched them get settled, Maggie hurried toward him. His blood ran cold as he strode across the churchyard to meet her.

"What's wrong? What happened?" he demanded.

Tears pooled in her eyes. Her face had paled. When she didn't answer immediately, Spence thought he would explode.

She looked up at him, and gulped hard. "Norman Kirby's daughter stopped me just now. She asked about going to the university and…and…and she wants to be…like *me*."

Spence's knees weakened from relief. Thank God nothing bad had happened to her.

"She said...she said some of the other girls wanted to do the same."

His worry for Maggie's safety gone, the impact of her words dawned on Spence. He smiled. "I guess that means there's really nothing wrong with being you," he said softly.

Maggie blinked back tears and caught his arms to steady herself. "The mayor stopped me. He asked if I would give a lecture about my travels at the Founders Day Festival."

Spence smiled broadly. "You'll give a hell of a lecture."

A single tear trickled down her cheek as she gazed up at him. "You were right. I don't have to be afraid to speak up, to tell people about myself, afraid they won't like me or that I won't fit in."

"You were never different from the other women here in Marlow, Maggie," Spence said. "Or anywhere else, for that matter."

She sniffed and smiled. "I guess I did fit in...all along."

"You bet you did." Spence drew her into his arms and held her tight.

When she pulled away a few minutes later, Maggie smiled up at him. "Thank you."

He nodded. "You're welcome."

"You deserve something special for all you've done for me," Maggie said. "But unfortunately, now you have to eat the lunch I prepared."

Spence chuckled. "It's a chance I'm willing to take," he said, and escorted her across the churchyard.

He spread out the blanket Maggie had brought among the other church members while she fetched their lunch. He checked to make sure Henry was behaving, then sat down with her.

"Fried chicken again, huh?" he asked, as she lifted the food out of the basket.

"I've decided it's my specialty," Maggie told him. "I'm going to keep cooking it until I get it right."

"I admire your persistence," Spence said. "Did you make a pie for the auction?"

"I did. But I had help. Emily came over last night," Maggie reported. "I can't wait to bake something all by myself."

Spence swallowed hard, forcing down a bite of chicken. "Me, either..."

Maggie couldn't help smiling. "You really are being awfully sweet about this."

"I like your cooking," Spence insisted with a nod of his head. "I swear I do."

Maggie giggled. If Spence eating her food wasn't unconditional acceptance, she couldn't imagine what it would be.

She couldn't imagine what her life would be like without him now. Maggie sat back on the blanket, her heart filled with the warmth of Spence's closeness. She couldn't imagine a day going by without him in it.

Nor could she imagine that what she felt for him was anything but love.

Could that be true? she wondered.

Or was she just fooling herself? Again.

"What the hell...?"

Spence mumbled another curse and shot up off the

blanket. Maggie scrambled to her feet. Good gracious, the man seemed to see everything that went on anywhere in town. She followed his gaze across the churchyard and saw Lucy walking toward them.

"Something's wrong," Spence said. "Come on."

Maggie quickened her pace to keep up with him. When they got to Lucy, she knew Spence was right.

Though dazed, pale, Lucy appeared calm. Eerily calm. Maggie knew now why Spence had asked her to come along.

"What is it, Lucy? What's wrong?" she asked.

Lucy just stared blankly ahead for a long moment. Maggie's stomach jolted. She glanced up at Spence and saw her own concern mirrored in his expression.

"Lucy?" she prompted again.

"I can't be in the pie auction," Lucy said. "I went home to pick up my pie and it's not there."

Maggie and Spence exchanged another troubled look.

"Where is it?" Maggie asked.

Lucy blinked once. "Raymond ate it."

"I'm so glad to see you here today, Henry," Maggie said.

"Yes, ma'am," he said.

He seemed a little nervous, but Maggie supposed that was to be expected. Dex stood only a few yards away keeping watch, as Spence had instructed.

The social was in full swing, but Maggie wasn't ready to join the others. After seeing the devastated look on Lucy's face, hearing how that dreadful husband had shattered her small dream, even Spence buying her pie hadn't lifted her spirits. She needed a distraction from her own thoughts. Henry filled the bill nicely.

"I appreciate the sheriff letting me come," he said. "I ain't been to church since before my mama...you know, since before she...died."

"How are things going at Mr. Grissom's workshop?"

"Good," Henry replied. "He don't yell at me, not even when I do something wrong."

"He's a nice man," Maggie agreed.

"Miss Emily from the bakery comes by the workshop sometimes. Last time, Mr. Grissom busted his thumb with a hammer when she walked in." Henry pushed his chin across the churchyard. "I think they're sweet on each other."

Maggie giggled softly as she saw Seth and Emily, winner of today's pie contest, sharing lunch. "I think you're right."

Henry glanced back at Dex, then took a half step closer to Maggie. He lowered his voice. "I got to tell you something, Miss Maggie."

She almost groaned, unsure how she'd bear up under another emotionally distressing situation today. But she couldn't tell Henry no.

She glanced at Dex. He lounged against a tree now, studying the tablet he kept in his shirt pocket.

"What is it, Henry?"

He hesitated, as if unsure how to proceed. "I know Sheriff Harding's kind of sweet on you, too, so I figure if you tell him something, he won't likely get too mad. 'Cause if I tell him myself, well, he might not take too kindly to hearing it."

"Hearing what, Henry?"

"I just think Sheriff ought to know," Henry went

on. "He's shown me a kindness—and he didn't have to. I wouldn't want something to happen, knowing all along I could have—"

"Henry, please. What is it?"

He glanced back at Dex once more, then leaned in a little. "It's my uncle Mack Donovan and Jess Wright, the other outlaw. Before I left the gang, they were making plans to move up to robbing banks."

Maggie gasped. "The one here in—"

"Yes, ma'am. They talked about robbing the one here in Marlow."

Chapter Twenty-Seven

"N̲o̲."

"But—"

"No."

"Spence, if you'll—"

"I told you no, Maggie," Spence said.

They stood on the boardwalk outside the jailhouse. Spence spared her nothing more than an occasional glance as he kept watch over the town.

"I can't arrest a man for eating an apple pie," Spence said.

"Why *can't* you arrest him?" Maggie demanded.

"Because there's no law against it."

"Can't you make up one?" Maggie asked.

Spence rolled his eyes.

"There are mitigating circumstances," Maggie insisted. "Lucy is devastated. She's holed up in her house. No one has seen her since the social. And her husband is an ogre. He thoughtlessly and callously ruined her only chance to be the final baking judge at the festival—something that meant the world to her."

"There's nothing I can do about it, Maggie."

She pushed her chin up a little. "I'd think that in your position as town sheriff you could be a little more inventive in your duties."

"You do, huh?"

"Show a little imagination," she told him.

"Aren't you supposed to be at work now?" Spence asked and nodded down the block toward the dry-goods store.

"But—"

"I'm not going to talk to you about this anymore," Spence said, turning his attention to the street once more.

The finality of his decision weighted his words. Maggie knew she should give up. And really, Spence had more important things to worry about than Raymond Hubbard destroying Lucy's opportunity to judge the baking contest.

Since Maggie had confided in him that Henry's uncle planned to hold up Marlow's bank, Spence had been on edge, making more rounds through town, watching for strangers, staying alert for any sign of trouble. His deputies were doing the same. He notified Mr. Harrison at the bank and some of the men in town who sometimes served as extra deputies of the possible attempt on the bank, but generally kept the news quiet so as not to cause panic among the townsfolk.

Spence had everything under control. Maggie still worried about Lucy.

"Well, fine then," Maggie announced, drawing herself up into a pose she hoped conveyed self-righteous indignation. "I'm going to work now."

He looked at her now. "Keep your wits about you, Maggie. If you see trouble—"

"—get on the ground and keep my head down. Yes, I know. You've told me about a hundred times this week."

He didn't seem put off by her sour reply, just stepped toward her. "I'll walk you to the store."

"I can walk myself," she informed him, still a little annoyed that he wasn't more concerned about Lucy. Of course, she couldn't blame him. But still…

"No," he said. "I'll walk you—"

"I got myself all the way from New York to Colorado," Maggie pointed out.

"Yeah, and we both know how well you managed that."

Maggie huffed. "Good day, Sheriff." She swept across the street without him.

Spence watched until she stepped safely onto the far boardwalk, but still, the knot in his stomach didn't ease. A knot of worry, he guessed, though maybe not.

For the past few months, he'd experienced a nagging sense of…something. He didn't know what. His visit to his folks, his return to Marlow hadn't relieved it. Instead, it had turned into something different. He still didn't know what. All he knew was that it got worse—or better—when Maggie was involved.

A wagon rolled past, loaded with one of the families who owned a farm just outside of town. Spence slid his gaze to the three riders who followed and recognized them as cowboys from the Frazier ranch.

He'd watched for days now. No sign of the outlaw gang Henry had ridden with. Spence knew it was possible the boy had made up the story about the impending bank robbery, but doubted it; Henry had no reason to lie. The gang might have changed their minds, or decided to hit a bank somewhere else, but he'd gotten no word of a robbery in either of the neighboring towns. Spence couldn't know for sure what the outlaws planned, but he would be ready, just the same.

Spence glanced across the street and saw that Maggie had paused to speak with Doris Tidwell. His belly tightened. He wished she'd get inside.

Another group of riders caught Spence's attention. He eyed them carefully. They looked familiar but he couldn't remember their names. He'd seen them in town often.

Spence kept watching. He had the advantage—a slight one, but that might be all he'd need. During the stagecoach holdup he hadn't worn his badge, so Mack Donovan and Jess Wright didn't realize he was a lawman. But he'd gotten a good look at the two of them. Spence would know them in a heartbeat. If he saw them first, recognized them, got the drop on them, the outlaws wouldn't have a chance at the bank.

"Sheriff?" Spence glanced back at Dex as he stood in the open jailhouse doorway. "I'm taking Henry down to Griss's workshop now."

Dex stepped outside, guiding Henry by the arm. The boy wore leg irons; his hands were tied in front of him. Though Henry continued to prove himself trustworthy, Spence wouldn't take a chance that the outlaws might attempt to free the boy if they rode into town; no sense making it easy for them.

"Watch yourself, Dex," Spence said, then looked at Henry. "You behave yourself, or—"

Henry froze. He gasped softly. His eyes widened. Spence spun around. Mack Donovan and Jess Wright approached on horseback, along with another man Spence didn't recognize.

Spence drew his pistol. Donovan swung toward him, saw his gun, his badge, pulled his gun and opened fire.

Spence crouched behind the water trough, firing. He caught the third outlaw in the shoulder, knocking him from his horse. Jess Wright's horse reared as he pulled his gun and returned fire.

Women screamed. Footsteps pounded the boardwalk. Shop doors slammed. Behind Spence, a moan. He glanced back. Dex lay just outside the jailhouse doorway, blood oozing from his forehead. Henry crouched next to him.

Spence whipped around and fired at the outlaws again. Donovan grimaced, grabbed his chest and tumbled backward off his horse. Spence caught Wright in his sights and squeezed the trigger. Nothing.

"Dammit..." Spence hunkered down behind the water trough to reload. A bullet zinged through the jailhouse window. Glass shattered. He flipped open the chamber. Dumped the empty cartridges. Reached—

Henry got to his knees. With his bound hands, he picked up Dex's pistol, swung it toward Spence. For an instant their gazes met. Cold, hard determination showed in Henry's eyes. Spence, unarmed, too far away to jump him. Helpless. Henry fired the pistol.

The bullet whizzed past Spence's ear. A soft thud behind him. A moan. He turned. Jess Wright towered above him on horseback, five feet away, a pistol aimed point-blank at Spence. Yet he sat there frozen, blood trickling from a small hole in his forehead. His arm dropped and he tumbled into the dirt street.

Spence whirled. Henry, trembling, threw the gun away. The boy had saved his life.

Spence rushed to Dex's side, just as the deputy roused, and saw that the bullet had only grazed his forehead. Spence rose and turned. Ian appeared. Shop doors opened. Men rushed out, hurrying to check on the fallen outlaws.

"Get the doctor!" Spence shouted.

One of the men nodded, and took off at a run.

Spence's gaze swept the street in both directions. No other outlaws. No one on the ground. No one else shot. No one—

Maggie.

Spence's heart pounded in his chest. Where was Maggie? Had she made it to the dry-goods store? Ducked into a different shop?

"Maggie!"

Across the street, Doris Tidwell stepped out of the alley, slapped her palms to her cheeks and screamed.

Two small feet stuck out from behind the water trough, the hem of a skirt fluttered against them.

Spence's heart slammed against his chest. He bolted across the street. Maggie lay facedown behind the trough. Spence dropped to his knees.

"Maggie!" He grabbed her arm and yanked her around.

Her eyes blinked open. "Why are you shouting at me?"

Spence gaped at her. "You're—you're all right."

"Well, of course I'm all right," she told him, sitting up, straightening her hat.

"Then why the hell didn't you get up!" he roared, flinging out his arms.

"Because you told me not to. Get on the ground. Stay down. Remember?"

"Oh, God..." Relief swamped him. Spence wrapped his arms around Maggie and surged to his feet, pulling her up with him.

She stayed in his embrace for only a few seconds, then pulled back. "Oh, Spence, that man could have killed you. If it hadn't been for Henry shooting him first—"

"You were supposed to keep your head down."

"I did," Maggie told him. "I only looked up once...or twice, maybe."

Spence grumbled a curse and crushed her against his chest again.

When he finally released her, Maggie said, "I'd better get down to the store."

"You're staying with me."

Spence dropped his hand to the small of her back and shepherded her across the street with him to the jail. More people were outside now, some to help with the dead and injured outlaws, some just to watch.

Dex was on his feet, holding a handkerchief to his injured brow. Henry still sat on the boardwalk.

"You okay?" Spence asked.

Dex nodded. "Just stunned me for a minute. Nothing serious."

Spence knelt in front of Henry, untied his hands and removed his leg iron with the key Dex passed to him.

"Thank you," Spence said.

Henry nodded. "Yes, sir."

Spence rose, pulled Henry up with him, and escorted him and Maggie into the jail.

"You two wait here. I'll be back when I can," he said, and went outside again.

When Spence returned, Seth Grissom was with him.

"Griss has agreed to take you in for a while," Spence said to Henry. "I'll talk to the judge when he gets here, explain things."

"Thank you, sir," Henry said and left with Seth.

"What about the outlaws?" Maggie asked.

"Wright's dead. Doc thinks the other two will make it."

Maggie sighed. "I'd better get over to Hank's store."

"No." Spence shook his head. "You're staying with me for the rest of the day."

Chapter Twenty-Eight

Maggie waited just inside the front door while Spence lit the lantern on the table beside the settee. Her little cottage came to life, the faint light casting shadows throughout the room, making it seem more homey than ever.

But maybe it was because Spence was there with her.

He closed and locked the door, then tossed his hat aside and looked down at her.

Terribly improper, it was, to allow him into her cottage this late in the evening. Dark outside, no chaperone. People would talk.

Yet after what they'd been through at the shoot-out, proper decorum hardly seemed important to Maggie. Nor did it to Spence, obviously.

She gazed up at him and had never seen him look so troubled. It startled her.

"I was scared today."

Maggie pulled in a quick breath. "You? Scared?"

"I thought I'd already lived through the worst thing that could ever happen to me," Spence said softly.

"Losing Ellen?"

He nodded. "But when I looked across the street after the shoot-out and saw you lying on the ground, and for those few seconds when I didn't know if you were safe or not...I was scared. For the first time in my life. Just plain scared."

"I didn't think you were ever frightened," Maggie said.

"I never used to be," Spence told her. "Until you came along."

"Me?"

"Now I'm scared all the time. Scared something will happen to you. Scared you'll get hurt. Scared...scared—hell, I'm scared all the time about you."

Maggie pressed her lips together thoughtfully. "Really? That's very interesting, because—"

"Oh, hell, Maggie, don't write this down."

She smiled gently. "I wasn't going to enter this in my journal. I was going to say that being frightened today is a reminder that you can't control things that happen."

He frowned. "I can control things."

"Not really," Maggie pointed out. "Today you expected the outlaws to ride into town. You'd warned your deputies. You were on the street, keeping watch. You were ready. And still, there was a shoot-out. Somebody could have gotten hurt, gotten killed...just like Ellen."

Spence drew away a little. "That was different."

"No, it wasn't. It was an accident, just as a shooting today might have been. You couldn't have prevented either one of them."

He looked away, seeming to really think about

what she'd said. A quiet moment passed and Maggie didn't speak again, giving him time to consider what she'd said.

"Maybe…maybe you're right," he said softly.

"I worry about you, too," Maggie said. "What do you suppose that means?"

"I don't know what it means." Spence shook his head wearily. "I don't want to think about it right now. I don't want to think about anything."

He pressed his palm against her cheek. Maggie's stomach warmed at the feel of his big hand against her face, and his fingers caressing her softly.

"I have a confession, too," she said. "Since I met you, since we…kissed…I started to wonder what it would feel like to think of nothing at all. To be completely empty-headed."

Spence looked a little startled by her words, then a grin pulled at his lips. He leaned in and whispered. "You'd like it."

"Do you think so?"

"I'd make sure of it."

Her stomach tingled as he lowered his head and kissed her softly on the lips. Then he pulled away a little.

"Do you understand what I'm talking about?" he asked.

Maggie's cheeks flushed, but she nodded. "Yes."

"And you want to—"

For an answer, Maggie rose on her toes and looped both arms around his neck. Spence kissed her long and hard, then pulled away.

"This isn't just part of that research project of yours, is it?" he asked.

"No," she said.

His eyes narrowed a little. "I don't want to do this if you think it's because that love goddess is making you."

"This is what I want. Me. Just me."

Spence smiled, then kissed her until her breath grew short. He lifted her into his arms and carried her to the bedroom.

In the dim lantern light, they kissed while their hands sought out buttons and fasteners and finally discovered the intimate secrets beneath.

Stretched out on the bed beside her, Spence threaded her dark hair across the pillow, then kissed his way down the length of her. Maggie gasped at his touch, yet didn't pull away. Instead, she moved closer, exploring him in the same way.

When he shifted above her, she welcomed him. He moved carefully within her, locking her in his arms, whispering into her ear. She caught his rhythm, joined as one, until the exquisite pleasure burst inside her. She grabbed his hair and called his name as he followed.

Lying beside him, beneath the covers in the dim bedroom, Maggie snuggled closer. "Spence?"

"You didn't stay empty-headed for long." He rolled toward her and draped his arm across her, pulling her closer. "Guess I'll just have to keep at this."

She giggled as he planted a kiss on her forehead, then froze as a knock sounded on the front door. They both looked in that direction, then at each other. Spence got up and shoved on his trousers as he left the bedroom. He jerked open the front door, not surprised to see Dex on the porch. The deputy at least had the good graces to look embarrassed.

"Uh, sorry, Sheriff. I, uh, I wouldn't have bothered you, but, uh…"

"What is it, Dex?"

"I think you ought to get over to East Street," Dex said, pointing in that direction. "There's a fire."

"A fire? What's on—"

"Nothing's on fire, Sheriff," Dex said. "It's more like a bonfire. But I think you ought to get over there. And bring Miss Maggie with you."

"What the hell's going on, Dex?"

"It's Lucy Hubbard. She started a fire."

The blaze was visible when Spence, Maggie and Dex turned the corner onto East Street. Bright orange and yellow flames blazed, sending sparks into the night sky. Lucy sat in a chair in her front yard, her hands in her lap tucked beneath a shawl, staring into the roaring fire.

The spectacle had drawn a number of townsfolk from their homes, but they hung back watching.

Maggie exchanged a troubled glance with Spence.

"Go find Ian," he said to Dex. "Tell him to get over here."

"Yes, sir," he replied, and hurried away.

As Maggie approached the fire with Spence, a chill passed through her, despite the heat. In the flames were the burning skeletons of chairs and a table, along with scraps of fabric. Lucy sat silent, watching them burn.

"We've got to get her away from that fire," Spence said to Maggie. "I don't know what she's liable to do."

She gulped, concerned for her friend's safety.

"Lucy," Maggie said gently, "tell me why you're doing this."

She didn't reply.

"Why don't you come home with me?" Maggie said. "We'll have some coffee and—"

A commotion from down the street took their attention. Raymond Hubbard strode up, the light of the fire reflecting on his angry face.

"What in the hell do you think you're doing, woman!" he demanded. He looked into the fire and uttered a string of curses. "That table and chairs belonged to my mama!"

Lucy's gaze left the fire and turned to Raymond. "You don't live here anymore," she said calmly.

"The hell I don't!" he roared. "You get away from there and—"

Lucy pulled her hand from beneath the shawl in her lap, picked up a shirt from the clutter beside her and tossed it into the inferno.

"Hey! That's my shirt!" Raymond shouted. He looked into the flames again. "That's all my clothes you're burning! I'm telling you for the last time, Lucy—"

She selected a pair of trousers, and tossed them in.

Raymond's eyes bulged. "You'd better quit right this minute, woman, before I—"

"I don't want to be married to you anymore. I want a divorce," Lucy said simply.

"A divorce! I'm not giving you no divorce and there's not one damned thing you can do about it!"

Lucy reached beneath the shawl and came out with a pistol. She pointed it at Raymond and pulled back the hammer.

Raymond froze. "Now, now, Lucy, you can't go

pulling a gun on somebody.'' He turned to Spence. ''Sheriff, I want you to arrest her for threatening my life.''

''Shut up, Hubbard,'' Spence snarled, ''before I shoot you myself.''

Lucy fished a packet of papers from beneath the shawl and passed them to Spence. ''That new attorney in town drew up these papers. They mean we're legally divorced. Tell Raymond to sign them.''

Spence opened the packet, leafed through the papers, then shoved them at Raymond along with the pencil that Lucy had put inside.

''Sign. Now,'' Spence said. ''Then get out of town.''

Raymond yanked the papers away, gave Spence, then Lucy, a menacing look, then scrawled his name and threw the papers in the dirt.

''All right, I'm going,'' he said to Lucy. ''And you'll be sorry, too, one of these days. But don't expect me to take you back.''

''On your way.'' Spence gave him a shove. ''And I'd better not find you anywhere near Marlow come sun-up.''

''You couldn't pay me enough to come back to this damn town,'' Raymond declared. With one last hateful look, he stomped away.

Maggie picked up the signed papers and took them to Lucy. ''That was a very brave thing you did,'' she said.

Lucy closed her fist around them. Her hand began to shake. ''I—I just couldn't take it anymore.''

''Lucy?''

Ian rushed up to her. Lucy flung herself into his arms and burst into tears.

Spence eased up beside Maggie. "I think we should go."

Maggie was glad to be at his side as they headed down East Street. The crowd of onlookers had drifted away, the windows in the shops were dark.

Save for one. Spence saw it first. He stopped abruptly. Maggie noticed it then and gasped softly.

Professor Canfield's Oddities of the World Museum, lit up like daylight.

Dex caught up with them. "I meant to tell you, Sheriff. Professor Canfield got back into town today."

Chapter Twenty-Nine

Time to go home.

Maggie paced across the kitchen of her cottage, twisting her fingers together. Professor Canfield had returned last night. Time to reclaim her artifact. Time to go home to New York.

When she and Spence had seen the lights on in the professor's museum last night, both had realized what it meant. Yet neither had spoken of it. Spence had walked her home, kissed her good-night on the porch, and left.

She'd lain alone in the bed, on the sheets that smelled of Spence, staring into the darkness trying to decide what to do.

New York no longer seemed as if it were her home. Did she even belong there anymore? Maggie wasn't sure.

She paced to the front window, staring out into the morning sunlight. Marlow. This little town—and the people in it—held a warmth she'd never experienced before. For the first time ever, Maggie felt as if she belonged…truly belonged.

But should she stay here? Was this sense of finally fitting in reason enough to stay?

Maggie turned away from the window as Spence floated into her mind. Was he the reason she considered staying?

Had he given her a reason?

No.

A heaviness settled around Maggie's heart. He'd been nice to her. He'd taken care of her. He'd come to her house, kissed her, eaten her chicken. He even said he worried about her.

But he hadn't said he loved her.

Maybe he would have done the same for any stranger in town. Maybe she was making too much of it.

Maggie uttered a bitter laugh. She was hardly "wife" material, as she demonstrated over and over with her cooking, her housekeeping. When Spence could have any woman in town, why would he want her?

Maybe the power of the love goddess controlled her. The idea caused Maggie to stop still in her tracks, yet she rejected it. Spence was in her heart, in her mind, in her soul. She didn't doubt her feelings for him, or that those feelings were hers alone.

Maggie giggled aloud at the joy of her realization, and she had to—simply had to—see Spence right away. She yanked open her front door to find him striding up her steps.

He froze when he saw her, his face drawn in tight, worried lines.

"I'm scared," he said.

"Again?"

Spence pushed past her into the house. She followed and closed the door, while he paced fitfully back and forth through the room.

"What's wrong?" she asked, thinking that something might have happened in town this morning.

"I told you. I'm scared." He stopped and looked at her. "I'm scared that you'll get on that stage and go back to New York. Scared I'll never get to see you again. Scared that the best thing that ever happened in my life will disappear."

Maggie gasped. "Does...does that mean you love me?"

"Hell, yes, that's what it means." Spence strode to her and pulled her against his chest. "I love you, Maggie. I don't want you to go back to New York."

She smiled up at him. "I don't want to leave Marlow. I love it here."

He narrowed his eyes. "And me?"

"Oh, I love you, too, of course," she insisted.

Spence smiled and kissed her on the lips, then lifted his head. "You're not still thinking this is all because of that silly love goddess statue, are you?"

"No," she said, shaking her head. "I figured if you can give up your old way of thinking about Ellen, I could change my ways, too."

"Good." He hugged her tighter. "So you're staying?"

"Yes."

"And you'll marry me?"

She smiled. "Oh, yes."

Spence kissed her again, this time long and slow, until she sighed and he groaned.

"I'd better go talk to Professor Canfield," Maggie said, "before..."

"Yeah." Spence backed away, the heat in his

body telling him exactly what she meant. "I'll go with you."

The streets of Marlow had come to life. Shopkeepers busied themselves sweeping the boardwalk, the townspeople went about their business. No sign of the shoot-out that had taken place yesterday; even the jailhouse window had been replaced.

A tremor of guilt shook Maggie's stomach as they walked past the Townsend Dry Goods store. She should report for work now, but didn't think Hank would really miss her.

"Do you think putting in a good word for Henry when the circuit judge comes to town will keep him out of prison?" Maggie asked, as they headed down Main Street.

"The kid saved my life," Spence said. "That will go a long way with the judge."

"I was thinking maybe Henry could have my job at the dry-goods store," Maggie said. "Shop work isn't really for me."

"You don't have to work at all," Spence said. "I'll take care of you."

"I can't do nothing at all," Maggie said. "I'm going to ask Professor Canfield if I can work at the museum."

Spence nodded. "You'd be good at that."

They reached the door of the Oddities of the World Museum and Maggie stopped. Spence paused beside her.

"This is what you came here for," he said. "If you can get Professor Canfield to return that statue, you can send it to your father, make up for your mistake."

A little thrill zinged up her spine. How proud he

would surely be of her for handling the situation herself. Spence gave her a wink and opened the door.

"Good morning, good morning. I'm Professor Canfield. Please come inside."

The short, round man waved them into the museum. Tufts of white hair circled his bald head like a halo.

His smile broadened. "Ah, Sheriff Harding. Good to see you again."

"Morning, Professor."

"Oh, Sheriff, it looks as if someone tried to break into my museum while I was gone," he said, nodding toward the rear of the building.

Maggie and Spence exchanged a quick look.

"I'm checking into it, Professor," Spence promised. "This is Miss Maggie Peyton. She's from New York."

"Ah, yes, Miss Peyton. You left a note for me. I found it last night." He swept his hand toward the exhibits. "You're just in time, my dear. I returned from my latest expedition with new and wondrous displays to delight the senses and excite the imagination."

"Actually, Professor, I'd like to talk to you about one of your artifacts, in particular," Maggie said.

He hung his thumbs in his vest pockets. "Oh? Which one?"

"The ancient South American love goddess," Maggie said.

Professor Canfield frowned and tapped his finger against his chin. "Love goddess…love goddess…I don't recall having a love goddess, ancient or otherwise."

Maggie walked to the back shelf and pointed. "It

sat right here. About a foot tall with big feet and outstretched arms.''

"I've got the thing down at the jail, Professor," Spence explained.

"Oh, yes, of course." The professor tilted his head. "It was a love goddess?"

"Well, yes," Maggie said. "It was stolen from my father in New York. It was my fault, really, my mistake. So I came here to get it and return it to my father."

"Oh, dear…" Professor Canfield's brows pulled together in a deep frown. "That might be a problem."

Maggie gulped. "But the artifact rightfully belongs to my father. He recovered it himself and brought it to New York. It should be returned to him."

"That's not what concerns me." Professor Canfield shook his head, worrying his lips together. "You see, the statue that sat here in my museum, well, it wasn't the original artifact."

"What?"

"I bought the original from a fellow down near Houston. He'd used it for target practice. Nearly destroyed it completely," Professor Canfield explained. "But I liked the look of it so I paid a stone carver to make me another one."

Maggie's head swam. "So…so the statue here in your museum was…?"

"A copy," the professor said. "Just a copy."

Maggie made a little mewling noise. Spence hooked his arm around her to keep her on her feet.

"Thanks, Professor," he called, and escorted Maggie out of the museum.

Her breath came in short puffs and her heart pounded as she gazed up at Spence. Then he laughed. And Maggie laughed, too.

"All this way," she said through her giggles. "And it wasn't even the real artifact."

"What are you going to tell your father?" Spence asked.

Even that didn't ruin her good mood. "I'll write to him, tell him the truth. Perhaps learning that I found a husband will soften the blow."

Spence offered her arm. "Let's get out of here."

"You still want to marry me, don't you?" Maggie asked, strolling at his side. "Even though I traipsed all the way across the country on a fool's errand?"

"Yeah, I'll keep you."

"I'm not much of a cook, you know," she reminded him.

Spence grinned down at her, displaying both dimples. "In a way, you're my own personal love goddess, because you cast a spell over me."

"Will it last a lifetime?" Maggie asked.

"It will," Spence said. "Even with your cooking."

* * * * *

HEAD FOR THE ROCKIES WITH

Harlequin Historicals®
Historical Romantic Adventure!

AND SEE HOW IT ALL BEGAN!

**Check out these three historicals
connected to the bestselling Intrigue series**

CHEYENNE WIFE
by Judith Stacy
January 2004

COLORADO COURTSHIP
by Carolyn Davidson
February 2004

ROCKY MOUNTAIN MARRIAGE
by Debra Lee Brown
March 2004

Available at your favorite retail outlet.

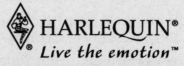

HARLEQUIN®
Live the emotion™

Visit us at www.eHarlequin.com

HHCC

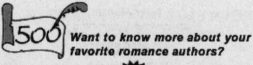